"That ancient vampire in the mountain—" I begin. "His family name was Montgomery."

Victor grows still, processing the information, and I'm not even sure he's breathing. I force out the words—

"Victor . . . I'm a vampire."

I don't know what sort of reaction I expected, but it certainly isn't a smile followed by a quick laugh.

"That's not possible, Dawn. I would know."

"Okay, maybe not a vampire, but a dhampir. Half-human, half-vampire."

"They're a myth. Like leprechauns, faeries, and werewolves."

"You thought Day Walkers were a myth, too."

That sobers him.

"Think about it, Victor, think about my blood. If it contained vampire, it would explain why for a time you had a craving for it after you tasted it. And our ability to share dreams," I continue, pressing my point. "Faith said that only happens with Old Family."

He walks over, pushes my hair behind my ear, and trails his finger along the crucifix tattoo on my neck. "You always hated the thought of becoming a vampire."

I force a smile. I imagine it looks pretty pitiful. "Ironic, huh?"

THE DARKNESS BEFORE DAWN NOVELS

Darkness Before Dawn

Blood-Kissed Sky

After Daybreak

A Darkness Before Dawn Novel

J. A. LONDON

HarperTeen is an imprint of HarperCollins Publishers.

After Daybreak
 For information address HarperCollins Children's Books, a division of HarperCollins Publishers, 10 East 53rd Street, New York, NY 10022.

www.epicreads.com

Library of Congress Cataloging-in-Publication Data
London, J. A.

After daybreak : a Darkness before dawn novel / J.A. London. — First edition.

pages cm

Summary: Seventeen-year-old Dawn reveals that she is half-vampire to persuade the vampires to unite with humans against the Day Walkers, before their world is destroyed completely.

ISBN 978-0-06-202067-3 (pbk. bdg.)

[1. Vampires—Fiction. 2. Orphans—Fiction.] I. Title.

PZ7.L8422Af 2013 2013000030

[Fic]—dc23 CIP

AC

Typography by Michelle Gengaro-Kokmen

13 14 15 16 17 CG/RRDH 10 9 8 7 6 5 4 3 2 1

❖

First Edition

For all our wonderful readers
who embraced the characters and the world we created.
You made all the difference.

Prologue

Sin watched them flee.

From atop the mountain, with his keen vampire sight, he spotted them clearly: Dawn Montgomery, who he knew would join him eventually, and his old friend, Michael Colt. Michael used a slender broken-off tree limb to stake the vampire coachman that had driven them here on Sin's command. He watched as Michael then unharnessed the lead horse and mounted it. Dawn, now aware of the vampire blood coursing through her own veins, pulled herself up behind him. Then they were galloping away from the mountain as though the devil were coming after them.

But the devil wasn't going to follow. Not yet.

Dropping his head back, Sin spread his arms wide, stared at the vast star-filled night sky, and relished the sensation of his power increasing. The blood of the ancient vampire upon whom he'd just feasted coursed through his veins. How long before he became imbued by the Thirst? Was it even possible? He had seen only the Lessers—humans-turned-vampires—succumb to its influence. Perhaps it was merely fantasy to believe it could have any effect on a born vampire, an Old Family descendant such as himself.

Yet even as he thought this, Sin smiled. No. It would happen. He could already sense the change taking hold deep within his heart. For years he had fed off other vampires with few knowing his dark desire to become one of the Infected. To many others, the Thirst was a myth. The thought of a vampire becoming a monster—developing an insatiable taste for his fellow kind, with human blood no longer serving to stave off his hunger—was the stuff of nightmares. Easier to deny its existence than to face its horrors.

But Sin basked in the reality, because in the Thirst he recognized limitless power. He would be untouchable, stronger than any other vampire. Then Dawn would realize how futile resistance was. She would take her place at his side and they could rule together.

Calmly, he watched Dawn and Michael flee farther and farther away. Sin looked across at the horizon. The sun would rise in a few hours and he would not fear it.

But the world . . . the world would fear him. For soon, all he saw, and everything beyond, would be his.

Chapter 1

With my arms wrapped tightly around Michael's waist, we ride out fast, eager to escape the mountains, desperate to escape Sin.

Warm liquid pools against my hands. Michael's blood. His chest is still bleeding, a four-strike wound from Sin's claws as Michael tried to protect me. I press my palms against him, trying to stop the flow. Before Sin clawed Michael's chest, he sliced open his cheek. The blood there has caked over, but the gashes must ache. We debated taking two horses from the coach, but Michael's injuries are weakening him. I wasn't certain how long he'd be able to ride if I wasn't holding him. If he falls, I doubt I'll have the strength to get him back on the horse. No way am I leaving him to the mercy of any vampires who are roaming the countryside.

Exhaustion threatens to claim me. I can't give in to its allure. I can only imagine how difficult it is for Michael to remain upright. We don't speak as the mountains behind us become mere ripples in the sky.

The clouds begin to change, lightening in shade, and then the moon fades. The sun rises, but it brings little comfort. It'll send most of the vampires into hiding, but it won't affect the Day Walkers.

Michael brings the horse to a slow canter, giving it a chance to catch its breath. "We should stop, check your wounds," I say.

Michael shakes his head. "Let's find some sort of shelter first. If I get off the horse, I don't know if I'll be able to get back on. Although . . . maybe you should go on alone, search for help. You'll be faster without me."

"I'm not leaving you."

"Dawn, you might not have a choice."

"I'm not leaving you, Michael." I make my voice as forceful as possible. I don't want to admit that he's right. We're the only ones who know the full scope and horror of Sin's plans. One of us has to return to Denver, to let the others know so they can prepare to meet the new threat.

Time passes. I don't know if it's minutes or hours. The sun beats down on us. It's so incredibly desolate out here. My mouth is dry; my lips feel as though they might crack if I talk again.

We have to find food and water, but where?

The horse slows to a plodding walk. Michael is drooping

in the saddle. How much blood has he lost? How much longer can he ride?

Michael directs the horse to a steep hill and, kicking his heels against its sides, urges it up. We arrive at the top of the rise and look out over the vast expanse spreading before us. Thirty years of war decimated it. Ten years later, nature is still struggling to reclaim what it once owned—much as we humans are.

Michael raises a hand to his brow to shield his eyes from the glare of the sun. "In the distance there." He points. "Is that what I think it is?"

It doesn't seem possible, but through the wall of shimmering heat—

"It looks like a town," I say.

The Vampire Human Treaty, or VampHu, outlaws the establishment of any town other than the twenty walled cities agreed to in the settlement that ended the war.

"Maybe it's a mirage," he says, and I can hear in his voice his reluctance to hope.

"I don't think so. I mean, would we both be seeing it if it were?"

"Guess not. I've heard rumors that illegal towns exist beyond the walls, but I never thought I'd see one."

I hate to be the bearer of bad tidings, but we need to be realistic. Without the walls that surround the major cities to protect them, the humans in that town would be easy prey. "It might be prewar, and the odds are that it's abandoned, but that doesn't mean we won't find water or food there."

"I could use a drink."

He could use a lot more than that. He needs medical attention. Maybe we'll find something that I can use to tend to his wounds.

The horse isn't as sure-footed going down the hill, and I hold my breath, hoping it doesn't stumble. But we make it safely to level ground and the horse trudges forward.

The town, so small it seems threatened by the enormity of the surrounding desert, grows steadily larger. I spot a windmill, hear the clacking of the blades echoing over the plain as the slight breeze turns them. The tiny buildings begin to take shape, their odd placement showing no evidence of planning, their even stranger form indicating a lack of craftsmanship. Walls curve and bend at unusual angles, stone is missing from key foundations, and the road through the town's center is little more than well-packed dirt. The only impressive things are the thick, clay roofs, which seem to be attached to the unstable walls by some miracle of architecture.

As we near, we get a genuine surprise: men, women, and children. They walk along boarded paths, talk to others in front of their homes. People are working: patching walls, gathering water from a well beneath the windmill, sorting a myriad of boxes. I see smiles. I hear the din of laughter and conversation.

We must look pretty sorry when we arrive at the edge of the town. Michael's bleeding has worsened, our clothes are torn and dirty, and our poor horse is panting like it's spent a year in the desert alone in desperate search of a cool lake.

A burly man with salt and pepper hair that matches his beard approaches. He must be a guard. A rifle is slung over his shoulder, and a sturdy stake-filled bandolier wraps around his barrel-shaped chest. With steel in his light blue eyes and his mouth set in a firm line, he gives us a measuring look before shouting, "Get Doc Jameson!"

A young barefoot girl with braids races off.

The man helps me slide off the horse, softening my landing. I nearly collapse when my feet hit the ground, my legs unsteady after the long ride. Michael tries to dismount, but his weakness is apparent as he begins to fall, and the man quickly catches him.

"Easy now," he says. "No shame in asking for help."

Michael leans on the man and we all walk into the center of town. People stop what they're doing to watch us. They're probably wondering what sort of trouble we've brought. I'm just as wary. How have they managed to exist in this isolated place?

A woman with red hair pulled back into a ponytail runs up to us.

"He's in rough shape, Doc," the man says.

"I'd say so." Her face sports a constellation of freckles. She's wearing a beaten and frayed lab coat. Maybe it was once white, but it's now the color of the dust. She doesn't look very old, and her movements are quick and efficient, her green eyes sharp as she surveys the damage.

"Get him inside," she says before turning her attention to me.

"I'm fine," I say, barely able to get the words past my moisture-stripped throat.

"Don't be brave just for your friend," she says, examining my neck, and I know she's searching for bite marks. "I can take care of you both. Follow George. I'll meet you in the clinic."

I would've followed George no matter what. Michael's hold on the guard loosens with each step, his strength sapped. I slip under his free arm, determined to get him where he needs to be, even if it kills me.

The outside of the building is crude and simple, like all the others, but the inside is clean and tidy. On one side of a living area is an open office with a large desk. On the other, strings of beads serve as a doorway to a shadowed room. George walks straight through an opening that leads into what must serve as their infirmary. No tile or white sheets greet us, but care has been taken to ensure the dust and sand from outside don't creep in. George lifts Michael onto an examination table that looks to be salvaged from some ancient scrap yard and hastily repaired.

When George leaves, I step forward, take Michael's hand, and squeeze it reassuringly. The gashes on his cheek look angry, swollen, and painful. I can only imagine how much worse the ones across his chest are.

Dr. Jameson marches through the door, followed by a girl who looks to be about my age. Her blond hair is pulled back into a long braid. There is purpose in her movements as she sets a bowl of water on the counter. The doctor begins washing her hands while the girl arranges towels and instruments on a small table near where Michael is resting.

A dark-haired girl enters carrying two glasses with clear liquid in them. She gives me one. "I'm Amy."

"Dawn," I croak, before drinking the water. It's cool as it travels down my parched throat.

"Drink slowly," the doctor orders.

But it's difficult. I never expected anything that didn't have a flavor could taste so good.

With a shy smile, Amy puts an arm beneath Michael's shoulders and lifts him gently, taking the glass to his lips. He finishes it off quickly. She settles him back down, takes my empty glass, and leaves the room. I realize the other girl is gone as well. But I'm not leaving. Maybe Dr. Jameson recognizes my determination to stay because she simply ignores me and steps over to the table. "Let's see what we've got here."

Scissors in hand, she proceeds to cut away Michael's shirt to reveal the crimson furrows. I cling to his hand, more for my sake than his. I can't believe he was able to help us get away. He must have been—still must be—in agony.

"Nasty gouges," Dr. Jameson says. "On your face and chest. What happened?"

"Got into it with a cat."

She shoots him a warning glare. "Now isn't the time for jokes."

Michael looks at me, hoping maybe I'll crack a smile, but I'm too worried.

"Someone swiped at him with steel-tipped claws." The weapon, so frightening, seemed like a natural extension of Sin's demented persona.

"You're lucky," Dr. Jameson says. "If not for your ribs, these wounds could have gone a lot deeper, sliced into your organs. You wouldn't be here now."

Dr. Jameson dabs alcohol over the torn flesh. I feel helpless while Michael takes in a sharp breath and cringes. He tightens his hold on my hand. He's nearly died for me so many times that I'm losing count. I wish I could do more for him.

"I'd love to offer you some anesthetic," she says. "But all I have is this."

She hands him a piece of wood, about the size of my forefinger, wrapped in rope. Michael places it in his mouth and bites down.

As she works a needle and thread through the wounds, she tugs tautly to close the openings. With every puncture, Michael grunts and tightens his jaw as he transfers the pain onto the piece of bark between his teeth. With my free hand, I brush my fingers through his short hair.

I lean over so he can hear me easily. "Remember when we were kids and we played on the swings? Go there, in your mind. Go to a place where there's no pain, no Sin."

He grows silent, and the doctor continues her work. I still feel the tension from his hand holding mine, but I can tell that my talking is distracting him. So I carry on, reminding him of all the good moments we've shared. He's been my best friend for so long. For a while he was more than that.

When Dr. Jameson is finished with his chest, she closes up the gashes on his cheek. "All right, all done," she says when she's completed her work.

I help Michael sit up.

"How do I look, Dawn?" he mumbles, trying to talk without reopening the wounds. "Am I still as handsome as ever?"

Fighting back tears for all he's suffered, I smile. He's made another little joke, but right now it's just a relief to know he's going to be okay.

"Chicks dig scars," I say.

Which he'll have. Forever. Four deep strikes across his cheek, nearly cutting to the teeth, sealed up by a railroad of stitches. In a few weeks they'll become small mountain chains of scar tissue. Then there are those along his chest, which the doctor is now covering with strips of gauze.

When she's secured the ends so the bandage won't unravel, she studies me intently. "Are you sure you're okay?"

"Just bruised a little."

She sits in a chair and sighs heavily, maybe slipping out of doctor-emergency mode finally. "So, who are you two?"

"Dawn Montgomery," I say. "Former delegate for the city of Denver."

"Impressive. And you?"

"Michael Colt. Bodyguard." Even away from Denver

he's careful not to reveal that he's a Night Watchman. They're a clandestine group, their identities always held secret so their families don't become the target of the vampires they hunt.

"Well, you two are certainly far from home. What brings you here? And is there trouble following you?"

A lot, but while I want to reassure her, I'm too tired and can't think of how to be diplomatic. "I'm afraid we're a magnet for vampires."

"Who isn't these days? But don't worry," she says, holding up her hand. "They never bother us here. I'll have Amy get you some fresh clothes and show you where you can wash up while I get Michael settled in a bed."

"I'm not leaving Michael."

"He'll be in the room through that beaded doorway," Dr. Jameson says. "You can join him there."

"I'm not leaving him."

"I'll be fine, Dawn," Michael says.

"No. We stay together."

With a wry grin, he looks at Dr. Jameson. "She's stubborn."

"I'm getting that. Come on, then. I'll have Amy bring the water to you."

With Michael moving gingerly, we follow her back into the front room and through the beaded doorway into a room with three cots and no windows.

"What is the name of this town?" I ask.

"Crimson Sands," Dr. Jameson says.

I imagine this place is in a delicate balance, teetering

on the edge of oblivion. The harsh landscape can dry out societies, dry out souls. How many towns have tried to be Crimson Sands and failed? How long has this illegal town survived, and how much longer can it?

"We'll get your horse watered and fed. I'll have supper ready for you when you wake up."

"Thank you. How long have you been living like this?" I ask.

"Five years."

"That's incredible."

"We survive by working together. Into bed now."

"We'll do what we can to repay you," Michael says.

"No need. Crimson Sands has flourished, relatively, on the kindness we offer each other. It's only right that we extend that kindness to those who wander our way. You could say it's our little way of reclaiming the world after such a devastating war."

"By showing that you never lost your humanity," I say.

"Precisely. Now please, no more talk. You need your rest. Just make yourselves comfortable and sleep as long as you like." She leaves, the wooden beads clacking in her wake.

With a deep sigh, Michael sits on one of the cots. "I think I'm safe here. You could get to Denver faster without me."

"You are turning me into an echo. I'm not leaving you. Now get some sleep and I'll keep watch."

"But—"

Before he can finish, the beads are clicking again. Amy

sets a large bowl on a small table. "Brung you some water and clothes."

"Thank you."

"I'll help him put on the shirt I found for him." She gives Michael another shy smile as she walks toward him. "Don't want to undo Dr. Jameson's handiwork."

While she's tending to Michael, blocking his view of me, I quickly remove my shirt. I wash my hands, face, neck, and chest. The gray T-shirt she brought for me is soft and faded with age, somehow comforting.

The beads smack again. Dr. Jameson is holding two mugs. "Decided you should have a little soup before you sleep."

She hands me one, then takes the other to Michael before leaving, ushering Amy out of the room as well.

I ease onto the bed across from Michael. I take a sip of the thick, creamy, tomatoey soup. "It's good."

"Yeah." He barely opens his mouth to take a long swallow.

"Are you in much pain?" Stupid question. I know he is.

"I'll be all right."

If he were dying, he'd say the same thing. Not only because stoicism is part of his training as a Night Watchman, but because it's in his nature to downplay his own suffering. Even when we broke up after going together for several months, he contained his anger and pain as much as possible.

I'm just grateful that we were able to become friends again after we separated.

Once we finish off the soup, I set both mugs on the table and return to the cot. "You try to get some sleep."

Reaching across, he touches my leg. "Are you okay? Sin and that old vampire in the cave laid some heavy stuff on you. Just so you know, I don't believe any of it."

I don't either. It's just not possible. "Thanks. I'm fine."

"I mean, your dad would have told you if you were . . . you know, a vampire."

If I was a vampire. I squeeze my eyes shut tightly against the obscene thought. I shoved back everything I was told. I wasn't ready to deal with it—not while Michael was bleeding, not until we were safe. Octavian, the ancient vampire in the mountain, claimed to be the last full-blooded vampire of the Montgomery clan. He claimed I was one of his descendants.

"Sin said I was a dhampir. Not exactly a vampire. More like some half-breed freak. But Sin has done nothing but lie to us. Why believe him now?" Especially when the truth could be so painful.

Michael pulls back his hand, rubs it on his jeans. He probably doesn't even realize what he's doing—wiping me off his skin. He still hates vampires as much as I used to. He lies down. "I don't think I've ever been so tired."

"Me either." I hear him snoring before I'm fully stretched out on the mattress, my eyes on the beaded doorway. I can't sleep, not for a while yet. I want to trust these people, but Sin has destroyed my ability to trust. He let us go so easily. What if he knew about this place? What if he has already made its citizens his disciples?

But if they answer to him, then why not just admit it? Take us captive?

Beyond the walls that surround us, I can hear the movement of people as they work: hammering, scraping, shuffling feet over the ground. It all sounds normal, safe. I fight to keep my eyes open, to remain on guard, but the past few days and the horror of last night have taken their toll.

If I give in and sleep, I could also reach out to Victor. Victor, the Old Family vampire who changed my life and worked his way into my heart. After being terribly wounded during a fight, Victor was forced to drink my blood in order to survive. Now we have a connection where we can visit each other's dreams. I shy away from the thought that this bond may be proof of my vampire heritage. What's important now is finding Victor.

I relax and succumb to sleep.

I feel like I've been floating forever. Then I find myself at a place that starts my heart racing.

The mountain.

I'm inside the cavern where Sin brought us, where I met the Old Family vampire who claimed to be my ancestor. The area is awash in blues as the moonlight spills in from a hole in the top. I see the throne where the ancient vampire sat. Now there is nothing except a pile of ash. The sun poured through earlier and destroyed his body.

A forlorn figure is kneeling before the throne, his fists clenched, his head bent.

"Victor!"

He turns toward me, and without a second's hesitation we embrace each other. Although I'm in his dream, I can feel him. He's solid, comforting.

"Dawn, you're alive. I was so afraid."

"I'm fine," I assure him. "But how are you here?"

Releasing me, Victor paces before the throne, combing his fingers through the ash of the vampire who once sat there.

"Jeff and I were here," he says. Jeff served as my bodyguard at the Agency. "After you came to me in the dream and told me Sin had taken you, I left Denver with him as soon as I could. But we were too late."

He throws a handful of ash onto the ground in frustration.

"We were so close . . . ," he whispers.

"It's okay," I say. "Our blood kiss has brought us together again. In this place."

Victor nods, still investigating the throne and its ashen king. "What happened here, Dawn?"

I rush toward him and grab his shoulders, forcing him to stare into my eyes with his deep blue ones.

"I'll tell you everything when you find us." There's no time to discuss it now. Our dreams are so fragile that either of us might wake at any moment. We'll lose our connection and the ability to communicate. "Michael and I are in a town, not too far from here. To the southeast. You'll see a windmill. Come for us."

"What about Sin? Does he know where you are?"

"I don't know," I say.

I touch his face. The bristle along his jaw scratches my fingers. I've never understood how I can experience all these sensations when we're together like this. "I need you, Victor. Please, get to us as soon as you can."

"I will," he says, and I feel him move sharply.

It's like his body is being pulled from me by some invisible string, jerking him across vast distances. My hand passes through the empty air where he stood just a moment ago.

He's woken up, breaking our connection. He'll find me. I know it.

I walk over to the throne and stare at what remains of the ancient vampire.

What if I am *a descendant of the lost vampire family—the Montgomerys—as Octavian claimed? It changes everything if I'm no longer human. What world do I fit in? The humans won't want me, and since the Old Families signed a death warrant to eradicate the Montgomerys, I'm pretty sure the vampires won't want me either.*

Like him, I may be cast out, forced into hiding, and left to live my life alone.

Chapter 2

Slowly my consciousness returns to my body from what feels like a journey of a thousand miles. Every time I fall into Victor's dream, upon waking I'm never quite sure I was truly there. The memories of that place, of holding Victor, of talking to him, gently re-form in my mind. I add details: the scent of his cologne, the softness of his hair tickling my nose, which I would have laughed at if matters weren't so urgent. I carry these sensations into the real world. His fragrance lingers; the press of his body against mine still warms me. Hopefully it was all real, and he heard my pleas. If so, he'll be here soon.

I sit up on my cot. The light in the room outside is entering slowly, hovering just at the edges. I hear the scratch of a pen from the next room. I don't want to think about how vampires have such keen hearing. My senses seem more attuned to my surroundings. Is it just my imagination? Or is it vampiric blood beginning to stir?

I rub my face, washing away the final cobwebs of sleep. Michael is still snoozing. I'm grateful he's able to escape the pain for a while.

I stand up, stretch, and walk toward the beads. As silently as possible, I slip between them, not wanting to disturb Michael.

The front room is as simple as I remember. The sparse furniture—a sofa, table, and chairs—was salvaged from somewhere. Everything is mismatched; the colors, shapes, and heights all from different styles, different eras. Holding a mug that seems to be handmade from clay, Dr. Jameson sits at a table, busily jotting down something.

I glance over at the window, nothing but a hole in the wall with a few metal slats making a crude cross.

"It's night?" I ask. How long did I dream? It seemed only minutes, but time has no bearing in that other world.

"Yes," Dr. Jameson says, making a few final flourishes before looking up. "You were out cold. Probably for the best, as you certainly needed the rest."

"Has anyone else arrived in town?" I ask, suddenly realizing Victor may already be here if enough time has passed.

"No," she says flatly. "Were you expecting someone?"

"Maybe," I say. "He isn't trouble," I quickly add. "A friend. A very good friend."

"Well, let's hope he arrives safely."

I nod, picturing him on the road, driving in his black

Mustang, looking for the windmill.

My heart jumps when I think of the Thirst, a madness vampires acquire when they begin taking blood from each other instead of humans. The blood of an Old Family vampire would be considered a treat to those Infected. What if he's ambushed? What if that's what Sin wanted all along?

No. No, that's impossible. Sin doesn't know about our dreams, about our ability to communicate. He couldn't know, could he?

"Help yourself to some food," Dr. Jameson says. "I imagine you're hungry."

"Starving," I admit as I take a chair near the desk and reach for a sandwich. It's filled with avocado, tomato, onion, lettuce. My mouth waters with the variety of flavors. "You must have a greenhouse."

"We do. It's relatively small, nothing like your city's massive ones, but it meets our needs. With plenty of sun and adequate water, all we had to do was gather up soil. It doesn't provide everything, and we still scavenge for old supplies in abandoned or half-destroyed ration factories. But we're working on becoming more self-sufficient. We've even managed to round up some dairy cows. Animals seem to be growing in number again."

Their blood is of no use to vampires and with no humans out here to hunt them down—

Maybe our ecosystem will finally right itself.

"What city did you live in?" I ask. "Before you came here."

She seems uncomfortable, tucking her hair behind her

ear, studying the notes she was making when I came in. "It doesn't really matter, does it?"

"Depends on what you know and what you've seen."

She laughs. "That's the delegate talking."

I give her a wry smile. "Yeah, I guess it is."

Settling back in her chair, she studies me intently. "You're a little young to be a delegate."

At seventeen, I'm the youngest ever. Victor's father, overlord at the time, personally requested me. The Agency, charged with protecting the citizens, had no say in the decision. The vampire hold over humans is that strong. What vampires demand, they get.

"My parents were delegates," I explain. "They were killed one night on their way back from Valentine Manor." I didn't know at the time that Sin killed them on Lord Valentine's orders. Valentine wanted me as delegate so he could keep a closer watch on me. He knew what I was. He wanted to use me, just like Sin wants to now. But I'm only going to share with Dr. Jameson the surface of my life, because I still have a hard time swimming through its depths.

"Valentine," she mutters. "The most ruthless of all the vampires from what I understand."

"He's dead now. His—"

I cut myself short as the door opens and the guard who first welcomed us strolls in. With his wide-brimmed hat and bandolier of stakes, George looks like a cowboy gunslinger stepping out of the pages of a bizarre western story that foresaw the rise of vampires.

"I hope you're enjoying your stay," he says, taking off his hat and wiping his sweaty brow with the sleeve of his blue-checkered shirt. His beard glistens with the day's hard work.

"Your hospitality has been amazing," I say.

He rests his rifle against the wall and sits down, exhaling heavily. I study him as he stretches out his legs and crosses them.

"A rifle *and* stakes?" I ask.

"We get vampires wanting our blood and bandits wanting to steal our water. Need to be prepared for both."

"Do you suffer many attacks?"

"We did at first. But I think everyone knows to leave us alone now."

"I didn't realize so many humans were roaming the countryside."

"More than you'd think. People get tired of being walled in and under the thumb of Old Family vampires."

Dr. Jameson stands up, goes over to a small pot, and pours coffee into three mugs, bringing them back to us.

"Thank you kindly," George says with a deep, slow drawl.

The coffee is strong and tastes rich; it provides the energy boost I need.

"Are you on guard duty tonight?" I ask.

"Every night."

"And every morning. You were the first one to greet us."

"That's right," he says. "Never was one to sleep much."

He takes another big gulp, then looks at the mug as if trying to decode its delicious secrets. He's probably been drinking this coffee every night, but I can tell Dr. Jameson appreciates his wonder.

"You always did make a good cup, Marjorie," he says.

She's about to reply when the door opens again.

"Someone coming down the road, George," the man announces. "In a car."

My heart jumps. Victor!

"A car?" George asks. "Must be one of those freelance vampire hunters. Not many people can afford a car these days."

"It's not a vampire hunter," I assure them, my joy evident. "It's my friends."

The man at the door studies me, then turns to George.

"Well," George says, "roll out the red carpet for 'em. This little lady here says they're her friends, so we'll treat them as such until they prove otherwise."

The man nods and leaves.

"Thank you so much," I say, not completely sure what I'm thanking them for. But before the door even shuts, I'm outside, George and the doctor right behind me.

In the distance, the dust is kicked up, flying into the night sky. The door behind me squeaks open one more time and Michael emerges.

"Who is it?" he asks, groggily rubbing his head.

"Victor and Jeff."

The car fishtails to a stop in front of us, the dust catching up to it and swirling around the headlights, creating mystic shadow puppets that stretch across the town square. Jeff steps out of the passenger's side, and Victor quickly emerges from the driver's side.

In spite of our audience, Victor and I race toward each other. I collapse against him, wrapping my arms tightly around his neck as he brings me nearer. I'm overwhelmed with a sense of relief at being this close to him again. His warmth, his solidity offer reassurance. Even though I was just with him in my dream, being with him in the flesh is so much more satisfying. I think of where I am: in the middle of nowhere, Sin just behind us, and a deeper night still to come. Yet it doesn't matter, because I'm with Victor.

"I was so worried about you," he whispers, and I feel his breath ruffling my hair as he holds me tightly.

"I know, but we're okay now."

Loosening our embrace, Victor looks me squarely in the eyes. I could stand here forever, relishing this moment. More breadth of wonder rests in his blue eyes than in the vast skies above us.

When Jeff finishes shaking Michael's hand and giving him a pat on the shoulder, he turns to me. "Hey, sunshine. Good to see you."

I smile, release a tiny laugh as I hug him. In addition to serving as a bodyguard for the Agency, he's been dating my guardian and mentor, Rachel Goodwin. He's become as special to me as she's always been.

I introduce them to George and Dr. Jameson, give a brief accounting of all they've done for us.

"Thank you for taking them in," Victor says. "I know

trust is a rarity in places like this."

"That it is. But even more rare is an Old Family vampire showing up," George says, an eyebrow raised.

Victor gives a wry smile and looks at me. Old Family vampires are elegant, suave, sophisticated. Comfortable with what they are. Humans who are turned—Lessers—never quite achieve that beauty. Victor may be dressed in jeans, a black long-sleeve T-shirt, and a leather duster, but there is something regal in his bearing. Confidence oozes off him. And if I'm honest with myself, he is quite simply gorgeous in a way that's impossible to hide.

"I hope that isn't a problem," Victor says.

"It doesn't have to be," George says. "So long as you understand we ain't under your *jurisdiction*."

"I'd never dream of it," Victor says.

"Well, that's settled, then. I can tell you're itchin' to have a talk with your little lady. When you're ready, come inside and we'll have a sit-down."

He heads back into Dr. Jameson's house. The doctor, Michael, and Jeff follow him.

The townsfolk have come over to examine Victor's car. They run their hands over the smooth surface and make noises of appreciation. Since the war, cars are rare and no doubt a curiosity for them.

Putting some distance between them and us, Victor guides me over to the side of the road and cradles my face. "I was so scared, Dawn."

Lowering his head, he kisses me tenderly.

The world falls away, and it's just us and the stars above

in this desolate place. We stand like a pair of wildflowers that somehow grew in this dry sand, and we breathe together, and move together, and entangle ourselves around each other.

Pulling back, he skims his knuckles over my cheek. "This is so much better than what we shared in the dreams." He shakes his head. "But there I could stay. In the real world, I have to walk away."

Victor said before I left Denver that we couldn't be together. That I'm the weakness his enemies will exploit. But it's too late.

"Walking away won't protect either of us now. Sin wants me to kill you."

His jaw tightens.

I continue, "It's the price I have to pay to keep everyone else I care about safe."

Victor stares at me, perhaps wondering if I would actually take Sin up on the offer. Not because I'm afraid, but because of how much I care for all my friends.

"I told him to shove it," I say quickly, and Victor laughs. "Maybe not in those exact words, but I think the message was clear."

I put my hand on Victor's heart, as though protecting it from any stake that would dare strike him.

"But what about Faith?" Victor asks. "And Richard. Does Sin have them?"

"No, no," I rush to assure him. Faith is Victor's sister. He sent her and his best friend, Richard Carrollton, to watch over me when I journeyed to Los Angeles to find out what

I could about the Thirst and Sin. "They escaped using the engine of the Night Train. Along with Tegan"—my best friend—"and Ian Hightower."

"Hightower?"

I sense his alarm. Ian Hightower is the most famous and deadly vampire hunter to ever live. More recently, he's been the guardian of the Night Train.

"Don't worry. We formed an alliance with Ian," I tell him.

"That must have taken some convincing."

"Richard was quite persuasive, and his killing some of the Infected who got on board the train didn't hurt. They're probably back in the city by now, don't you think?"

"Probably." I can sense him taking comfort in the knowledge that everyone should be safe. "If they made it out, what happened to you? How did Sin manage to capture you?"

I tell him about Los Angeles, how the outer ring of the city is nothing but weak and hopeless humans and the inner ring is overrun with Sin's Day Walkers. He was waiting for us. I explain that we tried to kill him, but he was too powerful and his followers too many. While the others escaped, I wasn't so lucky. I couldn't get to the train in time. Michael came back for me, but Sin's legions surrounded us.

"Why didn't Faith and Richard stay back with you?" Victor asks, accusation in his voice. He told them that I was more important than anything else, even their own lives.

"They couldn't," I say. "What we learned was too

important. If they hadn't made it, no one would know about Sin's army."

Victor nods, swallowing his anger, washing it away with reason and sense. "Then tell me about the mountain. The throne. The ash. When I got there with Jeff, I had no idea what I was even looking at or why Sin would take you to a place like that. What did it all mean?"

I'm not ready to go there yet. "It was nothing," I lie. "Just a—"

A thunderous sound echoes around me. The ground beneath my feet begins to tremble.

Victor and I spin toward the commotion. I didn't realize how far we'd wandered. We're standing at the edge of town. People are starting to gather at its center. The door to the doctor's house bursts open and George rushes out with Dr. Jameson and Jeff on his heels. Michael is striving to catch up, but he's still weak from his wounds.

"Come on," Victor says, grabbing my hand.

We run over to where George, Dr. Jameson, Michael, and Jeff are gazing at the growing dust storm in the distance. But what's causing it?

My mind races to Sin and his horde of Day Walkers. The thought of what they would do to the people in this town sends terror through me. Then I realize the car is what must have led them here. It's loud, its lights serving as a beacon in the darkness—

But it isn't Sin. As the four horsemen gallop into town, they stop and let the air settle into stillness around them. The beasts beneath them neigh and paw at the ground.

"Well, boys, it looks like the rumors were true," the obvious leader says. He looks to be in his late twenties. Like him, each of his friends is cloaked in a long coat, chaps, and gloves. "A whole town, somewhere in this godforsaken desert, just waiting to be drained."

Licking his lips, he proudly displays his fangs.

Beside me, Victor tenses and I know he's preparing to attack, to protect these people who gave us shelter.

George drops his large hand on Victor's shoulder. "Don't worry yourself. We can take care of these pests on our own."

He ambles forward with confidence. "Brave man," Victor murmurs, but I know he'll only honor George's request up to a point. He won't stand by while humans die.

"You boys should just head on out," George says. "Ain't no need for any trouble."

"There won't be any trouble," the vampire says, sliding off his horse, his spurs clinking as he lands. Judging by his attire, he was once a cowboy who herded the cattle that now roam free. When a human is turned, he tends to cling to what he was before, even when he lusts for blood. "In fact, we'll be able to take this town real easy."

The others dismount, their rumble of laughter and expectations at easy pickings echoing around them. But something incredible is already beginning to happen.

Rather than running off in fear, the townsfolk are surrounding them. The Lessers look around, unable to hide the strange nervousness they're feeling, obviously unaccustomed to any sign of bravery from humans. They wanted a town with inhabitants afraid of even one pair of fangs, let alone four.

"All right," the leader says, raising his voice in an attempt to calm his troops and intimidate the growing crowd. "The first person to step forward I will personally turn. No more running from vampires. You'll become one."

No takers. Not a single one. Instead, stakes are pulled from belts and boots. I'm impressed by the resolve of the townspeople to protect themselves.

"Last warning, friend," George says, placing his gun on the ground and pulling out a pair of his own metal stakes. "The dust in this town ain't sand. It's vampires. You hear me?"

"Maybe. But it'll all be blood by morning."

"Something's off here," Victor whispers. "I was distracted, didn't notice it before."

"What?" I ask.

Without a word, he pulls a stake from within his duster and steps slowly in front of me. With an Old Family vampire here, I feel better about our odds. Much better.

Michael and Jeff also have stakes in hand. Michael hands me one. I welcome its weight against my palm.

But I can't do anything as the outlaw leader, using his vampire speed, rushes toward an elderly woman. She tries to raise her stake, but the vampire is far too quick. The vamp stands behind her, arm wrapped around her neck, a knife at her throat.

"Don't," Dr. Jameson orders us quietly, but with

determination, and I realize each of us had taken a step forward. "This is our fight."

To my surprise the hostage woman's face is calm, serene, as though the vamp is simply holding her so they can dance. Why isn't she terrified?

"All right then, *friend*," the leader sneers. "We'll take one. Just one. Look at her: she'll be dead in a few weeks anyhow. We'll take her off your hands."

"You might've bitten off more than you can chew, son," George says, a glint of humor in his voice.

"Ha! I haven't done that in a hundred years," he says, the knife beginning to press into the old woman's wrinkled throat.

"That may be, but I can guarantee that you aren't gonna like the taste."

The old woman smiles, her fangs glinting. She opens wide and clamps down viciously on the vampire's arm. Releasing a high-pitched yelp, he backs away, dropping the knife and grabbing his gaping wound. The old woman immediately begins spitting out his blood.

Several townspeople move with such swiftness that the dust whirlpools around them. Only vampires move that fast.

George strikes with identical speed, and three others from the group converge onto the leader. I see the stakes, then they disappear, and I know the vampire is no more. A moment later, a dozen other townsfolk charge toward the other three, a beautifully timed choreography. Surrounded, the intruders scream. Then silence fills the air. When the townspeople step back, they look like petals opening to the sun, and the four vampires who rode into the devil's cavern thinking it was a treasure cove are left in a pile in the middle. Dead. Stakes through their hearts.

Victor didn't move at all but kept his hand on my arm, protecting me from this sudden outburst of violence.

"Don't worry," Dr. Jameson quickly says, approaching us with her hands up in surrender. "We're friends. Please, believe me."

"But . . . but they're vampires," I say. I look over at Jeff and Michael, who are just as still, just as shocked as I am.

"Half the town is, yes."

George asks for water for the elderly woman, and when it arrives, she quickly begins washing the vampire blood from her mouth. They must know of the Thirst and its dangers. Her actions are a preemptive step. A very good one.

"Are you—" I begin.

"I'm human," Dr. Jameson admits. "I'm the representative for all the humans here at Crimson Sands, while George leads the vampires."

"Every house here has two families in it," George says as he wanders over. "Humans, warm in their beds at night, and vampires, asleep underneath those very same beds during the day."

"But George, this morning, we saw you . . ."

"In the sun? Well, I'm a Day Walker. I know you haven't heard of us, but—"

"Believe me, we have," I interrupt. "We've even met your Maker."

"And you're still alive? I'm impressed. Seems like we have some catching up to do, then. Let's get these raiders taken care of first."

Several men make their way over to the bodies of the dead. They carry them off behind a small barn. Not a word is exchanged, just understanding. When the sun rises, more ash will blow through Crimson Sands.

Someone else gathers the horses and leads them toward a corral. People begin to wander back to their homes as though tonight's events were familiar and boring. But Victor stays by my side. If Old Family don't like change, this sudden shift has certainly made him tense.

When finished with his task, George returns to us.

"Come," Dr. Jameson says. "You'll probably want to hear more about our little town."

"That's an understatement," Michael says.

Chapter 3

Once inside the house, fresh coffee is poured for everyone. The four of us just stare at ours, while George and the doctor take alternating sips.

"There isn't much to tell, really," George says. "Vampires, Lessers to be specific, living together with humans. Peacefully."

"How many Day Walkers?" I ask.

"I'm the only one."

"That's why he's such a good leader," Dr. Jameson says. "He can walk between both worlds, as it were. A lot like you, Dawn."

My heart stops. Does she know? Does she know about Sin and the Montgomerys? Does she know that I'm a vampire?

"As a former delegate," she says, after a moment's pause.

"You know both worlds. Right?"

"Yeah," I say a little too quickly, swallowing hard. "Yeah. I know the rules of each."

"The difference is that in those walled cities," George says, "the blood is taken under threat. I know it's always called a donation, but it's pulled out of the veins by fear, nothing else."

"And here?"

"It's also a donation," Dr. Jameson says. "But here, the people *willingly* give it."

"Why?" Michael asks. To him, with his hatred of all things fanged, this must sound very strange.

"Because we recognize the value of our vampire friends," she says. "They protect us at night from the Lessers who would do us harm. In return, we protect them during the day from hunters and scavengers trying to make a quick profit off some vampire fangs."

It's a simple, beautiful system. But . . .

"Blood quota?" I ask, as though a delegate check sheet were right in front of me.

"Never needed it."

"Current blood supply?"

"Overflowing," Dr. Jameson says. "We have more than we need. I have to turn people away."

I think about Denver and its massive infrastructure, the blood banks, the initiatives, the propaganda posters, the thousands of citizens. All of that and we can't come up with enough blood. Yet here, they have plenty.

"We've never had a shortage," George says. "And we've

never had an incident of a vamp taking what doesn't belong to him."

"You mean taking blood straight from the neck," I say.

"That's right. Learning to control our urges took a little time, but now, we couldn't even imagine doing it."

"That's incredible," I say.

He just shrugs. "Out here we're kinda dependent on each other and grateful for one another."

Grateful for one another. I smile at that. I'd love to see that as a poster in Denver. Grateful for each other.

"Have you ever heard of anything like this, Victor?" Jeff asks.

"No," Victor says. "Not since the war anyway. Before that we tried living openly with humans, and you know how well that worked out. A system like this isn't sustainable. Once there are too many humans, or too many vampires, the power will shift."

"I wish you had more confidence in us," Dr. Jameson says. "But does your system of blood quotas and delegates work better?"

Victor turns to George. "So, you know my half brother, Sin."

The change in topic is abrupt, but I know Victor doesn't want to get into a discussion on the difficulties he has in getting donations from the citizens in Denver.

"I'm afraid so," George says. "He turned me back when he was still a young'un. But he's a different man now. I've watched him change before my very eyes."

"Tell us everything," I say.

"I was his second in command," George says. "I was one of the first Day Walkers he ever created, and I was loyal to him for a century, always by his side. I was a fool. I thought what he gave me was a gift. Eternal life. Terrifying strength and speed. But it came at the cost of taking blood from my fellow man."

He sips his brew, and we all stay silent, waiting for him to continue.

"I watched the madness slowly grow inside of Sin. He always felt like an outcast, and in many ways I suppose he was. He tried to reconcile with other Old Family, but they were all just like your father, Victor. They saw him as a freak of nature. The anger in his heart fueled him. He fed off human blood just as much as he fed off his hatred for the Old Families, for the vampires that turned him away."

"I should have looked for him decades ago," Victor says. "If I had, maybe I could have found him, reasoned with him. Stopped him from becoming a monster."

But George just shakes his head.

"There was no reasoning with him. He was born to hate. It's in his blood. And it only intensified once he controlled Los Angeles. I helped him. I stood by as he slowly turned the city of angels into a city of Day Walkers. I thought that would be enough for him. But I was wrong.

"He sent me out on a scouting expedition, searching for humans he could 'bless' as he called it, but I'd had enough. The farther I traveled, the less I wanted to go back. Then I discovered these folks and they welcomed me like I was one of their own. Before I was turned, I was a soldier protecting people. Returned to my calling here."

"But where does it end for Sin?" Jeff asks.

George doesn't look us in the eyes but instead takes another sip of his coffee, adjusts his hat that needs no adjusting.

"Complete domination of humans and vampires alike, with what he calls the Chosen leading the way," he says. "Handpicked Day Walkers, the best and most loyal, and he infects them with the Thirst."

I instantly think of Brady. That's what he became; it's what Sin turned him into. All traces of the brother I had once loved were lost within those blackened eyes.

"His goal is to have five hundred of them," George continues. "From there, he'll take them, along with every Day Walker, and march. Nothing will be able to stop him at that point."

"How can he possibly control these 'Chosen'?" Victor asks. "I've fought one before. It nearly killed me, and that was only one. Sin talks of hundreds? They'll overwhelm him."

"That's what I told him." George sighs heavily. "But he didn't seem bothered. His last words to me before I left were: 'Of course it's impossible, in my current form. But I have only begun.'"

I cringe as I remember Sin's teeth sinking into the neck of my ancestor, Octavian Montgomery. Sin knew what he was doing. Sin wants to be taken over by—

"The Thirst," I say. "Sin wants to become one of the Infected."

"Why would you think that?" Victor asks.

"We saw him drain an Old Family vamp," Michael says. "He seemed to think Old Family blood held the key to making him invincible."

Victor jerks his head around to stare at me, a clear question in his eyes: *Is that what happened in the cave?*

I give him a small nod. I can admit to that much, but the rest of it—

Not yet.

"Is it even possible for Old Family to become Infected?" I ask Victor.

"I don't know," he confesses. "I simply don't know."

"The real question," Jeff says, "is how long do we have? You said Sin wants five hundred of these Chosen before he moves out, right? Well, how many does he have? And how long will it take until he's ready? Months? Years?"

"Less time than that," I say. Sin told me that Brady was his perfect creation, so his plan to have an Infected army hasn't been in the works that long. But still . . . "Much less time." I measure my words carefully, watching Victor as I drop this bombshell: "Sin showed us his V-Process facility, the one buried beneath Los Angeles."

"Impossible!" Victor insists. "I personally destroyed them all after the war."

"Yeah, well," Michael says, disgust apparent in his tone, "you did a lousy job because Sin took us on the grand tour. It was horrible, but Dawn hasn't told you the worst part. In addition to using it as a quick way to turn humans into vampires, he's turning Day Walkers into the Infected. Five hundred of them? He'll have that in no time now."

Victor's stare grows cold. "We have to tear it apart," he says firmly. "Before we return to Denver."

"Don't you get it?" Michael asks. "All the citizens within the inner ring of Los Angeles are Day Walkers. They're protecting it. We'd never survive long enough to get to it."

Victor spins away from us, an angry flash, and I know guilt is gnawing at him. "We can't leave it standing so Sin can create more monsters."

"I agree, but we've only got enough gasoline to get us back to Denver," Jeff says reasonably. "It seems to me that our best plan is to get our butts back home, regroup, and figure out how we're going to stop Sin."

Victor gazes out the window. The sky is beginning to lighten. Soon it'll be daybreak. He'll have to retreat into the shadows.

Finally, he turns to face us. "You're right. Going to Los Angeles right now isn't the answer."

"I'm not comfortable heading out until the sun sets again," Jeff says. "If we get jumped by Sin or his Day Walkers, I want to make sure Victor can help us."

I can tell that Victor is anxious to get on the road, but he also recognizes the wisdom of Jeff's plan. He nods.

"You can stay in that back room," Dr. Jameson says to Victor. "It's angled so the sun can't get in."

"You are very kind," he says.

"I'm going to check on the car," Jeff says.

"I'll help you," Michael offers. As he's heading for the door, Victor pulls Michael aside quickly.

"Thank you," Victor says.

Michael comes up short. "For what?"

"For going back to protect Dawn in Los Angeles. She told me—"

"It's my job."

"You *made* it your job."

I think about Michael jumping off the train as it was leaving Los Angeles. He was seconds away from being free. Instead, he leapt into a swarm of vampires for me, knowing that he would probably die.

Victor's right. Michael didn't have to do anything. But he *chose* to. And that makes all the difference.

"Yeah, well," Michael says, "just know if you ever hurt her, I'll stake you."

"If I ever hurt her, I'd want you to."

I can tell that Michael doesn't know what to say to that. I don't either. Vampires aren't supposed to feel emotions, aren't supposed to love, but from the beginning I've known that Victor isn't an ordinary vampire.

After they've left, I pull Victor into the room without windows, the place where Michael and I slept on separate cots. But Victor and I lie together on the one farthest from the doorway, where the sunlight stops as though it knows it's not welcome in this tiny space. I can hear Dr. Jameson and George moving around, helping to get things ready for our departure.

Victor cradles my face, looks deeply into my eyes. I see the sadness and guilt in his. "He told you, didn't he? Sin told you everything about the V-Process."

I nod slowly. "The Victor Process. It was your creation."

"You have to understand, Dawn, at each city we conquered, the citizens were given a choice, turn or be killed. Immortality as a slave or death now. Most chose to be turned. The V-Process made it merciful and quick. But I came to regret it. So many Lessers were turned, more than we could expect a human population to sustain. It's the reason people were herded into cities, walled in. So we could control our blood supply and stop our Lessers from rising up."

"But how could you have thought this was a good idea for humans?"

"I saved millions."

"You turned them."

"They would have been slaughtered, Dawn."

"Look at what you've sown, Victor. If there weren't so many vampires, we wouldn't have a blood shortage. There wouldn't be the Thirst!"

"I had to," he says, containing his frustrations. "Humans were to be killed en masse. Women, children, men. The end goal, Dawn, was a world of a few thousand humans. That's all. A few *thousand*. That's all we needed to sustain a blood farm, to keep the Old Family vampires fed. Our armies of Lessers would starve until they were too weak to defend themselves, and then we would kill them too—their task complete."

"How did you convince them to change their plans?"

"By lying," Victor says. "I told them that the humans were too strong, putting up too much of a resistance. I told them that the easiest way to increase our numbers was by turning humans into vampires against their will. I . . . I preyed on your species' fear of death, how closely it clutches its precious, fragile life. I knew that given the choice between death and immortality, people would choose immortality, no matter what strings were attached. When the war hadn't yet reached a city, when the citizens saw it on television, they could hold high ideals and say, 'No! I would never convert! I will never be a vampire.' But when the walls fall down and we're marching through the streets and their families are taken away, crying and scared, that's when humans finally give in. It's inevitable."

Does he think this way about me? That I'm so easily broken?

"You're wrong," I say. "We humans are destined to die, which means we're willing to do it for a cause."

"I know," he says. "I couldn't stand by and watch everyone throw their lives away, because I know how short they are, and that makes each moment, each human heartbeat so precious. Without the V-Process, the war would have lasted decades longer, maybe centuries as we hunted down the remaining humans. By turning many, I saved so many more. The war was shortened, and lives were spared. You have to believe me, Dawn."

What is there to say? I do believe him. He always said he felt like a monster, and I see why now: because his grand scheme turned millions. But it was all for one purpose: to save as many humans as possible. Would I have done any different?

"What about your father?" I ask. "What did he think of your plans?"

"Oh, Father loved them. I found a way for us to achieve complete vampire domination easily and quickly. It sickens me now to think that I ever did anything to make him proud. He hated humans."

"Why?"

"Like most vampires, he could never find beauty in the world. He never saw the splendor of a flower or the wonder of a single shooting star. With his many years of living, these things were nothing more than facts and phenomena. Whenever he saw a human gazing up at the sky or holding a handful of sand, contemplating the aeons it took to whittle the stone down to these grains, he grew envious. Without beauty, he could live forever and never really live at all."

"And you, Victor, do you see beauty in this world?"

"I spent my whole life looking for it. But I never expected to find it. I especially didn't expect to find it trapped in a trolley car on a bad night after going to a party."

I smile with the bittersweet memory. I was the one cornered by starving vampires in a trolley car on a bad night after going to a party. That was the first time he rescued me. I know he isn't a monster, no matter what else happens or happened in his life.

I remember he once told me that he had created the world around us. I place my hand over his heart, am aware of its steady thumping. "You're not responsible for this world, Victor. Humans, vampires, we all had a role in creating it. And even after everything I've learned, you showed me that not all vampires are monsters. And that's so important." I feel tears burning my eyes and I blink them back. "More than you realize."

He strokes his thumb over my cheek. "What else happened in that damn mountain, Dawn? Is it the one you were dreaming about?"

Nodding, I bury my face against his chest, not ready to deal with that reality. He pulls me in close, holds me tightly. I inhale his spicy scent, absorb his warmth, draw strength from his comfort. I can't believe that while we were apart, visiting each other through dreams, I had considered they might prove a way for us to be together. Nothing is better than his solid form holding me near, nothing can beat his actual presence.

"Dawn . . ."

I'm still not ready. I may never be. Besides, Victor and I have bigger problems facing us now. Sin's army marching across the plains and deserts, destroying cities in its path, has nothing to do with what he told me in that mountain. What I saw there, what I learned, can wait.

Or maybe I'm just scared of what Victor will say.

"Just what Michael told everyone."

Victor brushes my cheek again, maybe knowing that I'm lying but not willing to push.

"What do you know about the vampire Sin drank from?" he asks.

I shrug. "Not much. His name was Octavian. He was Old Family. And ancient."

"Why do I get the sense that you're not telling me everything?"

I snuggle closer to him. "I'm tired."

"I won't push you, Dawn, but I want you to know that there isn't anything you can't tell me."

Maybe so, but there are some things that I'm not ready to tell him, because once the words are spoken, I won't be able to take them back.

Chapter 4

Victor is eventually pulled into sleep. I know how difficult it is for vampires to stay awake during the day. It's one of their vulnerabilities.

Once the sun is high and I hear more activity going on beyond the building, I decide to do a little exploring. Now that I know the truth of it, I want to observe this fascinating town more closely.

Outside, Jeff is going over the car again with one of Crimson Sands's citizens. He's wearing a plaid shirt, covered with dust and oil, his hands deep within the car's engine searching for something.

"Hey," Jeff says to me. "Michael is around back, looking at the windmill. He wanted to see you when you got up."

"Thanks. Is the car okay?"

"No problem. Just tightening a few screws."

He smiles. He looks so natural here. Maybe I can bring a little bit of that back with us.

The windmill is easy enough to find, and when I approach it, I'm surprised by how large the housing is. It whooshes with an oddly beautiful sound, a music made by man but composed by nature. Inside, the wooden slats are separated enough to let through beams of light. Standing beside a woman in overalls, Michael watches the turning gears and cylinders.

"All the water comes from here," she says, her hair tied in a handkerchief to keep it away from her eyes. "We pump it up from the ground."

Michael shakes his head in astonishment.

"It's really something else," I say, wandering over.

"You can say that again," he says. "This is Laura. She's been giving me the grand tour. And look."

He points upward at the complex machinery. Massive wooden gears, creaking and moaning, turn as the wind blows, compelling other gears to shift and wooden pistons to move. It's amazing.

"Couldn't have done it without our vamps," Laura says. "No way we could lift these things up, but we carved it during the day, and at night Charles, our vamp mechanic, was able to place them with a little help."

"You would have had to build an entire machine just to build this one," Michael says.

The woman nods. "Yup. But not with the vamps

around. We all donated a little extra blood to show our appreciation, had a small party at night once the water started pumping."

The gears mesh together and turn. I envision the human and vampire hands that crafted them also turning together, changing things for the better. So that all might live.

Later, we go to the donation site. A clean, sterile room, in a building separate from the infirmary. Dr. Jameson is inside, and so are *ten* other people! Ten! In a city of thousands like Denver, we're lucky if we can pull five a day.

"Is it always this crowded?" I ask her, somewhat in jest.

"Usually we have three to four."

"But after last night," a boy says, needle in his arm, bag filling with his blood, "we all wanted to chip in extra."

"You mean the raiders?"

"Yeah," says the man sitting beside the boy. "It isn't the first time our vamps have saved our butts."

"And it won't be the last," another chimes in. "And if any vampire hunters are thinking about coming this way, they'll have to deal with us first. No one messes with us."

Us. Humans and vampires.

For the rest of the day we walk through the town, including the classroom where the kids are taught and the tiny workshop where scraps are made into things that keep the place running.

"It's amazing," I say to Michael as we sit on a bench, drinking lemonade that a freckle-faced girl with braids brought us. "Just amazing."

He nods. "I thought Los Angeles had it figured out, you know? With the walls and how no one bowed down to Lord Carrollton. But it was just an illusion. They were all Day Walkers in the Inner Ring, helpless humans in the Outer. But this place is doing it right."

I wish Mom and Dad could see it. This is the kind of world they wanted but never had a chance to see.

It's late afternoon when I return to where Victor is sleeping. I want to get in a few hours of rest before we leave. When I burrow in against his side, his arm comes around me and I drift off.

When I wake up, the room is still shadowed and I watch the sunlight slowly arc across the floor, turning from yellow to orange to something even darker, as if fighting the night itself. It's a losing battle of course.

I find that this is the moment I've always loved, the turning of the earth, the setting of the sun, the precipice between day and night. It feels like infinite moments and possibilities are in those last drops of sun color. When I was a little girl, I'd watch the sun from my balcony until my mom got tired of calling my name and pulled me inside. It felt like she was tearing me away from some great secret, some holy excitement.

Victor is behind me now, his arms wrapped around me, his hands just above my own. Doesn't this mean something, the fact that we can lie in complete silence and enjoy every second of it? There is more truth in this silence than in hours of discussion with a stranger.

I close my eyes, fantasizing about Crimson Sands and making my life here with Victor. Why not? They've made it work; they've even thrived. Why not us? They'd be glad to have a vampire as powerful as Victor, lucky to have such a terrifying presence on their side, watching over them. And I have extensive knowledge of vampires, more than most will possess in several lifetimes. After all, it's supposedly in my blood.

We would build our own house, and in that house we could be like this every night, watching the sun slowly descend, its rays a beautiful theater for us to enjoy. And the sound of rare desert rains on our roof, the feel of it on our skin . . .

I want that so badly that it hurts sometimes, because it can never be. Not with Sin so close.

I can't put into words the anger I feel toward that monster. He took Brady, he killed my parents. Now he's taking my future. This new war has just begun, and I'm on the front lines with no guarantee I'll make it back. There's even less of a guarantee that *all* those I love will survive.

Those are the infinite possibilities in the sun painting across the floor, slowly disappearing from sight. The possibilities of victory over Sin. The possibilities of death for all of us. It's real and tangible now, and as Victor squeezes me, I know he's realizing the same thing. This moment, so precious and rare, must be enjoyed because it may never happen again. Once we step outside, once we go to Denver, what awaits us?

The sunlight disappears and softer light takes its place,

the glow provided by the kerosene lamps in the house.

"I like it here," I say quietly.

"Maybe we'll come back someday," Victor says.

"They're an example of how humans and vampires can live together. We can learn from them, Victor."

"The lessons will have to wait until we've dealt with Sin."

Rolling off the cot, Victor takes my hand and pulls me to my feet. He touches my cheek, gazes into my eyes. "I'll do everything I can to give you the kind of world you dream of."

Before I can respond, he's walking from the room. I'm not sure what I would have said. His words have left me speechless.

Outside, Michael and Jeff are waiting by the car. Dr. Jameson and George are on the porch.

"Here's some food for your trip," Dr. Jameson says, handing me a box. Inside, I can see some fruits and vegetables. And a bag of blood.

"Thank you," I say. "We really appreciate your kindness."

"Well, you certainly brought some excitement to our town," George says.

"Sin might bring more," I warn them. "Day Walkers, the Infected."

"We're already preparing," he assures me, gesturing with his head toward the edge of town. I turn to see several men laying down the first boulders of what will become a wall.

Sadness sweeps through me. I long for a world that needs no walls.

"Thank you so much for everything," I say again, not certain I can ever thank them enough. "I'll think about you often."

"Oh, don't get mushy now and say things you don't mean."

"But I do mean it," I say with conviction. "More than you'll ever realize. This place . . . it's the beginning."

"Of what?" Dr. Jameson asks.

"Of a new world."

Chapter 5

We head off into twilight, Victor confident at the wheel. With a vampire's reflexes, Victor is able to push the speed until it climbs over a hundred miles an hour. Jeff and Michael are sleeping in the back. Every now and then I can hear one of them snore.

"You're awfully quiet," Victor says. "What are you thinking about?"

"The darkness," I say. "And how I used to be so afraid of it." Because it brought out the monsters.

"And now?"

I shake my head. "Now I feel safe in it. I was trapped in that closet for so long, hearing Brady's screams when he was taken from me. He didn't want me to be afraid of the dark. It took years, but now I'm not."

Victor puts his hand on my leg and I feel his warmth.

"I've been thinking about your brother a lot," Victor says, and it catches me off guard. Sin turned Brady into a vampire, but he refused to drink human blood. He became infected with the Thirst. Is he going to talk about the monster that Brady became, how Brady attacked him and we had to kill him? "All I see are his eyes, and that little sparkle of humanity still in them."

My throat tightens with unshed tears.

"That tiny part of Brady was the one that saw you, Dawn. It was the part that gives you strength to this day. And it was the part that finally surrendered, knowing it was all so that you could carry on and make this world a better place."

I remember my hands, and Victor's, holding the stake over Brady's heart. Pressing down was the hardest thing I ever did. But it was the only way to free him. He hated what he'd become.

I turn to the landscape passing by almost as a blur. Yellow desert made gray by the moonlight, patches of blackened craters where the bombs fell years ago, our attempts to eradicate the vampires from above, to do what the sun hadn't. Now they're simply reminders of our failings, our reliance on technology and its inability to defeat the creatures older than us, creatures who were already at their prime during our infancy.

No one knows, not even the vampires themselves I imagine, how they came to be. But they've always drawn power from their immortality. What would take generations of mortals to learn and remember could be done so easily by their fanged counterparts.

The desert stretches forever, low-lying hills and mountains far off in the distance, so far they seem completely unreachable. I imagine walking toward them, only to always find them out of reach, just over the next ridge, just beyond the horizon, always *just* far enough away to hold their majesty.

So much like the vampire next to me. *Victor. How far away you always seem. Even when we're close, parts of your heart are shielded, secrets held that were never meant to be revealed. Will you ever give in to me totally? Is that even possible with a vampire, with an Old Family who has seen the world change for hundreds of years?*

After an hour of driving I sense Victor looking out suspiciously, his eyes darting back and forth, perhaps guided not only by sights but sounds I can't detect.

"What is it?" I ask.

"The Infected. In the distance over there," he says slowly, pointing across the desert.

I see sharp movements, violent and quick, running and bounding across the dunes. Gray and brown figures, wrapped in tattered cloth.

"I can't believe they're so far out," I say.

"I didn't know it was this bad," Victor confesses. "I thought we had more time."

It's like a tsunami that started in Los Angeles years ago, finally toppling Lord Carrollton, and is now moving across the country, heading east.

"Richard's father, Lord Carrollton, he's dead," I say quietly.

Victor curses beneath his breath.

"We went to his mansion. It was falling apart, but inside were so many Infected. They came after us. Richard drove like a demon out of hell and we barely escaped."

"Richard loved Los Angeles. He must hate what Sin has done to it."

"They should be in Denver by now, shouldn't they?"

He wraps his hand around mine. "They're fine. I would know if Faith was dead."

"How?"

"I'd sense it, but I don't."

"Speaking of sensing things, how did you know where to look for me in the mountains? How did you know I was in danger?"

He shakes his head. "I don't know. I just knew. It was like you were calling to me. Maybe I saw your dreams of the mountain through my own eyes one night, and I'd simply forgotten. But when I was there, I traced my hands along the wall, just as you told me you had, and I *knew* exactly where I was going."

"There's so much about the vampire world I don't understand."

"Even *we* don't understand it all."

Looking back out the window, I try not to think about my possible vampire heritage and how—if it's true—it will change everything, like a massive earthquake centered beneath my life. What will remain standing once it passes? Will it even be recognizable?

Even though Victor pushes the car as fast as he can, he can't outrun the sun. The car's windows are tinted, so the sunrise doesn't hurt him, but he's noticeably uncomfortable and has slowed down considerably. His vampire eyesight must be diminished even in the gentle predawn light.

As the sky begins to lighten, I can see the massive wall that surrounds Denver in the distance. I know we won't get there ahead of daybreak.

The gates into Denver are closed. They used to open when the sun rose, but that was before we knew about Day Walkers, before Sin came to our city at the behest of his father, Lord Murdoch Valentine. We thought he was a new student at our school. We befriended him.

"Jeff, are you close enough to get cell reception?" Victor asks. "I'd rather not lower these windows at the guard station to go through an inspection."

The city has one cell tower, located in its center. Its range is limited, its service sporadic.

"I'll give it a shot," Jeff says, pulling out his cell phone. He presses a button, waits—

"Clive, hey. We're about two minutes from the gate—yes, we've got Dawn and Michael. They're safe. . . . Great! I'll let them know." He moves the phone away from his ear. "The others arrived safely on the Night Train last night."

"Oh, thank God!" I feel like I'm floating up as a heavy weight lifts from my chest.

"Yeah, so listen," Jeff continues into the phone. "Victor's driving. Need you to alert the guards to wave us through . . . Okay, good. We'll see you soon." He hangs up. "We should be good to go."

The gate rises and a guard lets us pass without any trouble. Victor continues on to the more populated part of Denver. The center of the city. The rebuilding efforts began there, and they haven't quite reached the wall yet. Ten years since the war ended, and recovery is slow. But then with Murdoch Valentine ruling over us, we had little optimism or hope. Life under Victor will be different. Having seen Crimson Sands, I think by working together we can right all the wrongs of his father.

Jeff makes another call. "Hey, Rachel. We're back in the city. Dawn's with me, babe. She's okay. So is Michael. We're going to the Agency first and then I'll bring her to the apartment. . . . Yeah, okay. Hold on." He extends the phone to me. "Rachel wants a word."

"*A* word? I bet she wants more than that."

Jeff grins.

I take the phone and press it to my ear. "Hey, Rachel."

"Dawn, oh God, it's so good to hear your voice."

"Yours too."

"I'm going to head to the Agency—"

"No, wait. I don't think we'll be there that long. I'm really dirty, tired, and hungry. I just want to come home. But I want to see Tegan. Can you track her down?"

"I'll take care of it."

"Thanks, Rachel."

"Just know that you are never again leaving this city."

"I hear you." But I can't promise her that I won't leave. I don't know where fighting Sin might take us, and I still feel Crimson Sands calling to me.

We say goodbye and I hand the phone back to Jeff.

Victor slows the car to a crawl, not hindered by other vehicles but by people walking the streets, heading to work and school. I realize how little I've thought about my homework and tests and assignments. I'm not even sure if I'm still enrolled. Although it hardly matters. I've learned plenty of lessons out here.

In Los Angeles everything sparkled, but it was all fake. Here the buildings are drab, but I can see the sweat that was poured into each brick laid. Store windows display merchandise and signs written by hand. There's an authenticity to it and evidence of creativity. Michael eases up from the back.

"I didn't think anything would ever look so welcoming," he says.

"I'll be glad to be home."

"Words I never thought I'd agree with. I wanted to leave so bad." He thought things would be better away from Denver.

"We always think life will have more to offer somewhere else," Jeff says. "Sometimes leaving is the only way to appreciate what we have."

We pass by the massive Works, a series of buildings and

generators that provide lights to the city but also give it a dark foreboding feel as the smoke from the burning coal coats everything in soot. Then I see the Agency building with its glass and steel. It's the tallest and most pristine element in the city.

Victor enters the underground parking garage and pulls quickly into a vacant spot. The Agency has cars, but few others do. Gas is scarce. And there are no longer automobile factories. We just have to keep repairing what we have—which is the way of a lot of things these days.

We step out of the car into the well-lit concrete structure. We all walk to the elevator and ride it straight to the top. When the doors open, we're quickly whisked past the single receptionist and into the director's office. The large window that encompasses an entire wall, normally providing a perfect view of the city, is covered by thick blinds. No sunlight peeks through—in preparation for our arrival.

A few dim lights on the walls allow me to see the director. Clive looks as if he's aged ten years since I last saw him. He has less hair, his wrinkles have deepened, his tweed jacket drapes over his torso as though he's lost weight. He's always looked like a man who shouldered responsibility until it bent him physically, but now it looks like his back is broken.

"I'm so glad you're safe," he says. "You have no idea—"

"I do," I say. "It looks like you haven't slept since I left."

"Not a lot, no. I started second guessing my decision to send you, but when the others got back last night and told me what was going on in Los Angeles . . ." He shakes his head. "I fought alongside Matheson during the war, comrades in arms. I can't believe he'd allow himself to be turned by Sin."

Matheson was the Agency director in Los Angeles.

"I don't know if I can blame him," I tell Clive. "The alternative wasn't very pretty. The humans along the outer wall live a miserable existence."

"Given the choice between a miserable existence as a human or becoming a vampire, which would you choose?" he asks.

I don't say anything. The choice may no longer be mine. I may already be a vampire.

"That's what I thought," Clive says, misreading my silence. "Nothing would cause you to be turned. So I can blame him." He clears his throat, and I can tell that while he might not understand Matheson's choice, he still mourns his friend. "Although losing the Night Train in Los Angeles has been a blow, I have to admit I'm grateful that Ian is in Denver to offer his unique perspective on things."

The Night Train is the only mass mode of transportation allowed by VampHu. One train that services all the cities.

I glance over as Ian Hightower approaches. A legendary vampire hunter, he guards the Night Train. Or at least he did before everything except its engine got left in Los Angeles. Much like Clive, he seems to have aged years overnight. He's wearing different clothes, his others surely covered in ash from the furnace of the engine as it howled across the lonely stretches of isolated desert. But his eyes hold the same scars of a hunter's life, maybe even a few more after what happened in Los Angeles.

"I thought you were a goner," he says.

"Me too."

"I would've stopped the train and gone back, but I had to think about the others, and I thought you'd want me to protect them."

"You did the right thing," I say, meaning every word of it.

I hug him. He's resistant at first, upright and tight, his body stiff and cold, like it hasn't felt a soft touch in years. After a moment, he puts his arms around me. They are strong. Like my father's were.

When he releases me, Jeff and Michael move in to shake his hand. I glance over to the corner. Huddling together like the cool clique at school are the vampires: Victor, Richard, and Faith. Even when we're all together, there's a distance, a knowledge that they are different from the others. They look the same, more polished and beautiful maybe, but still human in appearance. Their hearts beat, blood runs through them, but that blood is so different, and they need our blood to sustain them.

I approach and Richard steps forward, circling me within his sturdy arms. He almost smells as good as Victor.

"I'm glad you're okay," he says. "We wanted to go back—"

"I wouldn't have been happy if you'd returned for me," I interrupt him.

He smiles. "As you well know, I live to please the ladies."

Faith growls. I think he flirts with me to tease her or maybe just to get her attention. It's always been obvious to me that he has strong feelings for her, but she maintains that vampires can't love. Although considering that her father was one of the most ruthless vampires to ever exist, I suspect she knows very little about the gentler emotions.

She stares at me, trying to decide what to do. So I give her a little help and open my arms. She flicks back her red hair, as if to say what the hell, and steps into my embrace.

"Victor would have never forgiven me if something happened to you. I never would've forgiven myself."

"You're sweet when you mean to be."

"I know. I should really stop."

She withdraws with a smile.

"So what are you two doing here?" I ask. "I figured you'd be at Valentine Manor."

Richard exchanges a glance with Victor, before looking over at Clive. "We were strategizing how best to handle things until Victor's return. Now that we know Sin has an army of Day Walkers—"

"It's worse than that," Victor says.

"How could it be worse?" Clive asks.

"He's using a V-Processing center to not only create *more* Day Walkers but to infect them with the Thirst," I say.

"What does he hope to accomplish?" Ian asks.

"He's creating an unstoppable force," Richard answers. Victor once told me Richard was good at strategy, so I'm not surprised he sees the potential of Sin's scheme. "He doesn't just want to control humans, he wants to control vampires."

"Exactly," Victor admits. "We learned that Sin has every intention of marching across this continent."

"With each city that would fall, he would gain more soldiers, more power," Ian says. "It's how the vampires won the war against us. There's no reason the strategy won't work again."

"So what's our next step?" Clive asks.

Right now, vampires and humans don't seem to exist; the line has been erased. In this room, it's *us* versus Sin.

"We need to go to the Vampire Council," Victor says. "We need to warn the Old Families. But more than that, we need to convince them we're at war against an enemy they've never imagined. They can mobilize and destroy the V-Processing center in Los Angeles; it's the heart of Sin's entire operation. It'll slow down his acquisition of Day Walkers and converting them to the Infected."

"Do you really think they'll listen?" Clive asks. "I've heard the Vampire Council is a collection of stubborn old fangs."

"Unfortunately, Director, you're correct," Victor says. "That's the reason we'll need Dawn to come with Richard, Faith, and me."

My heart stops, and I feel the warmth heating my cheeks. It's nerves. Very bad nerves. I always knew this was big, that Sin's plans were real and potent. But Victor wanting to take me to New Vampiria, to see the Vampire Council, suddenly brings home the enormity of all that is at risk.

"I'm not sure why Dawn needs to go with you," Clive says.

"Because of what she saw and learned from Sin. A report coming from her directly will carry more weight. She was in the V-Processing center, she saw it for herself. The Council is full of ancient vampires who believe the Thirst is a myth."

"Dawn, we just got you back," Clive says. "How do you feel about this?"

"I need to go, Clive. I want to go."

He sighs. I know he's not happy, but I also know he won't stop me.

"Well, the one piece of good news I have," Clive says, "is that Eris and her Day Walkers haven't been seen since you left. Maybe she's waiting for the right moment, but for now we can all breathe a little easier."

Eris came into Denver in a white carriage, walked straight up to the Agency in the bright sun, and requested I surrender myself to Sin. At the time we didn't understand. Now I see why: He wanted to reveal my past to me; he wanted to give me the chance to face the New World Order by his side. When I left on the Night Train, I thought I was protecting myself and my city. Instead, I ended up falling right into Sin's hands.

"Why do I have a feeling there's bad news?" Victor asks.

Clive clears his throat. "Blood donations are down."

"How much?"

"Nonexistent."

I see a flash of anger in Victor's eyes, and I understand his reaction. He wanted to be different from his father; he wanted to gain blood through peace not threats. But the second he leaves, suddenly there's no blood.

"Why not?" he growls.

"Hursch isn't encouraging anyone. That goes against his duties as the delegate. No one knows that better than Dawn. I think you should replace Hursch with someone more competent, someone who believes in what they do and understands the value of increasing the blood supply."

"I think delegates have outlasted their usefulness," Victor says. "I already have a plan in mind for getting more blood donations."

Oh, no, the microchipping. During one of our shared dreams, Victor told me he was considering it. When he saw how bad things were, how little blood was being given. *No, Victor, please, not here, not now.*

The door flies open and in strides Roland Hursch. I'm surprised his own slime hasn't stained his expensive gray suit or his perfectly styled hair. He spoke out publicly against me being a delegate every chance he got and now that he's finally got the job, he's making a complete mess of it.

"Unbelievable!" he shouts. "You should have informed me the moment Victor arrived."

"That's Lord Valentine," Victor reminds him with a stern voice that would be foolish to challenge.

Hursch gives a smile and mocking bow. "Of course, *Lord* Valentine. Why am I the last to know about his visit? Why are there other Old Family vampires in the Agency?"

Clive rubs his eyes, maybe wishing this would all just go away.

"Roland—" Clive begins, opening his eyes.

"That's Mr. Hursch."

Clive sighs. "*Mr.* Hursch. Perhaps now isn't the best time."

"He's come into our city and our agency. I demand a meeting with him right now."

Clive holds up his hands in an attempt to calm down his belligerent delegate. "Fine. Perhaps you are right. Faith, Richard, if you will be so kind as to wait outside."

"In the parking garage!" Hursch shouts. "Vampire ears are a little too keen."

Faith is about to protest when Victor gives her a sharp look and confirming nod. She shoots him a glare that says, "I'll do it, but I won't like it." Then she and Richard leave.

"Michael, Jeff, Ian. Could you three go speak with the head guardsman downstairs? I believe you may be able to give him advice on how to tighten the city's security." It's a ridiculous task, but Clive shows his diplomacy by not simply dismissing them.

"Dawn can go as well," Hursch says.

"She stays!" Victor and Clive declare simultaneously.

"Okay, then, Mr. Hursch," Clive says. "You have the floor."

"Thank you, Director," Hursch says, turning toward Victor. "One Old Family vampire in the city I understand; exceptions must be made. But three? And you wonder why no one donates blood? You remind them, with these reckless actions, that you have no respect for our walls or the citizens they house. It's an outrage! Why are you even here?"

"To discuss the actions I am taking in order to maintain a steady blood supply."

"Blood supply? We discuss that at the manor each week."

"I will be leaving for several days, Mr. Hursch, and as I find you unable to carry out my wishes, I am here now to discuss them."

Hursch seems to consider for a moment but can't think of the right response. Victor puts his hands behind his back and begins pacing, circling Hursch in the same way a shark might circle its prey.

"Your agency will be embedding microchips into one hundred citizens: young, healthy, and disease-free. I will provide these chips."

"Where will you get them?" Hursch asks, trying to keep his composure but losing it every time Victor comes nearer.

"Prewar technology; I've had them for years, though I never imagined using them. Then again, I never imagined dealing with such an incompetent delegate." Hursch swallows hard, perhaps expecting to be thrown against the wall for his arrogance, something I've seen Victor do before. "These chips will allow me to track the citizens and determine if they have given blood within the past four weeks. If they have not, I will send in my Lessers to take it through an IV."

"You can't do that."

"Watch me!" Victor yells, and Hursch cringes, his eyes only opening after Victor has walked away. "After several months, we will increase the number of citizens being microchipped to five hundred, and then one thousand, with the end goal of two thousand citizens giving regularly. In this way, my Lessers are fed, the Thirst is staved off, and everyone is happy."

He rejoins me, and even though he's still the Victor I love, his speech reminds me harshly that we'll never be able to see things quite the same. At the end of the day, he's a vampire overlord in charge of feeding his vampires, and even if vampiric blood runs in my own veins, I've spent my whole life with humans, and to me they'll always be people before blood sources.

I want to tell Victor that this isn't the way to do it, but I can't undermine his authority in front of Hursch.

"I expect to have a list of three hundred potential candidates by tomorrow," Victor says.

"It can't happen," Hursch responds. "I won't let it."

"Mr. Hursch," Clive says.

"You walk in here and—"

"Mr. Hursch."

"Make demands so impossible that—"

"Mr. Hursch!" Clive shouts so loudly that even I jump. "You may write a report as to your opinion on these matters and present it to me tomorrow morning."

"But—"

"Until then, you may leave."

Hursch looks at all of us with unbelievable contempt before turning on his heels and storming out, making sure the door slams extra hard on the way out.

After a few moments pass and we know Hursch won't be returning, Clive spins toward Victor. "Are you serious, Lord Valentine?"

"Very."

Clive nods, perhaps in understanding of Victor's position. It isn't far from his own as director. Protect those for whom you are responsible, at all costs.

"As you can imagine, I dislike this microchipping idea," he says. "It will spread fear and resentment. Vampires swooping in and taking blood, even if by IV, will recall memories of the war."

Reaching out, I take Victor's hand. He looks at me, and in his eyes, I see determination. He's thinking of his Lessers, but we all need to think of everyone. "You promised me the world I dreamed of. This isn't it."

"I'm sorry, Dawn, but at this moment, I see no alternative."

Clive clears his throat. "We have a special blood

reserve," he confesses. "No one else knows about it, not even you, Dawn. And especially not Hursch."

I'm a little offended, but maybe it was for the best. Delegates shouldn't know that an easy solution is right around the corner; that way they negotiate harder.

"It's two weeks' worth of blood," he says. "Once it's gone, it's gone for good and we will be bone dry. But if I release the reserve, will you reconsider this plan of yours?"

Victor stands still, not saying a word, only thinking. After a few tense moments, he agrees. "Yes. But donations must begin again."

"We are trying," Clive assures him. "Believe me."

"I do. With the blood situation temporarily under control, we can leave for New Vampiria tonight. I'm sorry it's such short notice, but time is no longer on our side."

"I understand. Meanwhile, we have an inner room where those of you allergic to sunlight can stay until nightfall. If you'll gather Richard and Faith with you, I'm sure they'd appreciate it more than a parking garage."

"I'm sure they would," Victor says.

As much as I'd like to stay with him, I know I have a lot to do to get ready for this trip to the Vampire Council. And a guardian to persuade.

Victor touches my hand. "We'll be outside your apartment a few minutes after dark. Be ready."

"Is there anything special I need to pack?"

"Something conservative to wear when you meet the Council members."

"Not the corset and Victorian garb I wore for your father?" It took hours to get dressed.

He grins. "No. A dark suit should be fine."

I'd love to give him a kiss, even just a tiny peck, but not with Clive here. I have to show him that I'm following Victor not because I love him, but because we're doing the right thing.

"If I could speak with Dawn, alone," Clive says.

Victor gives a short bow and leaves us.

Clive presses a button and the dark shades rise, letting in the bright sunlight. Before us spans all of Denver. I walk to the window and look out. I have a responsibility to the citizens of this city, no matter what runs through my blood.

If my father knew what he was, he put the citizens first as well.

"It was hard enough sending you to Los Angeles," Clive says, coming to stand beside me. "I really don't like the thought of you going to the Vampire Council."

"It's imperative that I go. I saw the V-Processing center and I can tell them that it's fully operational."

He seems to consider this answer, but it isn't quite enough. That's because one of the reasons I'm going is the vampire who just left the room. "Is there something you're not telling me?"

There is, and he can tell because he's known me for a long time.

"I think your father kept secrets, too," he says quietly.

Surprised by his words, I face him. "Why do you think that?"

"He told me that if anything happened to him, I should protect you from Valentine. But when Lord Valentine requested you serve as delegate, I put the city first."

"You had no choice. Valentine would have made the citizens pay."

"Probably. I trust this younger Valentine more, but not completely, because at his core he's still a vampire. Remember that, Dawn. Vampires can't be trusted. Anyway . . ." He sighs deeply. "I think it's time I gave you something."

He goes to his desk and unlocks one of the drawers. He opens it and pulls out a large cassette player. It's nice, not something patched together by the city's many junkers who scavenge for parts to re-create prewar devices.

"I've been debating for some time when to give this to you," Clive says, approaching me with it. "You'll want to listen to it in private. And keep it. I've never played it—it was always meant for your ears alone."

He hands it to me. It's heavy. Not just from the thick plastic and dust, but heavy with memories. I can't really explain how I know that. "It's from my father, isn't it?"

"Yes."

I'm torn between the need to hear his voice again and putting off what his words might confirm. This could explain everything about my heritage. Or he could simply be singing me a lullaby. Or he's saying goodbye.

Exhaustion settles over me.

"Try and get some sleep before tonight," Clive says. "And know if you change your mind about going, I stand by you."

"Thanks, Clive, but I have to do this."

"Somehow, I knew you were going to say that."

Chapter 6

Jeff pulls to a stop in front of our apartment building. Nothing ever looked so good to me. I wish I was going to have more than a few hours here, but I agree with Victor's sense of urgency.

As soon as Jeff and I step into the apartment—

"Dawn!"

Tegan pops off the couch, leaps into my arms, and hugs me hard. "I was so scared that I'd never see you again."

"That'll never happen," I say boldly. I don't want her to know that I'd thought the same thing. It's easy to be confident when all the dangers are behind you.

She pulls back, and I see that she's aged, too. She still has her pixie features and her cropped blond hair sticks up all over the place, but she's faced almost as many horrors as I have.

"My turn," Rachel says. With her brown hair pulled back in a ponytail and her casual clothes—jeans and T-shirt—I figure she's not going to work today.

I give her a fierce hug.

"You could have told me what you were really up to, instead of just leaving a note," Rachel chides.

"Clive ordered me not to say anything."

"Since when do you obey orders?"

I smile. She's been fairly tolerant of the issues I have with authority. "I was trying to protect you."

"That I believe. How about some coffee?"

I glance over to see Tegan and Jeff studying me like they expect me to fall apart. "Love some. But I'm going to shower first."

"It'll be ready when you're done," Tegan says.

"Great. Thanks. I won't be long."

I walk into my bedroom and close the door behind me. I set the cassette player on my desk. I'm desperate to listen to it, but I want to be completely alone without the possibility of anyone disturbing me. Knowing Tegan, she'll be in my room before I'm out of the shower.

I strip off my clothes. When they collapse to the floor, dust leaps off them, bits of Crimson Sands that have followed me into the city. Perhaps that's a good sign, and I can carry the spirit of that place with me, too.

The shower is amazing. The water pooling at my feet is a dark brown at first as I wash all the dirt from my hair and skin, but when it runs clear, I turn the heat up and let myself absorb the warmth and the patter of drops against my skin. It's almost like I can feel each individual droplet. How is that possible? Am I really changing? Becoming more like a vampire? I want to crawl out of my skin. I don't feel at home in my own body anymore. It's like I don't know it any longer, like I don't know me.

Tears sting my eyes. Crouching in the corner, I wrap my arms around my legs. In spite of the warmth, I shiver. I don't want to be a vampire. I don't want to have things in common with Sin. I don't want to be a monster.

Shaking off the morose thoughts, I fight back the tears. I'm still Dawn Montgomery. I know who I am, even if I don't know *what* I am. I'm the humans' last hope, even if I don't officially represent them, even if I'm no longer the delegate.

Fighting for them is in my blood, too. My parents did it. My brother did it.

With renewed resolve, I'm determined not to let Sin win, not to let him conquer me.

Standing up, I shut off the water. After I step out and dry off, I put on a pair of loose flannel pants, a tank top, and an old soft hoodie. I need the comfort right now. I walk into the bedroom.

Clothes are strewn all over my bed and Tegan is standing beside it holding up a red silk negligee.

"Jeff told us you were going to the Vampire Council. He and Rachel are arguing about it now, so I decided to help you pack. I don't do well with yelling," she says. "Where did you get this?"

I snatch it from her, ball it up, and shove it back into the drawer where I'd hidden it. "From Faith. She gave it to me when I was in the hospital recovering from Victor's bite. I think as a joke. She said hospital gowns weren't fashionable or something like that."

"You should take it," Tegan says. "You know. For when you and Victor are alone." She wiggles her eyebrows.

"We're not going to be alone. Richard and Faith will be there." I start sorting through the clothes, trying to determine what looks conservative.

"They won't be there all the time. And not in the same room . . . or bed," she emphasizes.

"I don't know what the arrangements will be, but red silk is not appropriate."

She sits on the bed. I guess now that she's made a mess, she feels like her job is finished.

"Have you and Victor . . . done it?" she asks.

I feel the heat rushing to my face. I shake my head.

"Do you want to?"

Do I? "I think about it, but he's a vampire. It makes a relationship hard." Even though I may be part vampire as well, I'm not ready to admit it—not even to my best friend.

"You gave him your blood."

"He was dying."

"Maybe he's *dying* to sleep with you."

I wad up a T-shirt and throw it at her. Giggling, she ducks. It seems like it's been forever since we've laughed.

"What about you and Michael?" I ask, turning the tables.

"What about us?" she asks, grabbing a shirt and starting

to button it up, like it can't be folded until every button is snugly in place.

"You seemed interested in him when we were in Los Angeles."

"I've always thought he was hot, you know that. Even when he was your boyfriend." She stills. "I hate what Sin did to his face."

"He clawed his chest, too. After you guys got out of the city and Michael tried to fight him."

"God, I can't believe I loved that guy." She studies me for a minute. "Is it because of what happened to me that you're afraid to trust Victor with your heart?"

"Victor is nothing like Sin. But the world around us is so intense. I just wish we had time to do something simple like go on a picnic."

She sits up, excited. "Maybe you'll do something special when you're in Vamp City. I bet they have fancy restaurants—"

"That serve blood?"

She scowls. "People live there, don't they? Someone has to take care of stuff and provide that blood. I bet they have theaters and plays. These are the oldest of the Old Family vampires; they probably lavish themselves in extravagance. They won the war. They're bound to have the best of everything. Museums, art, libraries. I'd love to see it."

I can hear the deep wistfulness in her voice. I wish I could take her so she could experience all these wonderful things the Old Family has collected. Even if they are like Valentine and abhor modern technology, they'll still have priceless heirlooms. Old Family are wealthy beyond imagining. They'll have exquisite clothes, marvelous homes.

"I should probably pack a nice black dress," I murmur. "And heels."

"Definitely," Tegan answers. "And wear your hair up. I really should go with you so I can fix it for you."

"I wish you could, but, Tegan, it's a city filled with Old Family. Would you really want to be there?"

She visibly shudders. "No. Just . . . just don't let them turn you."

Oh, Tegan, if you only knew . . .

"I won't. I promise."

Her cell phone rings. She pulls it from her pocket, stares at the display, and answers. "Hey, Mom . . . Yeah, I am. Now? Okay. Okay, I get it. Okay. Okay."

Hanging up, she rolls her eyes. "My mom. She's got me on a short leash. I've gotta go."

Even though Tegan would consider it a betrayal if she knew how I felt, I can't blame her mom. Tegan snuck on the train so she could go to Los Angeles with me. I'm sure her mother wasn't aware of her plans.

"I'm sorry your family was worried."

"They don't understand. You're my best friend in all the world. I couldn't let you go alone."

I squeeze her hand. "I'm glad you were there."

"Not that I did much good." She pouts. "Missed my chance to stake Sin."

"We haven't seen the last of him."

"I'll be ready next time," she says.

Unfortunately, I don't know if it's possible to prepare for any encounter with Sin. He's not exactly sane.

She gives me a big hug. "Please come back."

"I will. Count on it."

She opens the door.

"Hey, Tegan?"

She stops and looks back over her shoulder.

"You didn't answer my question about you and Michael."

"Would it bother you if I liked him?"

"I think it would be awesome. The two people I love most in the world loving each other."

She suddenly looks shy and vulnerable. "Then maybe. I don't know."

"He's a really good guy."

She smiles. "That I do know. And he's hot."

She leaves, and the sudden emptiness of the room descends on me. The tape recorder draws my attention, but I turn away and get serious about packing. Just enough clothes to get there and back. With four of us in the car, there won't be room for extras. I'm sure Victor can buy me whatever I need in New Vampiria—I kind of doubt they'll accept cash from a human. Actually, maybe a little shopping wouldn't be too bad. Old Family always dress so well. I'm bound to be introduced to designers, tailors, dressmakers.

I pack, unpack, repack about a dozen times. Of course, I'm just avoiding that tape player. I know why. Because I already know what's on it. Not the exact words. I don't know when it was recorded or where. All I know is that the voices on it will be familiar.

The voices will belong to my parents.

The sun is beginning to set, and I know I'm running out of time. If I'm going to do this before I leave, I need to suck it up and do it.

At my desk I keep repositioning the recorder, as if its exact placement will radically affect the outcome of what's on the tape. When I'm satisfied, I take a deep breath and hit play.

The wheels of the tape begin spinning. Static. Then Dad's voice.

"Is it recording?"

"Yes, William."

Mom!

"Are you sure?"

"Yes."

"I just don't want to mess this up."

"William, please, just—"

"Okay, okay. Hi, Dawn, it's Dad here. I'm sitting with your mom and, well, we just wanted you to know how much we love you."

"That's right, dear. Dad and I love you so much. And if you're listening to this, then . . . well, then we aren't there anymore for you."

"We're sorry, Dawn. Whatever happened, we're so sorry. When we signed up for the assignment as delegate, we knew it would be dangerous. We knew the risks, but we also knew the

reward. Because we aren't just representing Denver, we're representing humanity. Remember that. Your mom and dad are doing this so that, one day, you won't have to be afraid of the dark."

"Whatever happened, don't blame anyone, Dawn," my mom says. *"Don't hold any anger inside, because it'll only rot you, and you're too beautiful, too precious for that. And you're too beloved."*

"I want you to know that, no matter what, we always love you, Dawn. And our last thoughts were of you. We love you."

"We love you, Dawn."

"We love you. . . ."

The static rolls on and they're gone again. I shut off the recorder.

And I begin to cry. I put my head in my hands and let everything out. With each tear I feel them, with each deep, choked breath I hear them. I grab the sides of my hoodie and pull it tight around me, like they're right here, holding me. Hugging me.

I miss them so, so much.

I put my hands on the tape recorder, my wet fingertips smearing the tears over the buttons, and I whisper . . .

"I love you. I love you. I love you."

Chapter 7

"Dawn?"

Victor's hand comes to rest on my shoulder. I don't know how long I've been crying. I look up to see him crouching beside me, my balcony door open. He's always moved so silently. I wipe at the tears. "You could have come in through the front door. Rachel is expecting you."

He gives me a wry grin. "Old habits are hard to break."

He's come into my room through the balcony doors so many times. Climbing walls, leaping from balcony to balcony is no challenge to vampires.

"I guess it's time for us to go," I say.

He skims his fingers along my cheek. "First, tell me why you were crying."

I touch the recorder, explain what it is, and tell him that Clive gave it to me before I left his office that afternoon. "I think he felt guilty. I might have died without ever hearing them."

Victor tucks my hair behind my ear. "May I hear them?"

My heart stutters a little at his request. To share something so personal and special with him . . . It would be amazing.

Nodding, I rewind the tape and then press play.

"Is it recording?"

"Yes, William."

"Are you sure?"

"Yes."

"I just don't want to mess this up."

"William, please, just—"

"Okay, okay. Hi, Dawn, it's Dad here . . ."

We listen to the voices from the past, but somehow this time it feels like they're right here, talking to both of us. I imagine them by my side or all of us gathered around the dining table, maybe Brady is there, too, and we're just talking and laughing and eating dinner. There aren't any monsters, there aren't any Day Walkers, and the Thirst is still just an urban legend. I close my eyes and Victor puts his hand on mine. I want so badly for the world to be perfect. I feel the tears starting to come again, and when I open my eyes, the world is still the same. But when I look at Victor, it seems just a little bit better.

"They loved you very much," he says. "The human capacity for emotion has always humbled me."

I hesitate, then remind him, "You once told me that you love me."

"But I fear it pales in comparison with what humans can experience."

"You would die for me." He almost did.

"Without hesitation. What I feel for you terrifies me. I shouldn't feel it. And yet I do." Putting his hand behind my head, he leans me down for a kiss. His mouth is tender, gentle, a reflection of him. I love the way he kisses me as though I'm special. I grow warm as yearning takes hold. Maybe I should pack the red silk—

"Dawn . . ."

With a start, I break away from the kiss.

"Dawn . . ."

I look over at the tape recorder. It's still playing.

"I thought it was over," I say.

"I guess there's more on it," Victor says quietly.

*"This is Dad. There's something I never told your mother. Something I never told anyone. It's about your—*our*—heritage."*

My stomach tightens. I hold my breath, dreading what he might say.

"I'm so sorry I never told you, but I had to protect you. And, well, if we're not there anymore . . ." He sighs, and static plays out of the speakers as he exhales. *"It's better that you know than be left in the dark. I hid something for you, Dawn. I hid it in the place I've always hidden things. I . . . I love you, Dawn. I only wanted to keep you safe. And no matter what, you will* always *be Dawn."*

I watch the tape spiral, the magnetic strip wind itself up, containing my parents' words that were only meant to be heard if the worst happened. I listen, hoping that there's more. But the tape grinds to a halt.

No, I think. *It can't be true. What Sin told me. It just can't.*

"Does that mean anything to you?" Victor asks.

I nod, unable to get the words out, already feeling the tears beginning to well up.

"Dawn . . ." Concern is deep in his voice.

"I have to think. What hiding place is he talking about?"

"You're growing pale. Why won't you tell me what's happening?"

Because I don't want to be what I am.

I look around my room, and it's immediately obvious. I go over to the music box that used to house little presents from my father as I grew up: pieces of candy, tiny notes, maybe even a few quarters that I could put into my piggy bank and hear the *clink clink* as they fell. But how could there be anything else to it?

"This is where he always hid stuff for me," I say, Victor joining me. "There's a little hidden compartment, but the only things in it are things that I've hidden."

I open it and listen to the music play, the tiny disc somewhere inside the woodwork, turning slowly and playing its song. I've always listened to it, but I've never really looked at the box itself, just what was inside. I turn it over, examine it from every angle. I tap the green felt bottom. It sounds off. Then I gauge its depth in relation to the rest of the box, and that's when I realize:

"It's a false bottom," I say. "It can be lifted out. But how?"

I grab the tiny wooden divider that separates the box

into two compartments and try to lift from there, but it doesn't budge.

"Let me take a look at it."

Victor puts his hand on the box, his fingers lightly touching key points. The music stops.

"Wind it up again," he says.

I do so, and when I let go of the turn key, the music begins all over again. Victor closes his eyes and listens. It's like he's in another world, his vampiric senses picking up impossible things.

"There's a note," he says, "I can *feel* it. Whenever the music wheel hits that spot, it shifts something inside the box. I think it unlocks it."

I wait in silence as Victor listens to the song again and again and again, like a fencer waiting for that right moment to strike. His fingers clench the felt divider and then . . . *pop.*

The false bottom detaches perfectly, and Victor sets it aside. In the box, a tiny strip of leather is wrapped around a bundle of documents, everything secured with a rubber band. I pull it out and close the box; the music stops.

"Dawn, do you know what this is?" Victor asks.

I'm afraid I do, but I'm not ready to face it yet.

"We really need to get going," I say. "I can look at this later."

"We can take the time now."

I shake my head. "Not yet."

"When you're ready, just let me know. You don't have to face it alone."

I simply nod.

First we have to pass through the gauntlet of Rachel and Jeff. Needless to say, both were caught off guard to see me walking out of my room with Victor holding my duffel bag. But considering what my life has encompassed during the past month, I'm a little past the scolding-for-bad-behavior phase.

"The balcony," Rachel says, nodding, as though she just answered a question she'd asked herself about how Victor had gotten past her unnoticed. Then she quickly shifts into protective mode. "You'd better take good care of her."

"I can assure you," Victor says, "that if she comes to any harm, it will be because Faith, Richard, and I are all dead."

Instead of comforting her, his words only make her narrow her eyes. "Don't get dead."

Victor grins. "Trust me. I'm not planning on it."

Rachel embraces me tightly. "At least I get a hug instead of a note this time."

I squeeze her hard. "This is lots better."

When I release her, I clasp Jeff quickly. "Keep her out of trouble."

"I'll do my best."

Then Victor and I are walking out of the apartment, and I can only hope that it won't be too long before I'm back. We take the elevator down. I wave at the guard at the front door before we step outside. The car is waiting at the curb.

Victor opens the passenger door for me and I slide in. Faith and Richard are in the backseat. "Hey," I say.

"I never understood that term as a greeting," Faith says. "Isn't that something they feed to horses?"

Her words barely connect with me. My fingers are lightly tapping the leatherette on my lap. Victor tosses my bag in the trunk before getting behind the wheel.

"Took you long enough," Faith says. "What were you guys doing? Having a cup of tea before you left?"

With a sigh, Victor twists around in the seat. "Faith, don't be a pain."

She holds up a hand, palm out. "Excuse me, but I need to pack."

"I'll give you an extra five minutes."

"Fifteen."

"Done."

Trying to distract myself, I glance over at Victor. "So vampire siblings squabble, too?"

He grins. "All the time."

"But I'm the one who always wins," Faith says.

"You think that because I make it appear that you've won."

"I'd know if I won or not."

Victor winks at me. "I was willing to give you a half hour to pack, Faith."

"And I was willing to settle for ten."

Laughing, Victor reaches across the console and takes my hand. "This could be a long trip."

I force a smile before glancing out the window. I wish I could laugh with him, but I know what my father was trying to tell me.

My life, everything I've always believed, was built on a foundation of lies and I can feel it shifting beneath me, turning into dust, just as vampires become ash.

With my father's secrets taunting me, the drive to Valentine Manor takes an eternity. But then it appears, a looming silhouette outlined by moonlight.

It's huge. Looks like some sort of medieval castle. I used to hate coming here to meet with Lord Valentine, but now it's Victor's home and it doesn't seem quite as foreboding. Victor stops the car just shy of the ancient front door.

Everyone climbs out. I can sense more than see the Lessers hovering about in the shadows.

"I'll need to speak with my lieutenants and distribute the blood the Agency sent this afternoon," Victor says.

The Agency always places the blood in a refrigerated unit at the back of the house, delivered during the day. It is safer that way. Or at least it was before Day Walkers.

We walk into the house, and the butler approaches. He's the same one who always escorted me to Valentine. He's tall, slender, with hair that drapes down to his shoulders. He bows slightly. "My lord, welcome home."

"Eustace, was the blood delivered?" Victor asks.

"Yes, my lord. And your lieutenants are waiting in the dining hall for your commands."

"Very good. Please escort Miss Montgomery to the dawn room." He squeezes my hand. "I won't be long if you want to wait. . . ." His gaze drops to the leatherette and I imagine he's as curious as I am. He can also sense that I'm dreading what might be inside.

I just nod. I haven't decided yet if I want to be alone with the secrets.

He looks over at Richard. "I want you with me."

"Yes, my liege." He gives a little bow.

"Funny. Just come with me."

As he and Richard walk off down the hallway, Faith murmurs, "This is all so hard on Victor."

"You love him."

She jerks back. "What? No, vampires can't love. I've told you that. But I'm observant. I can see how he's aging."

"Would it be so awful if you could love?"

"Love is a weakness."

"I thought after our talk on the Night Train that you were going to give it a chance."

"Uh . . . no." She turns for the sweeping staircase. "I can imagine what drab things you might have packed. I'll see if I can find something a bit more fashionable for you."

She's taller than I am. More voluptuous. And she wears six-inch spiked heels that are better suited for use as a weapon than walking, but I just say, "Thanks."

She wiggles her fingers at me as she starts up the stairs.

I turn to the butler. "I can find my way to the dawn room."

"Still, please allow me to take you there."

I follow him down the hallway. He doesn't seem to be as stiff and formal as he was when I came here as a delegate. "Are things better under the new Lord Valentine?" I ask.

"He is more tolerant of imperfections," he says tightly.

He leads me into the dawn room, then backs out, closing the door behind him. My breath catches. I've only been here in the dreams that I shared with Victor. It's exactly as it was there. I saw this. I was truly here with him. How is it possible?

Faith told me that he redecorated the room after his father died. All the paintings on the walls represent sunrises. I set the leatherette full of documents on the coffee table and walk around the room, studying each work of art. Faith also said they were a tribute to me.

I give a little start when the door opens. Eustace walks in carrying a silver tray with a flowered tea set on it.

"I thought you might like some tea while you are waiting for the master," he says, setting the tray on the coffee table.

"Oh, yes, thank you." I amble over as he pours the tea into the delicate china cup.

"Would you care for sugar?"

"Yes, please. Three teaspoons."

"Ah, you like a little tea with your sugar."

"Sorry. Sweet tooth." I shrug. "And hot tea's not really my thing."

"Oh, my." The china rattles as he quickly picks up the tray. "My apologies. I should have asked what your preference was before I assumed—"

"No, it's fine." I hold out my hand, trying to reassure him.

"It's not fine. My responsibility is to see to your comfort.

Instead, I've managed to put us both in a very awkward spot."

"Maybe I'll like your tea."

He shakes his head. "No, I've made quite the blunder."

"Truly, it's not—"

Victor strolls in. Thank God. He studies us both. "Is everything all right?"

"My apologies, my lord. I have not adequately seen to her comfort. She does not favor hot tea."

Helplessly I look at Victor. I don't know how to console Eustace. Victor's lips twitch as he gives his head a small shake.

"It's all right, Eustace. I appreciate your attempt to make her feel welcome."

Eustace straightens his shoulders. "Who does not favor hot tea?"

"I know. It's quite impossible to comprehend."

"What shall I bring?"

"Nothing. We'll be leaving shortly."

"Very good, my lord." He begins walking toward the door.

"Eustace?" I call out.

He freezes, his back stiff. "Yes, miss?"

"Thank you very much for your kindness."

"It is my job."

With that he walks out, closing the door behind him.

"My father would have lashed him for bringing the wrong thing," Victor says. "Sadly, he hasn't gotten used to the fact that I never would."

"Your father got angry over tea?"

"He got angry over everything."

I realize he looks tired.

"Did everything go okay?" I ask.

"We have adequate blood for now. It'll keep the Lessers content until we return, but after that"—he shakes his head—"I'll deal with it when I get back."

He glances over at the pouch. "Did you open it?"

"No."

"It frightens you. Why? What is it that you think your father was talking about?"

"Not frighten exactly." I can see the earnestness and worry in his eyes. I feel like I'm treading water, on the verge of drowning.

"That ancient vampire in the mountain—" I begin. "His family name was Montgomery."

Victor grows still, processing the information, and I'm not even sure he's breathing. I force out the words—

"Victor . . . I'm a vampire."

I don't know what sort of reaction I expected, but it certainly isn't a smile followed by a quick laugh.

"That's not possible, Dawn. I would know."

"Okay, maybe not a vampire, but a dhampir."

"They're a myth. Like leprechauns, faeries, and werewolves."

"You thought Day Walkers were a myth, too."

That sobers him a bit.

"Think about it, Victor, think about my blood. If it contained vampire, it would explain why for a time you had a craving for it after you tasted it." Once vampires taste the blood of their kind, they risk becoming addicted to it until they are infected with the Thirst.

That totally wipes the smile from his face.

"And our ability to share dreams," I continue, pressing my point. "Faith said that only happens with Old Family."

I can tell that I've left him speechless. I've never seen him like this—he seems lost, whereas he usually takes command of any situation. Which means he's as confused and unsettled by all of this as I am.

He turns his back on me and takes a couple of steps away. Can he hear the thudding of my heart? Vampires have such keen senses that he must be aware of my anxiousness. Finally he faces me.

"What exactly did that old vampire say?"

I take a deep breath, not even sure where to begin. "That symbol in my dreams, the one on the document that my father discovered, the one you said was written in ancient vampiric—it's the name of the fifteenth Old Family—Montgomery. What legend referred to as the lost family. Apparently they had the ability to produce offspring with humans. The document was a death warrant against the Montgomerys, signed by the other fourteen families."

"Why exterminate them?"

"Why does Old Family do anything?"

He sighs. "Fear of change. Fear of things becoming different. Fear of anything they don't understand. It's why they hated Sin."

He walks back over, pushes my hair behind my ear, and

trails his finger along the crucifix tattoo on my neck. "You always hated the thought of becoming a vampire."

I force a smile. I imagine it looks pretty pitiful. "Ironic, huh?"

"Did Sin know about your heritage?"

I nod, swallow past the lump in my throat. "He shares it. His mother was a Montgomery. Esmerelda. I think that's why he—and your father—were obsessed with my family."

"Jesus, Dawn."

"I know. I—" I'm so overwhelmed with emotions that I can barely think. I wanted him to find a reason that my being a vampire was impossible. Victor cradles my face between his powerful hands. "This changes nothing," he says. "And it doesn't change what I feel for you."

"Oh, Victor." I wrap my arms around his shoulders and bury my face against his neck. "I'm so afraid that it changes everything. That I'll be alone. Not fully vampire, not fully human. Some half-breed freak. Like Sin."

"You'll never be like Sin," he growls. He threads his fingers through my hair, cradling the back of my head. "You're not like Sin."

Then he covers my mouth with his, kissing me desperately as though he has the power to change what I might be, as though he is just as afraid as I am of what all this might mean.

When he pulls back, his smile reassures me of everything, and suddenly all of this feels inconsequential. And I remember what my dad said, his final message to me: *You will always be Dawn.*

"Let's see what your father kept from you for so long," Victor says.

He holds out his hand. I slip mine into it, drawing strength and comfort from his touch. We walk over to the sitting area. Instead of selecting a chair, I drop to the floor in front of the table and fold my legs beneath me.

I take the band off and slowly unfold the leather. It cracks and whines as I lay it flat, then curls back slowly in protest. Inside are an assortment of papers, some original documents, some that appear to be copies, and some handwritten notes. I immediately recognize my father's handwriting on those. And at the top, a tiny piece of paper:

In some way, I always knew this was true.
And I suspect you always knew the same.
—Dad

I carefully take out each piece of paper, arranging it slowly and methodically on the table. To my surprise, I find a photo of all four of us: Mom, Dad, Brady, and myself, sitting around a table. I didn't know there were any photos of us all together.

I only look at it for a moment, not letting my memories go there just yet. I place it very carefully off to the side and return my attention to the documents.

The more I dig, the older the pages become. Until I get to the end and pull out a very, very ancient parchment. The writing on it is remarkably clear for the weathered state of the paper, the infinite folds and creases that come from hundreds of years of moving from place to place.

"Octavian Montgomery?" Victor asks.

"That's what he said."

Victor points near the top of the page and the name is clearly written out, both in Latin script as well as vampiric and others from the time.

"What is this?" I ask.

"A family tree," he says, tracing a line from Octavian upward to his ancestors, then following it down along a branching tree. Octavian is in the middle of these branches, his brothers and sisters and cousins . . . but then they all end, and only his line continues.

"The death warrant," I say. "The Montgomery family was almost wiped out."

"Octavian survived, and so did his son, and his son's children."

I follow the line down, but the branches never extend very far.

"It ends here," I say, at the final entry: *Maximillian—1802*.

That's when I notice what the other documents are. They're hospital records. And Maximillian Montgomery is listed as the father of a boy named Abraham Montgomery, born in 1832. As the records go on, they become more modern, including the names of the hospital, the names of the entire family. Then I recognize the name Lloyd Montgomery.

"My grandfather," I say. I don't have many memories of him. He came to our house once for the holidays, but the war was still raging. How he made it there I'll never know, or why he thought it was so important to risk his life in order to visit with us.

Unless he knew. I think about the note on top of the documents: *In some way, I always knew this was true.*

I try to imagine my grandfather talking to his son—my father—in the dark of night. They discuss what they always knew, what their years and years of vampiric studies pointed toward. They talk about being drawn to the night, just like their ancestors before them. Am I making this up? Is it imagined? Or is it a memory?

"Why have this?" I ask. "I thought the Montgomerys wanted to keep their heritage a secret."

"It's tradition to keep very detailed family records," Victor says. "In case there's ever a doubt as to who is the legitimate heir to the family. At least, that's what they say. We vampires, sadly, are obsessed with purity of the blood. This helps us keep a record of that."

"The Montgomerys weren't pure," I say. "And that's why they were hunted down like dogs."

I'm surprised at the anger in my voice. Until now, this always seemed like a strange conspiracy theory to me, dreamed up by Sin in his dark mind. But my father's voice telling me, his notes, all of this . . . It's true. I am the last Montgomery. And the anger comes from the realization that all these people, these dhampirs, were slaughtered. I can touch their names and know that the other Old Families wanted them dead. Especially the Valentines.

"Wow, look at this," Victor says, pulling me out of my thoughts. He holds up a piece of parchment, very similar to the family tree but shortened. It only contains Maximillian's name and those immediate family members surrounding him. It's in English and Ancient Vampiric.

"This is a Confirmation Decree," Victor says.

"What's that?" In all my vampire studies I've never heard of one.

"It's used as evidence to the legitimacy of a vampire's heritage; in this case the heritage of one Maximillian Montgomery. I'm not surprised. By this point, there would have been so little vampire blood in Maximillian that his father would've worried that no one would have believed he was a vampire. So he wanted to make sure he had a Confirmation Decree. And in order for this to have any weight in the vampire world, it *must* be signed by a vampire from another family."

"Why?"

"Because no one would believe a Montgomery if he said *his* son was an Old Family vampire with the same rights and privileges as other Old Family. By having *another* family put their reputation on the line, it makes their heritage claim legitimate. It's a dangerous undertaking. If you sign one of these and are proved *wrong*, then you're practically exiled, never to be trusted again in the vampire community."

Wow. Someone stood up for my family? Someone risked his life to make sure that Maximillian's heritage as an Old Family vampire was forever legitimized, as were his children's heritage?

"So who signed it?" I ask, needing to know who this

one friend among the sea of adversaries was.

Victor traces down the page but can't find what he needs. He starts looking through the other papers on the table. I'm about to lose hope when he pulls out the second page and continues reading. And then he stops, his finger on the name.

"Lilith Ferdinand."

"Who's that? And why did she sign this?"

"You can ask her yourself," Victor says. "She sits on the Vampire Council."

Chapter 8

"That's absolutely impossible," Faith says calmly.

We're in the car, racing toward New Vampiria. While I was sitting here in a daze, trying to puzzle things out, Victor explained to Richard and Faith about my *heritage* and the documents.

"Old Family are tall, elegant . . . beautiful," Faith continues.

"Dawn's beautiful," Victor grounds out.

"She's short."

"I'm not short," I say sharply, "and don't talk about me like I'm not here."

"Are you even five and a half feet?"

I clench my teeth.

"Most women are short compared to you," Richard says.

"Which is my point. If she had Old Family blood in her, she'd be tall or at least *taller*."

"She also has human. So that's where her height comes from."

"Okay, maybe, but she has no fashion sense. She wears cotton and flannel and . . . and hoodies."

In rebellion, I draw my hoodie up over my head and slouch down in my seat. The tone in her voice indicates that the only thing that could be worse would be if I wore clothes I took off dead people. I feel like my world is crumbling around me, and Faith is worried about my wardrobe?

Richard laughs, clearly amused. "You can teach her all she needs to know."

"I don't know that I have enough to work with. Remember those makeover shows they had on television years and years ago, before the war? Did you ever see one, Dawn? Maybe the Denver archives had an episode."

"No."

"The ones doing the makeovers were mostly vampires. We have such extraordinary fashion sense. But you have none. I just don't see Old Family in you."

"Really? That's where you're taking this? Victor tells you what we discovered and all you can focus on are things that don't matter?"

"Better than focusing on your death."

That has me tossing the hoodie back, sitting up, and twisting around. "What are you talking about?"

"Have we forgotten that there is a death warrant out on the Montgomerys?"

"I haven't forgotten," Victor says. "It's the reason that I told you and Richard what we found—so you'd be prepared for what we might face."

"What? You think they might try to kill me? That death warrant is archaic."

"Archaic—the very definition of Old Family," Richard says. "At least this explains Murdoch Valentine's interest in you. He knew what you are."

"As well as his interest in my father. Maybe that's why he requested him. But what did he hope to accomplish?"

"Maybe he just wanted to keep an eye on him," Richard says.

"Or maybe he had plans to secure your father's place on the Council," Faith muses. "You know, use him as a puppet whenever he wanted a vote to go his way."

"Wait a minute. Can I have a seat on the Vampire Council?"

"No," Victor says briskly.

"Why not?"

"Because it's too risky. With the death warrant still active, we have no way of knowing how the Council will react. So for now, we need to keep your heritage a secret."

"But my name—Montgomery—could cause questions."

"It's common enough, no one will make that connection. Our purpose has to stay focused on persuading the Council to mobilize against Sin. Your role is to provide an accounting of everything you've seen so we can convince the Council that Sin poses a danger to us all."

Reaching across, Victor squeezes my knee. "I know it's

hard. I'm sorry we couldn't give you more time to adjust to what you learned."

"I know. Our priority has to be Sin. I get that. It's the reason I didn't say anything to you sooner. Well, that and I didn't want to believe it." I force a small smile. "So, who is this Lilith Ferdinand anyway?"

"She's head of the Ferdinand family," Victor says. "The only woman on the Council. I haven't seen her in years, but she's strong, smart, always three steps ahead of anyone else. In fact, she's probably the only one on the Council who understands anything. No offense to Montague Carrollton."

"None taken," Richard says. "My grandfather is more interested in wine and human girls than governing."

"And she has to be strong," Faith says. "The Ferdinand family is split into two very distinct sides, each one thinking it should rule over the family. I mean, every Old Family has tensions like that, but the Ferdinands are particularly vicious."

"Why?"

"No one likes to speak about family matters," Victor says, "especially ancient ones. But from what I've gathered, about two thousand years ago, Lord Ferdinand was murdered by his own brother, and that brother took the throne."

"I thought that was pretty common," I say.

"It is, but remember how Richard served as my witness when I fought my father?"

"Yes, it was to ensure the fight was fair."

"There was no such witness in this case. The family was

split down the middle between those who thought it had been a fair fight and those who didn't. That fracture has never healed. Lilith has to watch her back every day."

It sounds like the one ally I have, the one vampire who might have stood by the side of the Montgomerys, is in constant danger. Why should I not be surprised?

But it seems like everyone's life is at stake these days. We're heading into dangerous lands, into the maw of the beast, looking for help. Behind us, a new monster, an ever greater monster stands on the horizon.

As the moon shines its ominous glow on the ever-wasting road, I realize we may not stand a chance against him.

The sky is beginning to lighten when we reach a monstrous Gothic manor outside Chicago. A dozen vampires in black trench coats stand guard. They're holding machine guns. I guess this far to the east, their only enemy is humans.

"Why are we stopping?" I ask. The car has heavily tinted windows that the sun can't penetrate.

"It's a struggle for us to stay awake during the day," Victor says.

"But I could drive."

"And if you run into any trouble that requires our help?"

"Yeah, I guess that could be an issue," I say reluctantly.

Reaching across the console, he wraps his hand around mine. "Right now we have the luxury of being able to spare a few hours."

I nod. He's right. What difference will a few more hours make?

As we climb out of the car, the front door of the manor opens and a tall, slender man with slicked-back black hair rushes down the steps. "Oh my God, I can't believe it! Company. Old Family. Victor Valentine."

He takes Victor's hand and pumps it. "I can't tell you how long it's been since I've had visitors." He looks at me. "And this is . . . not a vampire."

"No," Victor says quickly. "This is Dawn."

"Your blood diva?"

"Yes."

I jerk my head around to stare at him. He shakes his head slightly. Apparently in the worrying about the death warrant against the Montgomerys, we didn't get a chance to discuss how we would play things here.

"Ah, Faith, you are as beautiful as ever." The Old Family vampire who doesn't look any older than Victor takes her hand and begins raining kisses over it.

"Oh, Xavier," she coos. "You flatter me."

"As much as possible. I've not seen a female since my father sent me to watch over his territory. How fortunate you are, Victor, that your father wanted to oversee his own estate. Come, come, inside quickly before the sun catches us." He wraps Faith's arm around his and begins to lead her toward the house. Tossing her head back, she laughs and pats his shoulder.

I glance over at Richard. He doesn't look happy.

"He ignored you," I say. "That was rude. I thought Old

Family was all about etiquette and politeness."

"They're also about subtle insults."

With that caustic statement, Richard marches toward the house. I'm so accustomed to him being carefree and light that I don't know what to say.

"Xavier Romanelli gave him a cut direct," Victor says as he escorts me up the steps. "In the 1800s, it was a common way to show someone you disapproved of them."

"Why would this guy disapprove of Richard?"

"Because he's competition for Faith."

"Okay, I get that, but why did you tell Xavier that I'm your blood diva?"

"So he'll keep his fangs out of you. Vampires won't take blood from another's diva without permission. And it was simpler than trying to explain why I'm taking a human to New Vampiria."

Once we're inside, a footman closes the door behind us. I'm not surprised by the beauty of the surroundings. Marble, gold, statues, paintings.

Richard is leaning against a wall, arms folded over his chest, glaring at Xavier as he keeps touching Faith's arm, shoulder, hand, and cheek.

Xavier looks at Victor. "Faith tells me that you're going to the Vampire Council, but surely there is no rush. You could stay a night or two."

"I'm sorry, Xavier, we are in a hurry. We stopped here only to wait out the sun. We can rest on the floor."

Xavier puts his hand to his chest and drops his jaw, clearly insulted. "Don't be silly. I'm already having beds prepared." He looks at Faith. "You can't leave the moment the sun sets. You must at least stay for a night feast. I have the most marvelous cook, a Lesser who prepared meals for Napoleon himself. The food is a sensual delight. Please, it's been so long since I've entertained. And your diva must eat in order to nourish you properly. It's so important to keep her blood fresh."

He licks his lips a little, eyeing me. Faith catches this and jumps in front of him, and he stares right into her low-cut dress.

Faith smiles. "I suppose we could—"

"Faith," Victor warns.

"An hour," she says. "Where's the harm?"

"Wonderful!" Xavier shouts, and claps enthusiastically.

Because I'm Victor's *diva*, I'm given a room to share with him.

It contains a large four-poster bed with a canopy and heavy velvet drapes hanging down from it. A low fire is burning in the fireplace in front of a sitting area. Faith is right: Vampires have exquisite tastes whether they are decorating rooms or people.

"I need a moment," I tell Victor, and walk into the bathroom. I'm taken aback by all the gilded mirrors, vanities, and artwork. Okay, so maybe they aren't as infallible in taste as I thought.

I lean toward my reflection. It's the first minute I've had to really examine myself since we discovered what was hidden in the music box. I don't know what I expect to see. My black hair, my blue eyes, the crucifixes tattooed on either side of my neck. I pull my mouth back and run my tongue over my teeth. No fangs.

Somehow I thought I would look different. I thought I would spot something I'd overlooked before. I thought I would *see* some evidence of vampire.

"You're still you," Victor says right behind me.

I scoff. "I hate that you can do everything so quietly."

"Do you really?" he asks as he comes up behind me, puts his arms around me, and meets my gaze in the mirror.

"I hate that you can sneak up on me and I can't sneak up on you."

"You snuck up on me," he says. "Maybe not physically, but in other ways. I never expected to feel for you what I do."

"Even knowing what I am?"

He turns me around, cradles my face. "It doesn't matter what is coursing through your veins. You're Dawn."

I wish I could believe that. "How many times did I tell you that you couldn't escape what you are, that you couldn't escape being a monster because it's in your blood?"

"You've also told me that I'm not a monster."

He brushes his fingers along my hair, a soft but protective gesture. "We need to get some sleep. It's going to be a long drive."

Threading his fingers through mine, he leads me into the bedroom. The couch in front of the fireplace has been shoved back and pillows have been scattered about. Ignoring the bed, Victor guides me over, sits on one of the pillows with his back against the couch, and pulls me down so I'm resting on another pillow, my back to his chest.

"Thought you were tired," I say, my voice low, my heart doing little flips as he skims his finger along my neck and brushes my hair off to the side until it drapes over one shoulder.

"I am." He presses a kiss to my nape. "But we've had so little time together. I miss the way we were able to be together in the dreams we shared."

"If we go to sleep now—"

"Dream-sharing, according to Faith, only happens when the couple is separated by a great distance. But it's okay, because I no longer need to dream of protecting you; I can actually do it."

"For someone who doesn't believe in this stuff, she sure knows a lot about it."

"My sister is complicated. But then, all girls are."

"I'm not."

"You're the most complicated of all."

"Like you're not complicated," I tease. His arms close around my waist. I fold mine over his and grow somber. "What about us, Victor?"

He presses his head to my shoulder. "*We're* complicated."

"Do you still crave my blood?"

I hear him inhale. "It still smells sweet, but I can resist it."

I swallow, trying to understand the consequences, trying to understand more about what I am and how it might affect my relationship with Victor. "Sin turned Brady—a dhampir—into a vampire."

"Yes." He places his warm lips on the curve of my neck, right where it meets my shoulder. Pleasure pools through me. "So you're still not completely safe from me. I could turn you."

"But you won't," I say with conviction.

His arms tighten around me. "I won't."

I shift around so I can look at him. "You said I was your weakness, that your enemies would use me to get to you."

He gives me a wry grin. "Where Sin is concerned, it appears I may have been a bit narcissistic. He wants you for you. He has plans for you that won't go away even if I'm dead."

"Then where does that leave us?"

He traces his fingers over the curves and hollows of my face as though he treasures each feature. He leaves my lips for last, outlining them before stroking them, as though he's a painter filling in between the lines. "I don't know, Dawn," he says so quietly that I almost don't hear him. "I don't know where it leaves us."

He kisses me, gently, softly, as though I'm fragile. Or maybe he fears our relationship is.

"We need to sleep," he says. "Obviously dhampirs don't feel the weight of day in the same way that vampires do."

He struggles to his feet, pulling me up with him. We both climb onto the bed and position ourselves similar to the way we were sitting by the fire, my back to his chest, his arms wrapped around me.

As sleep drags me down, my mind wanders to the

Council and the thirteen hungry glowing eyes staring at me through the darkness. Then I feel Victor pulling me nearer, holding me more tightly, and all my worries subside, leaving only the possibilities of something better for us . . . once we've dealt with Sin.

I wake up to a steady knocking on the door. With a moan, I work my way out of Victor's embrace and sit up. The fire in the fireplace has died. I feel incredibly rested. Somehow I can sense that it's night.

Victor rolls out of bed, crosses the room, and opens the door. He chuckles. "No."

"Yes." Faith pushes her way in. She's wearing an elaborate red ball gown, something that was worn two hundred years ago. It's satin and lace. Bares her shoulders. It rustles with her movements. She's carrying something that looks similar, only it's deep purple. She tosses it on the bed. "Dinner tonight is to be formal."

My eyes widen. "You want me to wear that?"

"Xavier does. Leave, Victor, so I can help her get ready."

"Faith—"

"We promised him an hour," Faith says, cutting him off. "It won't kill us to be dressed for the occasion. Your clothing is in Richard's room."

"I'm not wearing any of it; what I have on is fine."

"Oh, Victor, relax, have a little fun."

"Fun? Faith, you may enjoy changing outfits every hour, but putting on clothes once a night is enough for me."

"I don't change clothes every hour." She sniffs. "Every half hour maybe. Now, go on, get out of here. We have work to do."

"But we are leaving as planned."

"Of course."

Victor gives me a smile filled with apology before walking out of the room and closing the door.

I crawl over the bed and touch the soft material, rubbing it between my fingers. I had to wear Victorian clothing when I met with Murdoch Valentine, but it was more suited to funerals than parties.

"I realize you'd be more comfortable if it came with a hood," Faith says.

I glance up at her. "It's beautiful. It's just that it's not me."

"When I'm finished with you, for the next hour, it will be."

Faith does more than help me get into the gown. She fixes my hair and applies makeup. When I look in the mirror, I can hardly believe what I'm seeing. Faith curled my hair so it's full and flowing down my back. The gown is cut low, a little too low. I tug—

"Leave it," she orders.

"But I feel like I could pop out of it."

She chuckles softly. "You won't."

The deep purple material makes the blue of my eyes brighter. They also appear more almond-shaped, exotic. Faith did that, with liner and shadow. My lips are a glistening vibrant red as though they are waiting to be kissed.

"I don't know, Faith."

"Trust me. Victor won't be able to take his eyes off you."

Faith is right. When we enter the dining room, Victor looks as though he's never seen me before. He strides over and gives me an appreciative smile. "You look—"

"Like Old Family," Faith says quietly.

We both jerk our head toward her.

Faith shrugs. "She wasn't nearly as difficult to clean up as I expected."

My face heats with embarrassment.

"Dawn is always beautiful," Victor tells her, then winks at me. "Even when she's wearing a hoodie."

Faith growls low, but with his words, the warmth turns to pleasure. I've never had to pretend with him.

Like Xavier and Richard, he's wearing a black dinner jacket that's long in the back. Swallow-tailed, I think it was called. His white shirt is pristine and he has a red cravat—an old-fashioned tie—around his neck.

"Faith, you look magnificent," Xavier gushes.

She bats her lashes at him. "You're so sweet."

"Come, a quick meal and then we shall dance."

"Xavier, we don't have time," Victor tells him.

"An hour, no more, I promise. You must indulge me. I'm so lonely here in this dank, dreary manor."

"We promised, Victor," Faith reminds him, and then lets Xavier lead her to the table.

"*You* promised," Victor mutters before offering me his arm.

"I guess this is the way vampires usually entertain," I say as we walk over to a ridiculously long table.

"We can't do anything simply."

Xavier sits at the head of the table, while Victor and I are on one side, Faith and Richard on the other. I can't complain about the food. I'm served steak and various vegetables. Everything is delicious. While vampires derive no real nourishment from food, they do enjoy the sensations of taste.

I glance over at Richard. He's not enjoying anything. Not eating, not drinking, not joining in on the conversation. Probably because no matter to whom Xavier is talking, his gaze is always honed in on Faith.

"The Council just didn't give any thought to the inconvenience of putting humans within walled cities," Xavier says before sipping from an ornate silver goblet that I'm pretty sure doesn't contain wine. "Someone has to watch them. But there is nothing except desolation around the cities. No one comes to see me. Do you have any idea how long it's been since I've seen an Old Family female? How can I court? How can I bond?" He takes Faith's hand and presses a kiss to it. "How can I entice her into being my mate?"

"Have you explained all this to your father?" Faith asks. "Maybe he can send one of your brothers to watch over the territory for a while."

With a pout, Xavier sits back. "I have. He doesn't seem

to care. I simply wait around for the sun to rise, the sun to set, and blood to be delivered. Night in, night out. Week after week. Month after month. Boring."

"Do you get enough blood?" I ask.

He jerks his gaze to me as though he'd completely forgotten that I was there. He furrows his brow. "You allow your diva to speak?"

"She's very knowledgeable," Victor assures him. "I'd like to know the answer to her question."

"Not as much as we used to. I shall have to punish them soon. But I don't want to think about that now. Let's dance." He gets up, goes to an old phonograph sitting on a table, cranks it up, and sets a needle on a disc. After a few moments of static the room fills with scratchy music. Xavier rushes over to Faith, bows slightly, and holds out his hand.

"Xavier—" Victor begins.

"I know. You must leave. But what is three more minutes?"

Faith places her hand in Xavier's. "Yes, Victor, what is three more minutes? Dance with Dawn."

She goes with Xavier to an empty space on the other side of the room, and they begin to glide over the floor with graceful movements. It's very different from the way I dance at parties. Xavier has a hand on her waist. Hers is on his shoulder.

Victor stands and extends his hand to me. "Dawn?"

I gaze at him, standing there, looking incredibly handsome, so enticing. "I don't know how."

"Just follow my lead."

I can't deny that I've always wanted to dance with him, to have a moment that seemed normal. I follow him to the uncluttered area. Taking me in his arms, he sweeps me over the floor.

I want to laugh with the joy of it. Gazing into his eyes, I can almost forget that the world around us is such a mess. It's only the two of us, keeping in perfect rhythm, even when the music skips and plays over, skips and plays over. A broken record.

I feel elegant and beautiful in this gown. I've never worn anything this elaborate before. If this were a fairy tale, I'd be a princess. But I stopped believing in fairy tales a long time ago.

"You're so beautiful," Victor says quietly. "I wish I could give you more moments like this, when there is nothing but the music and the two of us. No worries, no evil, no problems."

"Is this what Old Family life was like before the war?"

"We had balls and dances almost every week. But we had orchestras playing the music. Not scratchy old records that grate on the ears."

"Do you miss it?"

"I miss the peace of it. The laughter. The happiness. Everything changed when we came out of the shadows. We couldn't hold on to this any longer."

"Xavier is trying to."

"Yes, many do."

They hate technology and modern conveniences. I try

to envision what it was like back then, but I'm distracted by the candlelight in the chandeliers as the flickering flames cause light to flutter over Victor's face. The shadows ebb and flow. It's magical, lures me in, and I realize that I'm nearer to him than I was when we started. My skirt brushes against his legs. My hand has moved from his shoulder to his neck. I can feel his warm breath on my cheek. I could fall into the blue depths of his eyes. I wish we could stay here, constantly moving in a circle over the polished hardwood floor.

Victor lowers his head. His lips graze my ear. His voice is low, mesmerizing. "I'm sorry we can't have this forever."

My heart gives a little lurch. Is he answering my earlier question when I asked what would become of us? Or is he simply referring to the fact that it's as though we have no cares?

"What exactly is *this,* Victor? What can we not have forever?"

A hideous screeching fills the room and the music stops. I glance over to see Richard standing by the phonograph, holding up the needled arm.

"Hate to break up the party, but if we don't get on the road soon, we're not going to get to the capital before the sun rises," he says.

Victor steps away. I want to clutch him back to me. I want to keep dancing. I want to pretend that no dangers exist in our world. But these few moments were only an illusion.

"Stay the night," Xavier says. "Go tomorrow."

"We can't," Victor tells him. "Richard's right. We have to go."

Xavier turns to Faith. "Stay with me."

Faith smiles and pats his cheek. "I wish I could, but Victor will be taking his place on the Council. I must be there to give him my support."

"Afterward, come back. You'll never want for anything. I'll make you happy. We can dance every night."

Leaning in, she brushes her lips over his. "We'll see."

With that she turns from him, marches across the room, grabs my hand, and begins pulling me toward the door. "Come on, Dawn, we can't travel in these clothes."

It seems the moment of pretending all is right with the world has passed.

Half an hour later, we're hurtling through the night, Victor at the wheel. The tension in the backseat is so thick that I could pierce it with a stake.

"Richard, don't pout."

"I'm not pouting, Faith."

"Then don't be angry or whatever it is, because I don't like it."

"I'm not angry, either. I'd just forgotten, that's all."

"Forgotten what?"

"That you're all about flirtation. A new guy steps into your path and off you go."

"That's not fair."

"Isn't it, Faith? In Los Angeles, I thought—" He sighs. "Never mind. We have larger issues. I intend to focus on those."

I dart a glance back to see Richard staring out the window. I can't blame him for being upset. I know he and Faith have some sort of past. I know he cares about her. While we were in Los Angeles, they actually had a date. I thought maybe they were becoming a couple. I think Richard thought the same thing. Guess we were both wrong.

"This system that VampHu set up doesn't seem to be a good thing for anyone," I tell Victor. "It isolates humans and vampires."

"All humans, not all vampires. We travel as we please, and Old Family tend to socialize with one another whenever we get the chance."

"If they're not forced to watch over humans. Wouldn't it be wonderful if all the walls came down?"

He glances quickly over at me. "You're thinking of Crimson Sands."

I sigh. "Yeah, I am."

"Their way isn't practical on a large scale."

"I think it is."

"The Council will never go for it. VampHu, the walled cities, they are here to stay."

"We'll see," I murmur.

Chapter 9

The sky has turned from pitch black to shades of blue, signaling the sun's rise. It's a familiar color to me. How many nights have I seen it, waiting on the balcony for my parents to come home from Valentine Manor? I always held my breath when I saw the carriage coming down the street, heading home.

Now, I hold my breath again. Through the fading shadows, I can't believe what I'm seeing. I've only ever heard of this place, never seen a picture. The tallest tower looks as though it could pierce the moon and make it rain blood across the gray city. A place made like this, of stone and mortar, of towers and walls, would take decades if not centuries to build. Yet it's been completed in only a few years. And as we approach along the road, which has turned from mere dirt and gravel to deeply inset cobblestone, I see how this monolithic city was made. Those who crafted the stone march across the fields, an exhausted race of enslaved Lessers. Dawn is approaching, and their slumped shoulders and dragging feet indicate a need for blood. But where is it? This is the capital, New Vampiria. Shouldn't it be the most affluent of all?

Then, as we draw closer to the wall, my expectations of a Victorian era reborn are quickly dashed. The wall isn't a wall at all, but merely the outcropped buildings of the city, small cottages made of ill-fitted stone. Is that where the Lessers live?

In the blink of an eye we're inside the city itself, the road turning into a street that shoots straight to the massive tower in the center. On all sides we're surrounded by gray buildings, weathered far beyond what should only have been their short life. Trash litters the street, nothing like the clean upkeep of the Valentine house that I'd expected. Instead of well-dressed vampires, the envy of the Lessers that surround Denver, I see bedraggled vampires looking at our car as though it may offer hope in this place. When we zoom past them, their stares continue to be reflected in our mirrors.

"Not what you expected?" Victor asks, my silence telling him everything.

"It looks . . ."

I struggle to find the words, so Victor does it for me. "Pathetic."

"Yeah. Not at all like I'd imagined. I mean, it's the vampire *capital.* Where's the grace and elegance? Where's the spoils from the war that they won?"

"When we talk to the Council, you'll see why some of them consider the war a defeat instead of a victory."

"That's ridiculous," I say, angry that the vampires would be so arrogant that after nearly wiping humanity off the map they claim it wasn't enough. Did the VampHu, which my father helped create, not go far enough in giving the vampires everything they wanted?

"Look around you, Dawn," Victor says. "The world of isolated, walled cities is a strange one for humans. But a world running rampant with Lessers is stranger still for vampires. Now you'll see that our grip on humanity is not as strong as we'd like you to believe."

We pass under arches that connect buildings, walkways that act as tendons bringing the city together. But even from here, at this speed, I can see the cracks forming.

Victor turns down a street, away from the tower in the center.

"Where are we going?" I ask.

"We arrived too late to see the Council until tonight. They'll need to know of my arrival in the city first. It's been a long time since a Valentine has sat at the table. My father was the patriarch, but he remained on his throne at Valentine Manor. He hated this place."

"Why?"

"He didn't like what they were trying to do. He thought the Old Families shouldn't attempt to create human-like cities. I never agreed with him on things, but I did on that point. The heads of the Old Families live here, but it's like they're strangers in their own land. We were never meant to be like this. We were always meant to be in the shadows. Now that we're in control, we don't know how to be."

"Wow."

"That's why I'm afraid of Sin," Victor says. "He wants control. He wants power. And I think he knows exactly how to keep it."

Victor slows to a stop outside a three-story building. Nothing unique about it. It could easily be mistaken for one of the many that we passed. I remember what Murdoch Valentine once said to me: "We vampires have never had imaginations." I can see that now. Every building looks as though it was cast from the same mold, thought of by the same designer. But Victor must know this is the right spot as he gets out of the car.

"Should I be worried?" I ask. "I mean, the Lessers here look starved."

"No," Victor says. "The fact that you're with me signals to them that you're my . . . *companion*."

"I have a feeling that means something else in the vampire world."

"It does, yes. It translates into: You're for me. Not for them. Nothing else needs to be said."

I hope he's right.

Richard and Faith climb out of the backseat and glance around.

"It's been a while since I've been here," Richard says. "It's worse than I remembered."

"New Vampiria has always lacked charm," Faith says.

"It's the reason I've avoided it for so long."

We open the trunk, gather our bags, and follow Victor through a wooden door, half eaten away by rain and rot.

The inside has the same glow of oil and gas lamps that haunted Valentine Manor. It looks like something that was made out of necessity and desperation. None of the tables really match; there's no paint, simply the natural wood tones and textures.

Behind the front desk a vampire, clearly a Lesser, stands up. "Ah, Mr. Valentine. Oh, I do beg your pardon, *Lord* Valentine. Lady Faith, Mr. Carrollton. It's a pleasure to have you all again gracing our humble hotel."

"Thank you, Louis. We'd never dream of staying anywhere else. And please, call me Victor."

"I'm afraid my manners would never allow such a thing." Apparently his manners don't extend to humans because he gives me a once-over as though I'm something he'd scrape off the bottom of his shoe. It's obvious that, like Xavier, he considers me a blood diva. "How many rooms shall it be?"

"Just one. Your largest."

"Straightaway, sir."

When Louis takes the key off the rack, it becomes the only one missing; all the others hang silently. We're the only guests staying here. And judging by the dust that's gathered on those keys, we may be the first guests for some time.

We head up two flights of stairs, each board creaking and threatening to give way. The top floor is divided into two suites and we take the one on the right. Louis opens the door for us, gives Victor the key, and Victor passes him a very large envelope, which I suspect is filled with a different kind of payment. Blood. The only currency a vampire really needs. It's obviously much more than Louis normally charges and he tries to give it back, but Victor won't hear of it and practically pushes him out of the room to prevent any more protesting.

After we turn on all the lamps, we see that the suite is, much like the rest of the hotel, *humble*, as Louis put it. Brass fixtures on the walls and in the bathroom a giant bathtub with copper lion's feet. The windows in the main room are covered by thick curtains, closed against the encroaching sun. The bedrooms, however, are completely windowless; probably a wise idea for a hotel catering to those who scorch in the sun.

"We'll sleep through the day," Victor says. "This evening we'll meet with the Council."

"Come on, Dawn," Faith says, and strolls casually toward one of the bedrooms.

I look at Victor, and he merely nods.

"I can get another room," Richard says, and I realize that before we stopped at Xavier's, he probably would have shared a bedroom with Faith.

"No, I want us to stay together," Victor says.

"I'll take the couch, then."

Victor slaps his back. "We all need to be well rested."

With a shrug, Richard heads toward the other bedroom.

"You *are* pouting," Faith calls out.

"Don't start on me, Faith," he says before going into the room and slamming the door shut.

Victor gives Faith a narrow-eyed look.

She angles up her chin. "What?"

"Your timing isn't the best. If you wanted to make him jealous—"

"I didn't. I was just being nice to Xavier."

"Nice? If that was you being nice, I'm not sure I want to be there when you're really grateful. I'm surprised he didn't get down on one knee and propose."

"That would have been a bit premature."

"Faith—"

"I'm going to bed." She stomps off to the other bedroom and bangs the door shut.

Victor sighs and I can sense his frustration. I walk over and slip my hand in his. He looks down at me, smiles, and says, "We really don't need their drama right now."

"What happened between her and Richard so long ago?"

"I'm not sure. I hate to say it because she's my sister, but if anyone is at fault, it's probably Faith. Old Family females tend to be spoiled, used to getting their way."

"I can't see her with Xavier."

"No, neither can I." Victor leads me over to the couch and pulls me down beside him.

"Thought you said we needed to be well rested," I tease him.

"Are you going to be able to sleep?"

"Probably not."

He holds me. I wish we could pull the draperies back and look out over the city, but that will have to wait for nighttime.

"Are you disappointed with the vampire capital?" he asks, his fingers sifting through my hair. I can feel each strand being tugged, lulling me into forgetting the world around us, until there is only us.

"I thought it would be beautiful. Why didn't you tell me it was like this?"

"Because it *should* be beautiful. It's mortifying that it isn't. We consider ourselves superior, and yet we're reverting to the Dark Ages."

"I don't think it's *that* bad." I shift around to face him. "Victor, will I even be allowed into the council chamber?"

"Hopefully as my guest, yes. You'll be the first human to ever step inside."

"Though technically I'm not human," I say.

"You have a drop of vampirism in you, the remains of a legacy long forgotten."

"But it's still in me."

Victor sighs gently. "It doesn't matter. You aren't human or vampire; those definitions are beginning to lose their meaning. You're Dawn."

"Am I?" I swallow hard, hating to admit some secret part of me still hopes that everything I've learned isn't true. "I've been noticing some changes."

"Like what?"

"My senses seem sharper. I can make out things in the dark. My skin is more sensitive. My hearing is better.

Taste—the meal at Xavier's was really good, and I'm not entirely sure it was all because he has an excellent chef. Maybe it's all in my mind, maybe I'm just imagining it."

He brushes his thumb over my lower lip. "How does that feel?"

"Incredible. It's like sensations are shooting all through me."

He slides his fingers over to the tattoo on my neck, to the place where he buried his fangs. "When did you start noticing the heightened sensations?"

"After you took my blood. Octavian said that your bite awakened the vampire traits that exist in me."

The corners of Victor's mouth turn down and he studies me sadly. "I didn't know, Dawn. I didn't know taking your blood would do this to you. I'd rather die than have you be unhappy."

"I'm not unhappy." I squeeze my eyes shut for a moment. "Maybe I am a little. Mostly I'm confused. Do you know anything at all about dhampirs? What I can expect? A longer life? Faster healing? Will I want to sleep during the day?"

"I don't know. Someone on the Council might."

"They're going to hate me, aren't they? Hate what I am? That's why they killed the Montgomerys."

"Not because they hated them, but because they feared what they didn't understand."

I know he's trying to reassure me, but he wasn't there when the death warrant was signed. It all happened long before he was born.

"And you're wrong," he says slowly as though he's beginning to become lost in the sensations of touching me. "They won't hate you. Once they see how strong you are, how brave, how much you care for others—they'll love you as I do."

"But love's not enough. It doesn't hold you. You keep telling me we can't be together."

"And each time we're together, it's getting harder to separate."

He skims his lips across my temple. It's as though each cell comes to life. I lean into him, drawn to the promise of pleasure. His mouth covers mine, his tongue sweeps inside. Warmth spirals through me, pools in the pit of my stomach. My toes curl. Suddenly it's like he's kissing all of me.

As I shift around until I'm stretched out on the couch, he follows my movements, never breaking from the kiss. Although we've slept in the same bed, he's always done little more than hold me near, but I sense that his restraint might be slipping. I know he wants me. I want him. But giving into temptation will complicate our relationship further, would prove a distraction when we need to concentrate on destroying Sin. Still, I can't give up the hope that when all this is over, we'll have time to truly explore our feelings for each other.

Drawing back, he rubs his fingers in circles over my cheeks, his gaze holding mine. "I wish I could hold you while you sleep."

I give him an impish smile. "We could sleep here."

"You deserve a bed and a good day's rest." He rolls off

me, holds out his hand.

Reluctantly, I let him pull me to my feet.

"I have faith in you," he tells me. "You'll impress the Council."

"And if I don't?"

"We'll have to overthrow them because they're obviously idiots."

Victor's teasing words stay with me as I go into the bedroom I'm sharing with Faith. Okay, it looks like we're also sharing a bed. A big one, but still . . .

I expected her to be asleep by now. Instead with her back against all the pillows, she's sitting up in a slinky red silk tank and boxer shorts. She doesn't look up from the romance novel she's reading, which must seem more like an instructional manual to her than a story. I grab my duffel bag, go into the bathroom, and change into my flannel pants and tank top. When I step back into the room, she glances over and rolls her eyes as though I pulled my clothes out of the trash bin.

"Be sure you stay on your side of the bed. I don't want flannel touching me."

I suppose with her sensitive skin, silk feels a thousand times better. "It's soft," I say defensively.

"Whatever." She turns her attention back to the book.

I climb onto the bed, tuck my legs beneath me. "So what happened with you and Richard? I know you guys have a past."

She closes the book and glares at me. "What is this—one

of those girl bonding things that you humans do?"

"I'm just trying to understand what's going on."

"There's nothing to understand." She rolls over, turns down the gas lamp, and buries herself beneath the covers.

Although we have a dim light, my eyesight is sharper. I can clearly see her outline.

"Do you really like Xavier?" I ask.

"Of course not."

"Then why dance with him?"

"Because he was our host. It would have been rude not to."

Faith always tries to be hard and uncaring, but I sense vulnerability in her. "When we were in Los Angeles, I saw your face when Richard leapt through the window with Sin." It was a fall from a height that would have killed a human. "You were terrified, worried about him. You have strong feelings for him."

"Let it go, Dawn."

But I can't. I care about Richard. I know he's hurting. I think Faith might be as well. "You once said something about a night you shared together . . . when was it? A hundred years ago?"

"Ninety-eight, but who's counting?"

"Obviously you. And Richard."

That seems to get her attention.

"When I first met him," I say, "I was with Victor. And so much was happening in the city, and we had no idea what was going on, and Victor was planning to overthrow his father, and you know what Richard asked? He asked if you were okay."

With a long-suffering sigh, she sits up. "You're like a little parakeet I once had. It kept chewing on its cage, on the exact same spot, for two years. It drove me mad, so one night I opened the cage and the bird flew away. Do you know what happened next?"

"What?"

"The thing came back and kept chewing."

I laugh a little.

"I know you care about him," I say.

"The parakeet?"

"No. Richard."

"Don't be silly. I can't. I won't." She studies me for a moment. "We should do something special with your hair before we go to see the Council."

"Faith." Reaching across, I grab her hands, feel her tense up, see her eyes widen in alarm, but I'm not going to let go.

"What are you doing?" she whispers, and I wonder if she ever lets anyone truly touch her. Not in the flirtatious way that Xavier did, but in a comforting way.

"You can confide in me," I tell her.

"You're human. You have emotions. You'd never understand."

"Try me."

"We can't love."

"You love Victor."

"No. I . . . he's my brother. I don't want him to do

something that will get him killed, that's all."

"Because you care about him. That's love. What happened that night with Richard?"

She shakes her head, squeezes my hands. "He was sweet."

"Go on," I prod.

"We . . . he was my first. Oh, hell, he's been my only, but don't you dare tell him that."

She looks totally disgruntled.

"Your secret's safe with me," I assure her.

"It better be. I can take you out without even mussing up my hair."

I don't think I'd go down that easy, but I'm not going to fall for her change in topic. "So you regret that you were together?"

"Of course I do."

I wrinkle my nose. "He wasn't any good?"

"Richard's good at everything. But that night I was so nervous. He was tender, gentle, made me feel safe." She rolls her eyes. "Then he spoiled it all by telling me that he loved me."

"And you didn't believe him? Faith, I've seen the way he looks at you—"

"No, I did believe him. That's why . . . I want forever and we don't get that."

I stare at her, trying to make sense of her words. "You don't die. Of course, you get forever."

"Not when it comes to love. Don't you see? He won't love me forever, and when he casts me aside, it'll hurt. It's better not to fall into that whirlpool of emotions."

"So you're scared."

"I'm practical. My mother was cast aside. Victor's mother was cast aside. Sin's."

"Maybe Richard loves you enough to hold you forever."

"But what if he doesn't?"

"Sometimes you just have to take a chance."

"Yeah, well, right now, I think I'm taking enough chances. You are aware, aren't you, that we might not leave this city alive?" She pulls free of my hold, lies down, and presents her back to me. "And I need my beauty sleep."

"You know, Faith," I say quietly, "vampires and humans—we're not so different. We all want to be loved forever. It's scary to trust someone with our hearts, but if we don't . . . loneliness can hurt, too."

She doesn't say anything. Sliding under the covers, I stare at the darkness hovering around the edges of the room. So much is at stake tomorrow, but I somehow manage to slip into the black and fall asleep.

Chapter 10

I awake to the rumble of thunder. Through narrowed eyes, I watch Faith sitting at the vanity, clipping up her red hair with a diamond-encrusted comb. She's dressed in her usual attire of crimson leather pants and a scarlet silk blouse. Her heels match the outfit.

Sitting up, I freeze at the sight of a pile of clothes at the foot of the bed on my side.

"You'll want to wear those," Faith says as she rises gracefully to her feet.

I inch forward and touch the supple black leather. "I brought a suit of my own."

"This will hug your body, make it easier to move if we get into a fight."

I jerk my gaze over to her. "You really think that's going to happen?"

"We just need to be prepared. You'll also want to wear your hair up, show the ink on your neck." She tosses me a pearl comb.

I study it. It's beautiful, but I can tell that it's ancient, maybe as ancient as some of the vampires I'll meet today.

Faith walks to the door, stops. "I don't want anything to happen to you because you mean something to Victor, not because you mean anything to me."

She does care, whether it's for Victor or me. She just can't admit it.

"I get that," I tell her.

"Good." She glances back. "Dinner is on its way up, so hurry."

As I get dressed, I have to admit that the leather feels great against my skin and it moves with me. Because it fits so snugly, it doesn't get in the way when I test it with a few defensive moves. The top is a little low for my tastes, but Faith provided me with a sleek jacket that goes over it. Guess she knows me better than I realized. I wear my hair up like she suggested. Then I strap on the holster and stake that Victor gave me shortly after we first met.

I study my reflection in the mirror. I look kick-ass tough.

When I step out of the room, my gaze immediately goes to Victor. He's standing near the center window, the draperies pulled back. I can hear the rain hitting the glass and am vaguely aware of lightning flashing in the distance. But my attention is riveted on him. He's wearing a dark blue suit. The corner of a red handkerchief embroidered with two overlapping Vs peers out from the pocket over his heart. He looks Old Family, so incredibly Old Family.

He gives me a long, slow once-over. "Nice."

I tug on the jacket. "I'm not sure this is really me, but it doesn't hamper movement, so I'll live with it."

"Don't even think about swapping the jacket for a hoodie," Faith says.

I glance over my shoulder and see her sitting on the couch, wineglass in hand. Richard is standing off to the side, also drinking wine. He's wearing a suit very much like Victor's, only it's brown. It matches the leather in the narrow strip of braided hair that runs along the side of his head. I want to tell him not to give up on Faith, to persevere, but I suppose after ninety-eight years, his patience is probably wearing thin.

We all sit down to dinner. Rare steaks. The potatoes are covered in cheese. The others don't bother with those, which leaves more for me.

"I can't believe the hotel has a cook when it has no guests," I say.

"Louis prepared the meal," Victor says. "He kind of takes care of everything."

From my place at the table, I have a perfect view of New Vampiria. Every time the lightning illuminates the sky, I see the silhouettes of crumbling structures. In books, I've seen pictures of the world before the war. We lost so much. The very foundation of our society. For some reason, I thought the remnants of it would still exist here.

"What are you thinking about?" Victor asks.

"Tegan. She told me to go to a museum for her. Is there even one here?"

"There is. Maybe we can find time for it after we visit with the Council."

"Really?" Faith asks. "We're going to go sightseeing?"

"If we have the opportunity," Victor tells her.

"You're optimistic." She looks at me. "You do know that bringing a human into the Council chambers is punishable by death."

"What?" I set down my fork. The steak that was tasting so good is suddenly heavy in my stomach.

"Faith exaggerates," Victor says. "Besides, you're not completely . . . human."

"Have you heard from the Council?" I ask.

"Yes, they're granting us an audience at nine."

"And it includes me?"

"It does."

I shove my plate aside. This is exactly what I was hoping for, but I'm not sure I really thought it would happen. I think about the two months of training that Rachel put me through before I ever was alone with Valentine. Everything had to be perfect: my dress, my manners, my knowledge of etiquette. One wrong move and he would have killed me. The oldest of Old Family are not very tolerant of mistakes.

"Maybe we should practice, go over the rules of etiquette, make sure that I don't mess this up."

Victor takes my hand. "Just be yourself."

"And nauseatingly polite," Richard adds.

"Don't speak unless spoken to," Faith tosses in.

"Never turn your back on the Council," Richard says.

"Never raise your voice," Faith counters.

"Never insult."

"Never anger."

"Never trust."

"Never expect understanding."

"All right, enough!" Victor demands, and I think that, like me, he realizes that Faith and Richard weren't really offering me advice on the Council as much as they were referring to each other. "I need to know you both have our backs."

"My loyalty doesn't shift," Richard says.

"You're my brother. You can count on my support," Faith assures him.

"Good." Victor turns his attention back to me. "Speak with confidence. Don't let them intimidate you. You've *seen* what Sin is capable of. You know his plans better than anyone. You must convince the Council that we are on the brink of being destroyed."

I swallow, lick my lips. "Okay, no pressure there."

"Just remember that we're behind you," Richard says.

"Standing beside me would be better."

Victor smiles. "At this moment, you are our most formidable weapon against Sin."

The great tower in the center of the city seems to be the only impressive thing within New Vampiria. After driving through the streets and seeing the cracked walls on nearly every building and the trash that litters the gutters, I'm pleased that at least something lives up to the image in my head of the vampire capital. The tower was obviously built before anything else. With so much effort placed in its design and structure, it appears nothing was left for the rest of the city. Every stone is meticulously set. The buttresses holding it up are decorated with gargoyles and demons and winged creatures of mythology and dream. There are few windows in this great monolith, giving the pillar a dominating presence, something that lacks soul and contains only raw power.

We walk up the steps to the massive wooden doors, ten times as tall as they are wide. Two guards stand watch, their dark suits unbuttoned, revealing a bandolier of stakes. With us in his wake, Victor approaches them without hesitation.

"The human is my guest," he says to the guards. "She is not to be touched."

Victor pushes open the doors and we follow him inside.

I can feel the emptiness of this tower. Hallways that are far too long and ceilings that are far too tall create drafts, as though the building has its own weather pattern. Massive chandeliers hang above us, the long candles dripping molten wax as the flames flicker. They do their best to light this place but barely illuminate the floor, let alone the walls off in the distance.

Every step we take echoes.

"It's a long climb," Victor says as we reach a staircase at the end of the circular room, a staircase that winds itself up and up and up. Worst of all, it has no railings. One slip and it's a long way down. I suppose vampires don't have to worry about such things—like cats, they always land softly on their feet, no matter the height.

After circling the room three times we arrive on the next floor, an empty space, large and filled with couches without sitters, a bar without occupants, a pool table without players. It's sad, an unappreciated playroom. We continue the climb to the next floor: something of a library, though so few lamps are lit that it's difficult to tell. This tower seems more and more like a ghost house, one that never wanted to exist in the first place.

Eventually we do find life: a Lesser servant who quickly disappears around a corner, perhaps out of respect for Victor. A few floors later, we arrive at what is clearly the guests' quarters. I remember Victor said that humans aren't allowed in the council chamber itself, so this is where they must wait. Their purpose is to feed their masters. They are all young and gorgeous, carefully dressed and made up like dolls that have the audacity to live and breathe. Boys and girls, no older than myself. All of them wear thick, black collars to hide what I know are the bite marks of their masters. Some, slightly older, wear them on their wrists as well. Vamp bites leave scars if the vampire isn't careful, and I have a feeling that their masters aren't. After all, in a vampire's eyes, a human is easily replaced with another. As long as the heart beats and the blood flows, what's the difference?

I get glassy-eyed stares from some in the room. I realize

they think I'm one of them, merely a plaything and food source. I feel sorry for them, and I'm glad when we continue up the stairs.

We have to be near the top of the tower when the stairs end at a hallway. It's narrow and cramped, an odd choice compared to the rest of the grand, but empty, design of this place.

"Are you ready?" Victor asks me, already halfway toward a door.

"Yes," I say with so much conviction it frightens me. Because I'm not nervous. I have been every step of the way, but these last few are the easiest. The journey, which started back when I was a scared girl trapped in a closet as my brother was taken, will end behind this door that holds the most powerful vampires in the world. And I won't bow to them. They will bow to me. Because this city has shown me everything I need to know. The Old Families aren't powerful, they're feeble.

Victor gives me one final look, both hands on the massive doors. I nod and he pushes them open.

Chapter 11

The Vampire Council. I'm staring at it. The heart that moves the world is right in front of me. Thirteen vampires sit around a large, wooden table, a single chandelier hanging from the ceiling. On the walls, misaligned portraits of their ancestors, painted by some long-forgotten artist in an era left to history books. Thirteen Old Family vampires. Some are elderly, ancient even, with straggly gray hair that hangs on only by some miracle. Others are younger and appear to be Clive's age, even though they may be pushing five hundred. At least one is the same age as Victor but not nearly as handsome, his plump body giving way to a rotund and almost-teenish face.

And one woman. She must be Lilith. She's intimidating, reflecting an aged beauty that is timeless yet frightening. Her stare is stern and cold, as though she's uninterested in things that don't bleed for her. I'm reminded of a school mistress from classrooms that could only be found in a child's nightmare. I guess I was hoping for someone a little, I don't know, softer.

None of them stand up or offer us seats. They simply turn as little as possible to get a view of their new guests. It doesn't even seem like we interrupted anything, and I can easily imagine this group gathering dust while waiting for some important news to come their way.

"Forgive my absence," Victor says. "I should have reported immediately once my father was no longer head of the family. But I trust you received word from the messenger I sent."

Victor is speaking more formally, melding into the world in which he's lived for four hundred years. For his efforts, he receives a bored pause, while each of the Old Family look at each other, wondering who will bother speaking first. One of the oldest finally does.

"Yes, we were informed by your messenger that changes were afoot. Not exactly proper, but that isn't unusual for the House of Valentine."

"I beg your pardon, Lord Paxton?" Victor asks, a calm but immensely powerful tone in his voice that demands everyone be held accountable for what they say in front of him.

"Your father chose to abandon his post here and live near that *city*." He says the last word with disgust, as though it tastes bad on his tongue. "A very, very disrespectful thing to do."

"Perhaps he chose to spend time at a place that he could mold, rather than sitting in a room, waiting for the world to mold him."

"I never expected you to defend your father."

"I'll defend who I choose and it will be no business of yours."

"Watch your tone, young Valentine," a vampire who looks familiar says. "My grandson stands at your side. I would not have him painted with the brush of your impudence."

Now I recognize that he has Richard's eyes, his sharp features. He's the head of the Carrollton family: Montague Carrollton.

"Apologies, my lord," Victor says. "I would do nothing to disrespect your grandson or your esteemed family."

"Apology accepted." Lord Carrollton glances around. "Shall we speed these proceedings along? I wish to have some time with my grandson."

"Very well," Lord Paxton says. "Young Carrollton, you stood as witness to this Valentine's rise?"

"I did, my lord."

"Was it an honorable battle?"

"It was, my lord. No one interfered. It was father and son. I give you my word."

"Lady Faith, were you also in attendance at your father's passing?"

"I was."

"Did you find fault with it?"

"I did not, my lord," she says, her confidence matching

her beauty. "My father brought on his own demise by challenging my brother. In fact, he taunted him, forced him to take action."

"Then it seems, Victor Valentine, that you have earned the right to take a seat at this table, to be named the head of the Valentine house."

"Do not be so hasty," the chubby-faced Old Family says, "to give such power to such arrogance. Barging in here after a long absence is perhaps forgivable. But to have the audacity to bring a human in here as well, I'm afraid, is intolerable."

"Lord Asher, in this instance, tolerances must be given," Victor says.

"Is that so?" he scoffs.

"It is." Victor stares at Asher, daring him to challenge him, to say anything else. But Asher simply leans back, as if bored with this conversation. I'm surprised he retreated so easily.

"Who is this young woman, then?" Paxton asks.

"Allow me the honor to present Dawn Montgomery."

I hold my breath, waiting for their reaction. There's a slight murmur at the sound of my last name from the oldest council members. They may be wondering: Is she *the* Montgomery? The fifteenth family of myth? Or does the name mean nothing at all to them, eradicated from their memories just as my ancestors were removed from life?

"She was the delegate for Denver," Victor says, and the whispers die down, my position as nothing more than common human reaffirmed in their eyes. "She, along with

Richard, Faith, and myself, has uncovered information of grave importance. A plan that could threaten all of vampire-kind is already unfolding. We need the Council's help to stop it."

Over the next half hour, we tell them everything: Sin, Day Walkers, the Chosen, Los Angeles. Victor speaks with confidence and often passes the explanations to me. Whenever I begin, I hear the groans of the Old Family, as if disgusted by my human breath in this room. But then I realize that I once dealt with the Bloody Valentine, I've faced down Sin, I've spoken to the oldest vampire in the world. And when I remember these things, I'm not worried anymore, and I become a delegate again. Not a delegate for Denver, but for all of humanity.

"Using the V-Process, Sin is creating powerful monsters that he could use to gain control of all the territories."

Lord Carrollton sighs. "I see the boy holds a grudge."

"I should think the humans would welcome a change in leadership," Lord Paxton says.

I shake my head. "He'll reduce our lives to a despair worse than what we now endure. I've seen the Chosen. Victor fought one, and it nearly killed him before he—we—were able to destroy it. Richard has dealt with them as well. Sin's plan is to have five hundred. Humans can't defeat Sin alone. We need you; we need to all be on the same side if we're going to stop him."

"This is nothing but myth and conjecture," Asher says. "If you had come by yourself, Victor, perhaps we would have believed you. But to bring a human with you to bolster your case, I'm afraid that you have lost all credibility with this Council."

"Do not speak so quickly or harshly," Lord Carrollton says. "Human words carry no weight here, but Los Angeles is Carrollton territory. Richard, what do you know of this?"

"The Thirst is rampant outside Los Angeles. The Infected hordes are rampaging through the countryside. I went to see Father. We—Faith, Dawn, and I—went to see him. I'm sorry to report, Grandfather, that my father was killed long before we arrived. All his Lessers are Infected."

Lord Carrollton closes his eyes for a moment and sighs heavily. "I should have followed Murdoch Valentine's example and overseen the territory of Los Angeles myself."

"With all due respect, Grandfather, I don't think it would have made a difference. It is as Dawn has indicated. The Chosen are formidable foes."

"Let us assume that this is all true, just for the moment," the eldest-looking vampire says. "What do you propose we do, Victor?"

"Lord Delacroix, in times of great danger, the Old Families will each send one child to fight for the whole. I ask that now. We need to go to Los Angeles and destroy the V-Processing center."

"Wasn't it *your* duty to get rid of the V-Process?" Asher asks.

Victor wastes no time with his response. "This one was built without my knowledge. Had I known, it would have been destroyed with the others."

"Your lack of knowledge is no concern of ours. This is your fault, not the Council's. Now you ask each of us to send a child to fight for you, a fight that is yours and yours alone?"

"You fail to see the larger picture," Victor says. "Unsurprising coming from the Asher family. Perhaps I should have brought a coloring book so you could busy yourself while I discussed serious matters with the Council."

"How dare you!"

"Enough!"

It's Lilith Ferdinand. Her tone is powerful, slicing through the bickering. Everyone holds silent for her.

"You have made your case, and a very good one at that," she says. "And you are correct: In times of great danger that affect us all, the Old Families will band together in such a way, but we do not go to war lightly. If that is your proposal, then it is time we vote on it."

My heart thumps and I'm sure they can hear it.

"All those in favor of Victor Valentine's proposal that we each send a child to fight with him, to destroy the V-Processing center in Los Angeles, in order to stop this army of Day Walkers and Chosen from growing any further—raise your hand."

Some do.

"All opposed?"

The others follow.

"The Council has spoken," Lilith says. "Seven to seven. I'm sorry, Victor, but we cannot help. The Council is divided, so we may take no action."

No. This can't be.

"Perhaps we didn't make our case well enough," Victor says, taking a step forward. "We can't beat him alone. If we lose, all is lost."

"You're a bit dramatic," Lord Asher says.

Am I going to do this?

"You are forcing us to take on this darkness by ourselves."

"We did not create the darkness," Lord Paxton says.

Am I really about to say this?

"You spoke," Lord Paxton continues. "We listened, we voted—"

There's no choice.

"The house of Montgomery didn't vote," I say. "As its representative, I vote yes."

Everyone around the table looks as though they were just blinded by the sun—except Lilith. She is studying me, perhaps seeing me clearly for the first time.

"There is no longer a house of Montgomery," Lord Asher says.

"There is. And I, Dawn Montgomery, descendant of Octavian Montgomery, claim my family's seat on the Council."

Chapter 12

Victor is immediately at my side, taking my hand. With that simple touch, I feel his support and belief in me. I know he didn't want me to reveal my heritage, but now that I have, he won't let me stand alone. My love for him grows and I squeeze his fingers.

I wait a moment, gauging the Council's reaction. There isn't one at first, but slowly a smile appears on one of their faces. And then another. And another. Soon, the smiles turn to laughter, polite and soft at first, before becoming loud and boisterous. They turn toward one another, enjoying the joke in front of them.

All except for Lilith, who gives the smallest smile as she arches an eyebrow. She's holding my gaze, communicating with me. *They're all fools,* she seems to be saying.

"Whoever said the Valentines had lost their sense of

humor a thousand years ago?" Asher asks.

The laughing continues, but I know what will make it stop.

"I am Dawn Montgomery. *The* Montgomery. The very last. I am Old Family."

Reaching into my jacket, I pull out the Confirmation Decree, the vampiric family tree, the modern records and place them on the table, carefully, with all the respect they deserve. With them, I have the power to turn the tide.

Before I can pull my hand back, the closest vampire, Asher, grabs my arm tightly. I see the anger in his eyes and the fangs beginning to lengthen in his mouth. But if he was fast, Victor is faster, and much quieter. His long lean fingers are clutching the man's wrist.

"It's bad manners to touch an Old Family member without permission, Asher," Victor says. "Some have been killed for less."

"And yet you touch me as well. What is this game you're playing, Valentine?"

"There is no game. See for yourself."

Victor releases his hold after Asher lets go of my wrist. Even though it hurts badly, I don't rub it. To reveal any weakness is to put us all in danger.

If Victor is nervous about me speaking so boldly, he doesn't show it. I have no doubt that he'd throw his life down right now if it came to it. He isn't holding me, but I can feel his presence so strongly that he might as well be. Stealing a glance at him, I see pride and admiration.

One of the men eagerly grabs the parchment and reads.

When he flips the page, I can tell he's going over the signature again. And again. And again.

"Do you care to explain yourself, Lilith?" he asks, tossing the paper toward her.

She glances down at it before passing it to the Council member to her right. That man reads it, is left in stunned disbelief, and then passes it along. So on and so on, until Asher gets his hands on it. Somehow it angers me that his grubby little fingers trace the story of my lineage. And his eyes stop on Lilith's signature, just as Victor's had.

"What. Is. This?" he demands, flinging the parchment to the center of the table, where it lies stranded.

With a calm, collected voice, Lilith finally speaks. "Have you never seen a Confirmation Decree, Byron Asher?"

"Of course I have! But not one for a family that was eradicated a millennia ago. Do you realize the damage you've done to your family by signing such lies as these!"

"You dare question the authority of my signature?" she asks, ice in her voice. She's clearly used to dealing with men just like Asher. "In front of the Council, in front of all the families, you *dare* to question the honor of the Ferdinand family?"

"I question *your* honor, not your family's—"

"I *am* the House of Ferdinand and have been so for five hundred years, longer than you've lived."

Asher says nothing, perhaps realizing he can't win this one alone.

So it is Lord Delacroix who speaks, his tone measured and controlled.

"Lilith, no one here would think to question your loyalty or honor, but we must also inquire as to why you have signed a Confirmation Decree for a family that also has a death warrant signed by all of us."

"By our ancestors," she corrects. "And I have to explain myself to no one. If anyone here wishes to challenge the legitimacy of this document, and of Dawn Montgomery's claim as Old Family, then they must challenge the legitimacy of the entire House of Ferdinand. Here and now."

"Let's not get carried away," another says. "Lilith, you may explain yourself in due time to all of us. But until such a time, and for the integrity of the Council, I must insist that Dawn Montgomery remain, as it were, a human, and unable to take seat at this Council."

"No," I say. "I demand the seat that was stolen from my ancestors."

He looks at me, and his reasoned voice has given way to a cold stare. "Child, need I remind you that there is still a death warrant on all Montgomerys. That name, perhaps, may not be one whose weight you are ready to bear."

"Oh, enough of this!" Asher says. "Have you all gone mad? Are we seriously entertaining the thought that this girl—who contains but a single drop of Montgomery blood—should be allowed a seat on the Council?"

"That's exactly what we're entertaining," Lilith says. The room goes silent again, which seems its natural state. As time passes, Lilith looks for challengers, and when no one speaks, she does. "We've been very rude to our guests. Please, Dawn, Victor, Richard, and Faith, if you would be so kind as to join me in my study, we may discuss this further without constant interruption."

She stands, and in her movements I can see the obvious grace of Old Family women. Faith has it, but Lilith's is even more refined, as if each step were practiced a thousand times before letting it show in public.

She leads the way out of the chamber and back down the stairs, all four of us in tow. In the room where all the companions wait, I see an incredibly striking young man stand up as his mistress enters. Lilith simply waves him down and he obeys, knowing it isn't time for him yet.

Her study is down a hall and up another staircase, and when she pulls back the door, I'm impressed by all the worldly objects crammed into a single space. Paintings and tiny sculptures and strange artifacts from across the globe line shelves and desks. At the far end is a great Gothic window that looks out onto the night, and I realize then just how high up we are.

"I knew you would come eventually," she begins, turning toward us. "As soon as you stepped through that door, I knew. You look like a Montgomery; I could place you anywhere."

"Lady Ferdinand," I say, giving a little curtsy, "I thank you for your kind words in the council chamber."

"Oh dear, there's no need to curtsy for me. You are Old Family after all."

"Is it true?" I ask.

"Yes. I'm sure you have so many questions, but first, let me tell you my role in this bizarre drama."

We listen as Lilith tells us about the Montgomery family, words that I can hardly imagine I'm actually hearing, but they seem only to confirm everything I've always known was deep inside me. I clutch Victor's hand and scoot up to the edge of the seat, not wanting to miss a single syllable she utters.

The Montgomery family could produce dhampirs, she tells us. Half human, half vampire. This ability, as well as these unusual creatures, was feared by all the families and a death warrant was signed, led by the Valentine house.

"My great-grandfather, Errol Ferdinand, refused to sign the death warrant," she says. "And it was of such importance that until it was signed by everyone, excluding the Montgomerys of course, it could not be acted upon. So Errol was murdered by his own brother."

"And there was no witness," I say.

She smiles, strokes the necklace she wears, the Ferdinand family seal secured at the bottom. "I see you've been getting some history lessons. There's a bit of a debate as to whether a witness was involved. I doubt it, but others in my family would disagree. Nonetheless, our clan was torn apart after that. Errol had not yet become ash when the death warrant was signed by the new Lord Ferdinand."

"I'm sorry," I say.

"Thank you, child." Lilith walks over to a painting of a very handsome young man, whose features are much like her own: strong, confident, and at the same time chilly.

"Errol's son, my grandfather, Gustav, hated what had happened. The death warrant issued for the Montgomery family represented to him all that was wrong with us: our fear of anything different. The other families' obsession with blood purity was so great that they would eradicate an entire family. And for what? They placed such value on blood yet were willing to spill it so easily. Centuries passed, and Montgomerys were killed. Gustav eventually ascended the throne, killing the vampire who killed his father."

Lilith traces her hand over a long, metal dagger just below the picture, and I wonder if it was with that very weapon that Gustav reclaimed the throne.

"After that, Gustav made it his life's goal to find any remaining Montgomerys and protect them, just as his own father would have protected them had he been given the chance. It took him a century of looking, but he found him. The one Montgomery who had escaped. Gustav visited him in the loneliest cabin in the deepest woods, so far from all things. Around a small table a pact was made: The Montgomery line could continue. One son each generation, to be born to a human mother. In that way the blood would become diluted, but the name would always remain."

"Why would he do that?" I ask. "Going against the death warrant would have been a crime. Right?"

"Yes, and punishable by death. Which is what happened to him one night. Killed by a Valentine who suspected the pact had been made. I'm afraid that's where the rift between our two families began, Victor." She nods toward him. "I hope we may close that chasm."

Victor nods in return.

"Even two thousand years ago," she continues, "the Ferdinands knew that one day there would be a war between humankind and vampires. Our differences are too great. But when they heard of the Montgomerys' ability to conceive with humans, the Ferdinands saw their salvation. The Montgomerys could act as a bridge, bringing together both sides. In such a way, a war could be prevented. But when that death warrant was signed, my ancestors felt that we had in fact sealed our own deaths. We always thought that if we could save the Montgomerys, perhaps we could save ourselves."

In the painting, Gustav's eyes speak something else now. I think the painter captured it: hope that he'd made a difference.

"So it was that the Montgomery line continued, albeit slowly. They were always in danger, but as time passed, their name was forgotten by most families as sons killed fathers to acquire power—we are a bloodthirsty lot. All the original signers eventually perished. Those who came after began to think the Montgomerys nothing more than a myth. But the Ferdinands had made one more promise: They would forever remind the son of Montgomery of his lineage and of his pact to carry it forward. It has been my duty, for five hundred years now, to visit the son of the Montgomery line and to tell him of his true heritage."

"You mean—"

But she holds up her hand before I can continue, knowing that what I was going to say would pain me too much.

"I never met your father," she says. "I was unable to

reach him in time, and for that I'm deeply sorry. But I did meet *his* father and told him the truth. It's amazing. Every time I spoke to a Montgomery, they were rarely shocked. In many ways, I think they've always known. Even more telling is their ability to hold it forever, to keep it secret." She sighs deeply. "Now *that* is the mark of Old Family."

"And that's why you signed that Confirmation Decree."

"That's part of the reason, yes. But there's another, and this is where our little tale takes an interesting twist: No doubt you've seen the Montgomery family tree, and no doubt you've seen the branch that held two children. Maximillian Montgomery had a son and a daughter: Esmerelda. The first female Montgomery ever born. With her, I saw the chance to finally bring the Montgomerys back out of the shadows. I thought enough time had passed since the warrant was signed; I hoped that the Montgomerys would be embraced. Already the fear of war was growing.

"And so I played matchmaker as it were. Esmerelda was quite simply beautiful, and she had enough Old Family blood in her that she was irresistible. And so I persuaded her to pursue one Murdoch Valentine."

At this she gives an incredibly wicked smile, and I give one back.

"Your father, Victor, was notorious for taking human companions. Imagine his surprise when he took Esmerelda and found several months later that she had become pregnant with his child."

He would have been floored. With the exception of the Montgomerys, humans and vampires can't have children.

But Esmerelda had enough Old Family in her that she could carry Murdoch's son. A son who would grow up to become . . .

"Sin," I say.

"That's right. A horrid name given to him by Murdoch. He hated the child from the outset. And he hated him even more when I arrived at his doorstep with the Confirmation Decree, showing that Esmerelda was part of the Montgomery family. Imagine his anger at knowing that he helped to continue that blood line by complete accident, a family his own ancestors had tried to eradicate."

"No wonder he hated Sin."

"Yes, and his hatred only grew when he found the child's gift of day walking. He hated him so much that he did away with the boy's mother."

I cringe at that. Victor puts his arm around me.

"I'm so sorry, Dawn," Lilith says. "I had no idea Murdoch would do that to her. The Valentines were the most powerful family, and they led the charge to compose the death warrant. I thought that if Murdoch's son were a Montgomery, he would have to do the only honorable thing: embrace the Montgomerys, call an end to the destruction of their family. I thought, at the very least, he would protect Esmerelda. But I was wrong on all counts."

I think back to the family tree I saw but now fill in the lines myself. Esmerelda Montgomery and Murdoch Valentine, the parents of Sin Valentine. But there was another branch to that tree.

"Esmerelda's brother," I prompt.

"Yes," Lilith says. "The Montgomerys were always to have at least one *son* to carry on the name. And so a boy named Jonathan was born, and he was your ancestor.

"I've kept watch on the Montgomerys from afar," she continues. "By my count only three remain. You. Sin. And the last full-blooded Montgomery, Octavian. You should meet him. I'm sure he can provide many answers for you. I heard he was somewhere far west of here, somewhere in—"

"The mountains," I say.

"That's right." She pauses. "The mountains."

I shake my head. "He's dead. I met him when Sin took me there. He said that we were the last remnants of an Old Family bloodline. He said that, just before killing Octavian and draining his blood."

Lilith nods, her hands clasped together as though mourning at the man's funeral.

"I'm sorry to hear that," she says. "But I'm afraid Sin is more insane than you imagine. The hate inside of him festers without bounds, and it was a hate that began at the hands of your father, Victor. It pains me to say this, but in some ways you shoulder the blame for what Sin has become."

I'm about to defend Victor when he says, "I know. I knew my father had another son, but he rarely spoke of him. I also knew how strict my father could be, especially if it was a child he did not want. I could have gone back. I could have taken Sin away somehow. But instead I was young, afraid of my father's wrath, and just left him there."

"But we can still right it," I say. "Sin is beyond salvation, but we can still stop him."

"Perhaps," Lilith says. "But for that, I believe we must reenter the council chamber. And Dawn, your right as an Old Family vampire I will defend with my life, but that may not be enough to get you the seat you deserve. I see that now. The Council may demand that only full-blooded vampires be allowed onto the Council. But we shall see."

"Lilith, I don't know what to say. Everything you've done . . ."

"I've only played a small part in this. I've set the stage, I've put the actors out, but you, Dawn Montgomery, will now step into the leading role."

Chapter 13

Back in the council chamber our welcome isn't exactly warm. No telling what they've been talking about since we left.

Lord Paxton rises. "Miss Montgomery, we have examined your documents. We cannot deny that you have some trace of vampire blood in you, but you are not a vampire. Only a full vampire may sit on the Council. Are you willing to be turned?"

"No," Victor says adamantly.

"Why, young Valentine? If she would join us, then surely she would want to be like us."

Victor places his hands on my shoulders, turns me, and gazes into my eyes. "I'll die before I let you be turned."

"There's no need for me to be turned," I say, speaking with the conviction of truth. "I have Old Family blood in my veins. I can trace my lineage back as far as anyone at this table. Those facts alone give me the right to be here."

"She is right," Lilith says, standing as well. "She is of the Montgomery family. Her blood gives her a right to sit on the Council."

"Perhaps," Lord Paxton says. "But the concern exists that she will be more interested in her human side than her vampire. Dawn, you've spent your entire life living in the world of humans, yet if you would have a voice here, we need to be assured that your loyalty would be to us vampires. Perhaps a test is all that is required. Would you be willing to agree to that?"

"No," Victor says at the same time that I say, "Yes."

Victor turns to me. "You don't know what the test will be, Dawn."

"I know I can't vote if I'm not sitting on the Council. We need their help to defeat Sin." I face Lord Paxton. "I'm willing to be tested."

"Tomorrow night, then. Leave us now, all of you. We have much to discuss."

Victor, Faith, and Richard bow. Because they do, I bow as well. Then we turn and walk from the room.

No one says anything as we drive back to the hotel. When Victor parks the car, we all climb out, so silent, so somber, like the city. The rain has stopped, but a heaviness weights the air.

I look at the decrepit hotel. I can't face going in there right now. "Can we walk for a while?"

"We need to talk," Victor says.

"We can do that while we walk." I start out, not waiting for them, but I'm aware they're following. Victor quickly falls into step beside me, his nearness protecting me from any vampires who think I might be "unclaimed property."

We walk along in silence. I want him to take my hand, but I know he's upset with me. Vampires are out on the streets, but they give us a wide berth. A few are Old Family, descendants of those we just left. But most are Lessers. They bow as we stride past them.

"I can't believe that you agreed to a test without even knowing what it is," Victor finally says.

"I didn't really have a choice."

"One vote on the Council isn't going to make any difference."

"Eight to seven, it will make all the difference in the world."

"We could've reasoned with them, laid out our case in more detail and convinced one of them to change their vote."

I turn sharply and he stops in his tracks. I stare up at him. "Old Family are stubborn. They would've debated for a decade before finally noticing that their heads were in a guillotine. Sin could be weeks, maybe just days from marching. There's no more time for talk."

He puts his hands on my shoulders, squeezing me lightly. It feels nice.

"I know. But they'll never see you as equal as long as you're not a full vampire."

"Before we went to the Council, you said it doesn't matter what's in my blood, but it does. You saw the Council's reaction. Can you imagine when the citizens of Denver find out? Whenever they see me, they will only see the fangs I don't even have. They will only see the enemy."

He moves his hands down until they're wrapped around my own. "I don't see the enemy in you."

"But can you see how screwed up everything is? Vampires don't want me because of my human blood. Humans won't want me because of my vampire blood."

"You don't have to tell humans about your heritage."

"But if I don't, am I admitting to being ashamed of the vampire in me?" I break free of his hold and start trudging forward again. "In any case, I'll figure out what to tell the humans when we return to Denver. Right now, my issue is the vampires. Any idea what sort of test they'll give me? Don't suppose I'd be lucky enough to discover that they're talking about a multiple-choice quiz to test my knowledge of vampires."

I'm trying to make light of it because I don't want Victor to know how worried I am that I made a big mistake in accepting their challenge.

"I doubt it," Victor says, his tone serious and concerned. I could probably tell him a real joke right now and he wouldn't laugh. "A seat on the Council isn't often vacated. Tests are never required to fill one that is. I have no idea how the Council will test you."

He has no imagination, but I do. I imagine it'll be difficult and dangerous.

"Maybe it'll just be an inquisition," I muse.

"They tortured people during the Inquisition." He slips his hand into mine. "Tell them you changed your mind, you don't want a seat on the Council."

I look up at him. "We need my vote to get the Old Families to rally against Sin."

"We don't need them. We can fight this by ourselves."

"But at what cost?"

We both grow silent, and I try to distract myself from my worries by taking mental snapshots of the city so I can describe everything to Tegan. She'll be so disappointed to learn that there's no beauty here. A few gaslights are glowing, and I'm not sure why. Vampires don't need them. Maybe humans wander the streets at night as well, although I haven't seen any.

"When are you going to stop being angry about Xavier?" I hear Faith say from several feet behind us.

"I told you, Faith, I'm not angry."

"You give a good imitation."

Richard doesn't respond, and I can sense Faith's frustration building. Finally, she hisses low, "All right. What did you want me to say when he asked me to stay?"

"'I can't because it's not where Richard will be.' I wanted to be the reason you wouldn't stay with him. Not Victor."

"You are! Don't you understand? I'm scared, all right? I don't like that I think about you all the time. I don't like that during the past ninety-eight years I compare every guy I meet to you."

"You do?" I hear the genuine surprise in his voice.

"Does that make you happy?"

"Yes, it does."

I hear a fist pounding into flesh and can't stop myself from glancing back. Richard is holding Faith's wrist. I have a feeling she punched his shoulder.

"I hate you," she says.

He cradles her face. "Do you really?"

She shakes her head. "But you'll stop wanting to be with me eventually."

"Stop wanting to be with you? I love you, Faith."

"Vampires can't love."

"If vampires can't love, then they can't hate. If you can hate me, you can love me."

"You'll break my heart."

"Why would I do that? In ninety-eight years, I've never met anyone who intrigues me like you do. You're stubborn, spoiled, and you try so hard not to be loved."

"Dawn says love is worth the pain, but I think it could kill me."

"It won't. Trust me." Then he lowers his head and kisses her. Leaning into him, she winds her arms around his shoulders. With her heels, she's almost as tall as he is.

As they begin entwining themselves around each other, I look away. "Maybe you should tell them to go back to the hotel."

Victor grins. "I think they'll figure it out. You probably won't be sharing a room with Faith this morning."

"That's okay. She snores."

His grin broadens. "Did you want to go back to the hotel?"

"No, let's walk a little more." We never have any time just for us, and while New Vampiria isn't romantic, it is quiet. A light mist begins to fall.

"Before the war, there was a beautiful field just over there," Victor says. "It was so green and lush. I wish you could have seen it."

Where he's pointing, I see dilapidated buildings. "We lost so much in the war."

"Things that can never be replaced," he says. "I don't even know if they can be rebuilt."

"They have to be. We must have a world that's better than this depressing place."

"There's that optimism I admire." He stops and faces me. "If the field were still there, I'd take you on a picnic. I'd—"

A scream rends the quiet. I jerk around, trying to determine where it came from. Faith and Richard are nowhere to be seen. I guess they did return to the hotel.

Then the terrified scream comes again.

"There!" I yell, and dash toward the mouth of an alley. As my legs churn, I yank out my stake from my holster. Although it's dark in the alley, just enough light is filtering in that I can make out the silhouette of a girl pressed against the wall, fighting off a guy.

"Hey, asshole!" I shout.

With one arm across her shoulders, he keeps her pinned

in place while he slowly turns his head to glare at me. He's emaciated, too thin. His cheeks are hollow. Dark half-moons rest beneath his eyes. Hissing, he reveals his fangs. "I'm hungry. You'll do for dessert."

"Help me," the girl pleads.

I glance quickly back. Victor's not here. What happened to him? Crap! Terror slices through me. Was this some sort of trap?

"Please!" the girl cries out, bringing my attention back to her.

I need to find Victor, but I can't leave the girl to this monster. I start running, gathering my energy and strength—

I take a flying leap and kick him hard, knocking him back, freeing her. "Run!"

She doesn't have to be told twice. I hear her rapid footsteps as she escapes, leaving me to face the vampire. He quickly comes to his feet.

"I guess you just became the main course."

He comes for me. I duck, shove him back. Hunger has made him weak, but also determined. We start circling each other.

He lunges. I swipe my stake across his chest. He leaps back to avoid it. Snarls.

"When was the last time you had blood?" I ask.

"What do you care?"

He rushes forward—

I leap to the side, then swing out a leg, knocking him off his feet. He lands hard, and I jump on top of him, pinning him, squeezing my knees against his arms, holding him down. I place the tip of my stake on his chest, above his beating heart. He roars.

Then surrenders. I feel him going lax. It could be a trick, but I think of the starving humans I saw in Los Angeles. I think about Crimson Sands. I think about the world I want to live in instead of the one that I do.

"You can have some of my blood," I say, shoving up the sleeve on my jacket.

"Dawn, no," Victor says.

I look back to see him standing there. I wonder where he was, but that's a question to be answered later.

"I don't have enough vampire in me to infect him with the Thirst. I have enough human blood in me to sate his hunger until he can find a legitimate blood source." I glare at my defeated vampire. "He'll kill you if you take too much."

"I wasn't expecting your generosity." With a sudden powerful move, he shoves me off and is standing over me.

From out of the shadows emerge cloaked figures. I leap to my feet, my stake at the ready. I was right. It is a trap. I start easing back toward Victor.

"We've seen enough," a voice I recognize from earlier in the night says. Lilith pushes back her hood.

I feel Victor at my back, his hand resting on my waist. "This was your test," he whispers softly.

I jerk my attention up to him. "You knew about this?"

"No. When you rushed toward the alley, I found myself surrounded by the Council's guards. Then I knew."

I glare at Lilith. "You said the test would be tomorrow."

"And you would have been expecting it. I believe you humans call something like this a pop quiz."

"What a stupid test! What if I'd killed him?"

Lilith smiles. "Hardly likely. Warwick is our best warrior."

Looking at him now, I can see that it was his loose clothing and makeup that made him appear emaciated. He's standing tall and confident. Yeah, my killing him probably wasn't going to happen.

"The girl?" I ask.

"One of my divas," Lilith tells me. "She was never in jeopardy."

"So it was all fake."

"All except your reaction."

"Well, did I pass?"

"We were testing your loyalty to vampires. The correct answer was to let the starving vampire have the girl. Your solution was *unanticipated*."

"She failed," Asher announces. "Her loyalty first was to the human. It will always be to the humans."

"Yet she showed empathy for the vampire. Unusual, most unusual. The Council must discuss this matter further. We'll give you our answer tomorrow night."

"Shouldn't I be involved in this decision?" Victor asks.

"You are recused because of your involvement with the human."

With that they disperse like silent wraiths into the night.

Victor puts his arms around me, draws me near. I can feel the rapid thudding of his heart.

"What if I had managed to kill him?" I ask.

"They'd have killed you. Vampire tests always hinge on life and death."

Lesson learned: Never agree to take a test without knowing the scoring system.

When Victor and I step out of the alleyway, Faith and Richard rush up to us.

"Sorry we couldn't get to you sooner," Richard says. "But guards swooped in on us."

"Too many to overpower," Faith adds. "Then they just let us go. What happened?"

"Dawn was given her test," Victor says.

Richard gives me a look of admiration. "Since she still breathes, I assume she passed."

"Did everyone know that not passing the test would have meant the end of my life?"

Richard shrugs.

"Someone could have said something," I tell them, irritated.

"Then you would have worried and nothing would have changed the outcome," Faith chimes in, a little too carefree.

"It's all moot now," Victor says, taking my hand and leading us away. "The Council is trying to decide if she passed."

Victor explains what happened.

"And if they decide she didn't?" Faith asks.

"I don't know," Victor admits.

"You mean they might still kill me?"

"Not without going through me," Victor assures me.

"Us," Richard clarifies.

"I'm deeply touched," I begin, "but if all of us are gone, who's going to fight Sin? We can't let him win."

"He's not going to win," Victor says adamantly. "And we're not going to die."

I take comfort in his words, then something else occurs to me, baffles me. "How did they manage to arrange a test so quickly?"

"They probably began discussing it when we were with Lilith," Richard says. "The diva and Warwick would have been at the Council building."

"Makeup can be quickly applied," Faith says.

"They knew where we were staying," Victor adds. "I sent my message to them from here."

"And if we hadn't gone walking?"

"They would have improvised. In some ways we are archaic and slow, but strategy and traps we've always excelled at."

When we get to the hotel, we go straight to our suite. Exhaustion hits me. I'm chilled and trembling from the dampness of the night and the fight in the alley.

"I'm going to take a shower."

Everyone looks at me with concern. Probably because I'm acting like a human.

I go into the room I'm sharing with Faith, grab my

bag, and walk into the bathroom. Okay, so it's not going to be a shower. Not sure why I didn't notice before that the claw-footed bathtub doesn't have a showerhead above it. Turning on the faucets, I let the sound drown out everything as I peel off the leather. It really protected my skin during the fight. Maybe I should look into getting another outfit.

Sinking into the warm water, I feel my muscles loosening, relaxing. I refuse to believe that the Council would kill me. I gave the human and the vamp a chance at life. How can they fault that? I want the vampires to be better than that. I want them to be our allies. I want them to have a spark of humanity. Because a part of them is in me.

"Daddy," I whisper as tears sting my eyes.

How did he feel when he realized what he was, what we were? I wish he'd told me while he was alive. I wish I could have talked to him about it. I just wish I'd *known*.

I see a small pool of red, widening and fading. Lifting my hand, I notice a tiny scrape. It must have happened during the fight. I watch the blood drip into the water. Just a couple of drops. Not human. Not vampire. Dhampir.

In anger, I press my thumb to the wound until it stops bleeding. It's blood. Just blood. It doesn't define who I am. I'm Dawn because of the things my parents taught me. They taught me compassion, they taught me to fight for the underdog. They taught me to believe in a world where everyone could live together. Where humans didn't fear the night and vampires didn't fear the day.

The Council needs to understand that my blood gives

me a right to sit at the Council table. And if they're too boneheaded to understand that, I can still fight for a better world.

Getting out of the bathtub, I dry off and slip into my flannel.

When I step into the bedroom, a guy dressed all in black is standing before me holding two stakes. The room has no windows, but it does have a fireplace. And his face is covered in soot. I sigh deeply.

"What is this? Another test?"

He slowly shakes his head. "I'm here to fulfill the death warrant."

Chapter 14

Crap!

The good news is that someone obviously believes I'm a descendant of the Old Family Montgomerys. The bad news—someone believes I'm a descendant of the Old Family Montgomerys and the death warrant is still in effect.

The worst news: My stake is in the bathroom. Going back in to retrieve it means getting confined in a small space—

I grab a vase from a nearby table and throw it at him. He ducks. It crashes.

He charges.

The door bangs against the wall and a blur of movement takes the vampire down. But he's agile and quick.

He's back on his feet and rushing toward me—

"Dawn!" Faith yells, and I look over to see a stake flying toward me.

I grab it, drop to the floor, and roll away from my attacker. Victor slams into him again. I see a stake going for his side—

"No!" I jam mine into the vamp's arm, pinning it to the floor.

He roars out in agony, but with renewed strength, he manages to toss Victor off, throwing him against me. He pulls my stake free and then is again on his feet facing us.

"Put down the stakes," Victor orders. "We won't kill you."

He shakes his head.

"Four against one, the odds aren't in your favor, my friend," Richard says. "Do as Lord Valentine says."

The vampire lifts the stakes and plunges one into his own heart. He crumples to the floor.

Victor curses as he rushes forward to kneel beside the fallen vamp. "Who sent you?"

The vampire merely smiles before closing his eyes forever.

"Why did he do that?" I ask, stunned that he'd take his own life.

Victor stands. "Because he knew we'd question him about who wants you dead."

"It had to be someone on the Council," Richards says. "They're the only ones who know about Dawn's heritage."

"But who?"

"Asher," I say. "He doesn't want me on the Council."

"I doubt it's him," Victor says. "More likely, it's someone who has been very quiet."

"The truth is that it could be anyone," Richard points out.

"Whoever it was," Faith muses, "this guy was afraid of disappointing him."

No kidding.

When Louis brings up a servant to help clean up the mess, he apologizes profusely that our evening was disturbed.

"No one has ever been attacked in this hotel before. I don't understand it. It's the younger generation. They have no respect or manners."

By the time he leaves, the sun is rising. Victor is concerned that whoever sent the assassin might send a human to finish the job, so he and Richard agree to take turns keeping watch. The bedroom doors are kept open, which I assume is a disappointment to Faith and Richard, since they're sharing a bed.

I'm in Victor's room. He's standing in the doorway, looking out. I want to talk with him, keep him company, ask him if he thinks coming here was still the right thing to do. I don't even know if he has the answer, so I turn away and find it in myself. Yes. And with that circling my mind and the exhaustion of the night's events, I drift into slumber.

When I wake up, it's night and we go through the same routine: dressing, eating, driving to the monolithic tower. Only this time we'll be waiting for their judgment.

Or at least I'm waiting. It seems Victor has something else on his mind. He stalks to the center of the council chamber and sets his hands on the table.

"I'm not sure that I made it clear last night, but Dawn is under the protection of the House of Valentine. An attack against her is an attack against Valentine."

"It was a test," Lilith says. "Warwick knew not to kill her or harm her in any way, I assure you."

"Perhaps he did, but the vampire who was sent to our suite at the hotel apparently didn't get the memo. He said he was there to fulfill the death warrant."

Lilith is obviously taken aback. She opens her mouth, closes it. Looks at me. Then she turns to Asher. "Did you know of this?"

"Absolutely not."

"Only the Council members know she is an Old Family Montgomery," Victor says. "So someone in this room sent the assassin."

Lilith stands and glances at the other twelve Old Family. "Who? Who did this thing without consulting the others?"

"The signed death warrant is still in effect," Richard's grandfather says. "No consultation would have been required."

"But we were treating her as a guest. It is not proper to attack one's guest."

"It is not proper to ignore a death summons."

"Was it you then, Grandfather?" Richard asks.

The old man holds his gaze. "No, but I understand why the action was taken."

"I demand whoever sent the assassin claim his actions," Victor says, "and accept my challenge."

"You would champion her?" Lilith asks.

"Yes."

I'm confused, not sure what's going on. So many of the vampire rituals have been kept secret from us. I touch Richard's arm. "Rich—"

"Shh."

I want to punch him. Turning to Faith, I see the sadness and worry in her eyes. She just shakes her head.

Asher stands. "Young Valentine has made the challenge. It cannot be ignored. Who sent the assassin?"

At the end of the table, a vampire who looks to be about the age of Victor's father stands. He is olive-skinned with coal black hair. "I did."

"Lord Romanelli, do you accept my challenge?" Victor asks.

He smiles cockily. "I do, young Valentine."

"Excellent."

Victor quickly takes off his coat, pulls out a metal stake, and tosses it toward Romanelli, who snatches it from the air with frightening speed.

"I see no need to take this outside," Romanelli says, removing his coat.

No. No. I can't let this happen.

"I agree. Let everyone watch," Victor says.

"So there is no question."

"Stop it!" I shout. "I refuse to let more blood be shed over a piece of paper."

"A piece of paper?" Romanelli says in shock. "It was *signed* by us to carry out your death."

"It was signed by your *ancestors*. By people you've never met to kill people you would never cross. Have any of you read it? *Can* any of you read it?"

I look around the table and see something I never imagined: nerves. They look from one to the other, each member hoping someone is still fluent in Ancient Vampiric and has read the document from top to bottom. But no one can.

"You just do it because that's what you're told," I say. "That's all. You did it out of tradition, without any thought, without a moment's hesitation. You are all enslaved by a piece of rotting parchment. And for what! What will it get you? Pride? Fulfillment? It will get you *nothing*! When I saw this city, I could tell how fragile it was, but I knew that this tower was solid, and I knew that I would find strength within the mighty Council that every human had feared for so long. But look at you all. You command empty space. You are masters of falling walls. And all you care about is making an ancient ancestor proud by fulfilling some mandate from a decree written over a thousand years ago.

"That's the difference. You vampires may have strength and immortality—at least until one of your own puts a stake through your heart. But in the end, living for centuries is your downfall. Because I'm proud that I'll die one day. I'm proud that my heart will stop beating forever. I have seventy years on this earth if I'm lucky, and I'll be damned if I waste a *second* of it fulfilling the desires of some distant relative from a thousand years ago who I never even met."

Silence. Wonderful, blissful silence. I felt the words from my heart, and in them I spoke not of my hatred toward vampires but, for the first time, of my love for humankind.

Victor slowly puts his stake back into his belt. To my surprise, Romanelli follows, albeit much more slowly.

"I often wonder," Carrollton says, "if the passage of all these centuries has brought us any true wisdom at all."

That gains gasps from some, contemptuous silence from others—but smiles and nods from a few. Including Lilith.

"We can see your passion, Dawn," he continues. "The death warrant was signed by all families, save the Montgomerys. It can only be removed by the same action. A unanimous vote."

Unanimous? Romanelli just tried to kill me! How could he possibly vote to get rid of it now?

"Then I call the vote now," Lilith says. "And I ask that all who raise their hand remember this: Now is not the time to create division amongst us. My family has suffered enough from this death warrant, fracturing us into two halves. I'd hate to see something similar happen to this Council."

Her words may be subtle, but their meaning is clear: The Ferdinands intend to stand by the Montgomerys. With a warning look at all the members who are now seated, and a knowing smile to Victor, she speaks words the Montgomerys have wanted to hear for so long. "All those in favor of rescinding the death warrant so that it may no longer burden us, raise your hand."

Some do it quickly, others more slowly. Asher takes his sweet time. But Romanelli's hand stays down. Until Victor looks at him, and another challenge is issued, only this one is more severe. Instead of them dueling, Victor seems prepared to go to war against the family who would threaten me. And as Romanelli looks at Lilith, he must realize that he'd be facing two enemies.

He raises his hand.

"Then it's unanimous," Lilith says. "The death warrant is forever stricken and the Montgomerys may now move in peace and be prosperous."

"Thank you," I say, the words seeming insufficient to express what I'm really feeling: incredible relief. "Now, my seat on the Council? The test? What did you decide?"

"You are a bold one, that much is clear," Asher says. "The Council has not yet decided."

"You haven't decided, Asher," Lilith says, "but I have. I was impressed last night and even more so now. She possesses an inner strength, tempered with compassion. We need fresh blood here. Young blood."

"We need no such thing. Strength in purity. You know that."

"Your opinion has been noted," Lord Paxton says. "But the fact remains: Dawn Montgomery has provided evidence of her Old Family heritage. She passed our test in ways that exceeded all of our expectations. And the death warrant has been rescinded. There is nothing to debate and nothing to vote on. Dawn Montgomery, please take your seat."

With a deep breath, I walk around the table and take the empty chair beside Lilith. It's simply a chair. Yet it carries with it so much power. It's the place where my ancestors should have sat all along. I have the opportunity to carry on their work, to affect the future of both humans and vampires.

Victor eases into the vacant chair beside mine. His presence calms my racing heart. Without him I wouldn't be here. I'm going to fulfill Lilith's dreams for the Montgomerys and serve as a bridge between the humans I've always loved and the vampires I've only recently learned to accept.

Lord Carrollton makes a special request that under the circumstances, Richard and Faith be allowed to remain. They stand at the back of the room, near the doors.

It is Lilith who first speaks, and her voice seems to resonate stronger now that I sit here with her.

"Shall we call for a new official vote in regard to

Victor's proposal? Now that we have a new member on the Council?" Lilith asks.

Asher's mouth drops. "You can't be serious."

"Very."

He looks like a man who can't quite get out of the absurd dream he's found himself in.

"Have you all gone mad?"

"Do you have a better plan to destroy Sin, Asher?" Victor asks.

"Destroy him? I suggest we join him."

"Never!" I shout, amid mutterings and the din of whispered conversations.

"We have no choice," Asher says.

"Sin may slaughter you before you even have a chance to speak," Lilith warns. "You fail to realize how twisted Sin's father was and in turn how twisted his own son became, having been locked in dungeons and cellars his whole childhood."

"He'll need us, don't you get it? Old Family blood is rich; one bag could probably feed his entire army of Chosen. He'll continue to march and kill everything in his path, including this Council. But he may need one of us for our blood. Just one . . ."

"And that will be you?" I ask.

"Why not?"

"I won't spend one more night as a coward," I say. "How in hell can you spend an eternity as one?"

"Listen, *girl*—"

"Madame!" Lilith shouts. "You will call her Madame or Lady. She is a Montgomery."

"First you want me to see her as Old Family. Then you have the audacity to give her a seat on this most sacred Council. And now you ask me, an Old Family vampire who has walked this earth four hundred years, to address her as Madame?"

"We aren't asking," Lord Paxton says. "We are demanding."

Asher looks around for support from the other Old Family, but none give it.

He chuckles lightly to himself, shaking his head in disbelief. "I've never seen such desperation. Maybe Sin is right: We've become weak. We're no longer needed. He is the future. He and his army of monsters. I'll take my chances with *him* over this insane Council. He'll decimate you all, but my blood may be spared if I act fast enough. While you try to save the bits of precious sand still in the hourglass, I'll be busy becoming allies with the man who's holding the hammer above it, waiting to smash it all to bits."

"If you leave now, the Ashers will have no say until a replacement is found," Lord Paxton says.

"I don't care! And neither will my clan. You'll doom us all."

"We were already doomed, Asher," Lilith says. "Before the war, before the humans even knew of our existence, we were already nearing the end. We vampires are immortal, but we stay the same. It is the humans who have become something more; it is the humans, with their few precious years, who try to change themselves for the better. We have forever, and we still can't do it. This war, VampHu, these cities were not the result of our victory, but the result of us exhaling our final breath."

Everyone is silent as she speaks. It's a truth they must've known in their hearts, a truth that has been created over hundreds, maybe thousands of years. And if we're all in awe of its reverence, Asher certainly is not.

"Damn you. Damn you all."

He leaves the room, shutting the door behind him. The Asher seat stands empty.

After a few moments, Lilith says, with a wicked smile, "Shall we call a vote as to Victor's earlier proposition?"

Hands are raised. Without Asher and with me, the vote is eight to six in favor.

"We shall each send a child to Denver," Lilith says. "One who can fight. But to gather an army of Lessers to accompany them will take time."

"Which is a luxury we do not have," Victor says. "We must act quickly to stop the creation of more Infected Day Walkers."

"You speak truth. What do you recommend, then?"

"Often, during the war, a small group of Old Family could do more than an entire army of Lessers. Our purpose is clear: to destroy the V-Processing center. I can achieve that with fourteen Old Family."

"And no Lessers?"

"We'll be able to move faster without them. Meanwhile you can begin assembling the Lessers and working on a means to ensure we have adequate blood. When the time comes and we have to face Sin's army, they'll be ready."

"I agree with your assessment," Lord Carrollton says. "As this began in Los Angeles, under my son's watch, it seems only fitting that Richard command those we send to do our bidding."

Richard bows his head. "I would be honored."

"Are there any objections to Richard leading the charge into Los Angeles?" Lord Paxton asks.

Silence.

"So it shall be. And, Victor, as we have you to thank for the V-Process—"

"I'm representing the Valentines," Faith announces.

Victor comes out of his seat. "Faith, I can't expect you—"

"Denver needs you."

Looking at her, I also suspect she doesn't want to let Richard out of her sight.

"And what of the Montgomerys?" Lord Romanelli asks.

"She is alone," Lilith says. "She is exempt from this."

"If she sits on the Council, if she has a vote, she is not exempt," Lord Paxton says. "She must go to Los Angeles or relinquish her seat on the Council."

I angle my chin. "I'll go to Los Angeles."

Beneath the table, Victor squeezes my hand. I know he's not happy about this, but I'm grateful that he doesn't say anything to undermine my authority on the Council. He knows as well as I do that I have to be seen as strong.

"We should be able to have our representatives arriving in Denver within three nights," Lord Paxton says.

Three nights? Then I'll be heading back toward hell's gates.

Chapter 15

As soon as the Council adjourns, we head out. We don't even bother to drop by the hotel to get our things. We have everything we need, everything of importance. We're not going to stop off at Xavier's either. We're going to drive straight through.

"That didn't turn out exactly as I expected," Victor says, and frustration vibrates in his voice.

"The truth is," Faith says, "someone has to keep an eye on Richard, make sure he behaves. I'm better equipped to do that than you."

His jaw clenches. He's not upset with Faith. He's upset with me.

"You should have stepped off the Council," he says in a flat voice. "Without Asher there, we had the votes to go to war."

"I proved that I had the right to represent the Montgomerys. That means at the table and in battle."

"And when we battle humans again? What then, Dawn?"

"With a seat on the Council, I'll die before I'll let that happen again." Reaching across, I lay my hand over his where it's gripping the steering wheel so hard that I can see the whites of his knuckles. "Victor, if I had sacrificed my place on the Council to avoid going to Los Angeles, I would have proved what many of them believed: that I wasn't worthy to be there in the first place."

"And how do you think Clive is going to take your returning to Los Angeles? Are you going to make up some story about why you have to go?"

I grow melancholy as I watch the skyline of the city grow smaller and smaller in my side view mirror. I wanted the vampires to be worthy of defeating us, of being more than they are. But just like the humans, they're struggling to survive. Like the humans? Not like us.

Because now I'm neither human nor vampire, but trapped between the two. I'm not sure where I'll fit in when we reach Denver.

"No," I say somberly. "I'm going to tell him the truth."

As usual my credentials get us through the gate, past the narrow-eyed suspicious guards. But as we roll through Denver, I can sense the thick tension in the air. Occasionally I see the bright orange flames from a large fire pushing up against the night sky as though its goal is to devour the stars.

A few people are out, running, darting through the streets. I hear screams, shouts.

"What's going on?" I ask, but then someone charges toward the car, trash can in hand.

Victor swerves the car just in time, his vampire reflexes missing the pedestrian who throws the metal tin at the car, where it bangs off the hood. He was aiming for the windshield.

I turn around in my seat to see him raising his fists in anger and others joining him. In their hands are their weapons of war: crowbars, baseball bats, and lit torches.

We round the corner and I see an old junker's shop where I once went with Tegan to get her phone repaired. The front window is smashed, people running in and out, holding their stolen goods tightly to their chests. The looters make quick work of everything, like ants eating a rodent to the bone. Little remains but empty shelves.

"This looks bad," Richard says. "I've seen some riots in my days, but this one—"

Splat!

Rotten fruit hits one of the side mirrors and Faith noticeably gags.

"Let's just get to the Agency in one piece," I say.

A huge explosion makes the night seem like day for a few seconds. I look upward and see the fiery smoke churning out of the Works. A careless worker? Sabotage? But why?

Victor speeds up and it takes all his concentration not to hit the rioting pedestrians who wander aimlessly through the roads, unreadable signs of protest in their hands.

We park in the Agency garage and go inside. Although the guards know me, they still call Clive to get his okay to send us up.

Clive looks weary, downtrodden as we step into his office.

"Dawn," he says, his voice rough and scratchy.

"Clive, what's happening?"

"I'm losing control of the city." He walks over to the wall of blinds and hits a button. They begin to retract slowly in a motorized fashion, starting at the middle and moving apart, giving us a good view of Denver. The vast city, with its maze of structures and surrounding wall, has its own mood. And the mood now is chaos.

The fires I saw from the street are more visible from this height. Portions of the city are aglow. Moving closer to the window, I press my hand against the cool glass as though I can erase what I'm seeing.

"You remember when I said Eris may have been waiting before she struck?" Clive begins. "Well, I think her waiting is over. The Day Walkers are everywhere. More than we knew, more than we could have imagined. People are terrified. They hear rumors that there is a nest of vampires in an abandoned building and they set fire to it. Without evidence. The fire department is having a difficult time keeping up. The Night Watchmen are fighting with citizens as much as with vampires. We don't have the staff or the resources. I've never wanted vampire intervention, but now we need it. Tell me the Council is sending help."

I glance back at him, wishing I could relieve his burden. "They're sending Old Family to Los Angeles, but we didn't know this was happening in Denver. Is there any sign of Sin here?"

"No. Just Eris. She's releasing Day Walkers into the city somehow. Not that it would be very difficult. It's only ever been a skeleton crew guarding the walls during the day. We always relied on the sun to keep the vamps out. But now that's not an option. We simply can't cover the entire wall night and day."

"How many have died?" I ask.

"Twenty, by most accounts. Half by vampires, the others by the fires started by those who feel powerless."

"Don't they know that isn't helping?" I ask.

"They don't think we're listening. They think we're making deals with the Day Walkers."

"That's ludicrous!"

"Of course it is," Clive says, stepping away from the window. "But it's Hursch who's telling them, so they're hanging on to his every word. He finally got his shot to be delegate and the city is falling apart. So he has to make a scapegoat out of someone. We've always been the easiest target, and even though we're now his *employer*, he gladly blames us."

"Fire him," I say. It seems like the obvious solution.

"I did, but he considers himself a delegate of the people now. He says he'll deal with Victor himself. He's always been seen as a radical hero, and that mystique has only grown since Eris arrived."

"Has Eris made any demands?" Victor asks.

"To surrender the city."

Victor curses harshly. Vampires aren't supposed to be controlled by emotions. Maybe he's been hanging around me too long, because it's obvious that he's livid. A big chill runs up my spine.

Faith and Richard are doing little more than staring out over the city. I can't tell what they're thinking.

Clive looks at Victor. "When you took the throne from your father, you told me things would be different, that there could be cooperation. Prove that to me now. Help us."

I turn toward Victor. I imagine running through his mind is every possible way to rid ourselves of Eris and her Day Walkers. But vampires lack imagination. His method will involve a direct assault. I think we need something a little more subtle.

"Do you have a way to contact Eris?" I ask Clive.

"Yes. She left a messenger in the city so she could be contacted when we're ready to negotiate our surrender. Why? What do you have in mind?"

"I think a little confusion might disrupt the Day Walkers and give us an advantage," I say, a plan forming.

"Confusion is often the best weapon if deployed properly," Victor says. "Do you have an idea?"

"Yes. It's time to cut off the head of the snake. It's time to go after Eris directly. We need to know exactly how she's getting the Day Walkers into the city and where they are."

* * *

Time isn't on our side. I don't know what Sin's plans are. He may be on the march already, his eyes set on Denver, the center of the entire country. If Denver falls, the country will be split in half, giving him greater power and leverage. So we have to act fast and secure the city behind the walls, then get the blood back into the countryside. From what I see, that all hinges on getting to Eris. How we deal with her I suppose will be her choice.

With everyone hovering around Clive's desk, I make various notes and jot down strategy, explaining as I go, adjusting as the others toss in their thoughts and ideas. My plan involves surrendering to Eris, asking her to take me to Sin so we can negotiate terms. I feel like I'm in the second phase of the war that never quite ended, despite what VampHu said.

"I don't like it," Clive says. "I say when we get her into the city, we capture her then."

"Too many Day Walkers are in the city," I remind him. "If anyone learns she's our prisoner, word will be sent to Sin. He'll unleash his army of Infected. The citizens of Denver won't stand a chance."

"What do you think, Richard?" Victor finally asks.

"I have a feeling that the Day Walkers, while smart, depend on Eris to give them orders. Their campaign to spread fear would be disrupted, *they* would be disrupted. If she goes, so do they."

"Then it's settled," I say.

"Dawn, this is risky. We don't know what she's capable

of or if she's planned on this all along," Victor says.

"I know. But we have to take the chance. We can't wait for her, or Sin, to make the first move."

I run my plan by them one more time, and we tweak it here and there, preparing for the worst-case scenario. Unfortunately, that scenario would be the deaths of everyone in this room. But if we don't strike now, then when?

Chapter 16

An hour later Clive sends word to Eris. When the sun has risen high enough to chase the vampires back into the shadows, we're both standing at the window, basking in the heat when he says, "She's coming."

I see the luxurious white carriage that carries her wherever she goes. Behind it is another one, no doubt carrying additional guards. They both come to a stop in front of the building and I watch as three hulking Day Walkers climb out of the first carriage and hand her down. More guards clamber out of the other carriage and take positions, obviously alert and ready for any danger.

"Everyone always thought we were making deals with vampires when really we weren't," Clive says. "And now, we're doing exactly what everyone always accused us of."

"Is the press release ready?" I ask.

"It's being typed up now." He checks his watch. "I go on air in thirty minutes to alert the citizens that you've surrendered to Eris in exchange for the Day Walkers leaving. I don't like this, Dawn."

It's not the first time he's protested or I've replied, "I'll be fine."

The moments stretch for eternity. Then she enters the room.

She looks like the sun's daughter walking through the doors, an expression of extreme arrogance on her face. With her are the three Day Walkers, good looking, obviously well fed, unlike so many others. They're calm and composed, not lusting after my blood, merely waiting for orders, looking around the room to make sure an ambush isn't in wait.

"Miss Montgomery," Eris says in that fake-polite voice I've always detested, "I hear you will be negotiating the city's surrender. Sin will be pleased."

"You'll take me to him?" I ask.

She tilts her head slightly. "To him and his army of Chosen. Shall we be on our way?"

"After you."

"Don't try anything. My guards are very fast and very deadly."

"I'm sure they are."

"Trained by Sin himself."

Which means they don't fight fairly.

I give Clive a determined look. "We're doing what we have to do, Clive. Don't feel guilty; it'll get you nowhere."

I hope he can read my subtext, that if something goes wrong, he can't blame himself. I knew what I was getting into when I came up with this daring idea.

Once outside, I'm given a hand up into the carriage. It's as luxurious on the inside as I'd imagined. It's clear that Eris would accept nothing less than plush, red velvet seats and a full burgundy leather interior.

She's lifted in as well and sits across from me, then the two Day Walkers join us, the third one taking his seat on top with the driver. With a whipping sound and the neigh of the horses, we begin clopping down the streets. The mighty carriage glides through the day.

The day. I knew Eris would want the meeting only when the sun was out. Only during the day can she neutralize any threat from Victor. Walking-in-the-sun bitch.

The gates of the city open up and we head down the long road. I wonder in which direction she'll ultimately take me. I assume west toward Sin, unless he is no longer there. Perhaps he's just over that hill or that mountain, nearer than we thought, in which case I'll be in a hell of a lot of trouble.

Looking out the window, I see the city walls slowly descend out of view as we make greater distance. They seem so fragile now, more fragile than ever. The Day Walkers are inside, walls or no. I can't keep my mind from returning to Crimson Sands and its unwalled foundation. Their strength comes from the citizens, vampires and humans, not from stone masonry on the outskirts trying desperately to hold the night at bay.

"Don't you love the sun," Eris says, looking dreamily out the window as it cascades beautiful light into the carriage.

"I enjoy the night more," I say.

"I would assume as much coming from you. After all, you are a vampire."

"A drop of Montgomery blood in my veins barely constitutes me as a vampire."

"But the potential of that single drop is infinite."

"You've been listening to Sin too much," I say, trying to paint her master as some myth-spinning madman. Anything to get her doubting, anything to keep her off balance.

"Once he turns you, you'll have a shift in perspective," she says. "So many Lessers are uncomfortable in their own skin. Do you know why? It's because they long to feel the sun. Everyone thought that the difference between humans and vampires was that we need blood to survive. No—that isn't the biggest difference. You humans ate animals, feasted on flesh and blood just as we do. In fact, you slaughtered them in a most uncivilized manner. So, no, it isn't the blood that made vampire Lessers different. It's the sun. Without it, the human soul shrivels and dies and all that's left is the choking reminder of the beautiful daylight they once felt but are forever denied."

"Are you implying that you still have a human soul? Because I'm not so sure of that," I say.

"I'm saying that Day Walkers retain more humanity than Lessers. We are superior. You will see that. Your humanity won't be lost, but only enhanced, coupled with the power and immortality of a vampire."

She's trying to sell me on the idea, though I know what Tegan would think: Eris is trying to sell *herself*. Maybe she isn't convinced, even after all these years, that she's happy with what she is.

"Of course, you'll be lucky if he decides to turn you now," she says. "He knows you went to the Council. Don't you remember the offer he gave you?"

"Kill Victor and he'll spare my friends."

"And you spat on his generosity. You've already shown your disloyalty. I have no idea what fate you now face." She smiles, hoping I'll be afraid of this ominous warning. But I'm not. "Rest now. We have many miles to cover."

That's the best thing I've heard from her so far, because that means the night will come before we arrive, and that is what we need the most. The night.

Despite Eris's suggestion I stay awake the entire time, watching the sun slowly dip down. It's funny, I've always enjoyed sunsets, though I've known the dangers they bring. Now, however, the opposite is true: The setting sun brings my salvation.

The night grows older and we continue riding. I figure it's been nearly twelve hours of nonstop traveling when we finally come to a halt. I look out the window, expecting to see Sin's devilish smile, the frightening metal claw attached to his arm, the one that scarred Michael's face and chest. Instead all I see are ruins of what were once buildings.

"We have to let the horses rest," Eris says, the carriage door opening and the Day Walkers exiting. She takes my arm and not so gently escorts me outside.

The air is cool and I quickly gauge our surroundings. We're barely off the main road.

"We'll stay here for the evening," Eris says. "Don't worry. The Lessers out here won't dare come near us."

"I wasn't worried," I say, knowing that if anyone should be worried, it's her.

The horses attached to the carriages are unhitched and led to a small stream running not far from the main building, or at least what was once a main building.

"This place used to be a hydro plant," Eris says, as though reading my mind. "That tiny stream was once a massive river. This building drew energy from it and powered the nearby cities. Vampires hid here during the war until it was bombed by you humans."

"Looks like we did a pretty good job," I say.

She glares at me, annoyed. "We've put a great distance between us and the city. Us and your friends. Don't annoy me. My hand might *accidentally* slap your face."

"I notice we went north. I figured we would go west, back toward Los Angeles."

"Yes, so would everyone else. I couldn't take the chance that Clive had set up an ambush down the western road, so we'll be taking the scenic route."

Clever, but I'd expect nothing less from her.

I start walking among the ruins. I'm Eris's prisoner, but she doesn't need to chain me. With her speed, and the Day

Walker guards as well, I could never escape. Not by myself anyway.

Concrete shells of buildings rise up like a strange forest, nothing but the gray slabs. The metal cables that once held them together now stick out as though they are exposed bone. Bits of rubble, both large and small, litter the ground and I have to watch my step. Inside the main building, or what's left of it, I see the remnants of a fire where scavengers once made camp. Cinder blocks circle the ashes.

"Terry, get up high and keep a lookout," Eris shouts.

One of the Day Walkers brushes past me and quickly scrambles up the building, using the wall and the remains of floors to bounce from one place to the next, until he's scaled the three stories in a matter of seconds.

Sitting at the top, he looks out over the land and I wonder what he sees. I sit on one of the cinder blocks and wrap my arms tightly around myself to ward off the chill. A Day Walker comes up to me and places a blanket around my shoulders and then lights the fire with a match.

"Thank you," I say.

"We wouldn't want you dying of frostbite," he says.

"You could just turn me and save my life before that happened."

But he shakes his head. "Only Sin will have that pleasure. Not only would you be robbed of the wonders of walking in the sun, but he would have our heads."

So I sit and wait, hoping that the horses will need a full night's rest before continuing their journey.

"Eris, something's coming," Terry says from atop his watch post.

My heart jumps.

"What is it?" she asks.

"A car. Heading this way."

Eris clamps her jaw tight, her words a hiss between her teeth. "Your friends?"

"I have no idea."

"Let's hope not. For their sake."

She moves away and gathers the other Day Walkers, each one checking to make sure their stakes are in their belts, in their boots, across them in bandoliers.

"Eris . . ."

"Talk to me, Terry."

"They're definitely—"

A vicious black shadow, fast and unforgiving, knocks him from his perch. One moment he's there, the next, he's falling to the earth, a trail of blood flowing from his body. When he lands with a thud, a stake is lodged in his heart. I look back to where he was, but the shadow has moved on.

"Spread out!" Eris yells.

The headlights of the car appear closer, barreling right down at us, its engine echoing through the vast space. When the car is near the camp, it stops and slides, the doors flying open, and figures tumbling out, stakes at the ready.

Terry's fall put the fear into their hearts, and the arrival of Old Family vampires, Richard and Faith, sealed their fate. Michael and Ian do their part. They may not have the speed and strength of their fanged opponents, but they have experience, they have technique. Day Walkers fall quickly to the ground. Each one has a stake squarely in his chest, and their eyes are closed, never to see another sunrise.

Eris looks around nervously. Jumping to my feet, I sprint toward her, intending to tackle her.

Her beautiful figure becomes a blur, a white cascade in the wind, shadows and mirrors, on a direct collision course with me. She stops dead just within arm's reach of my throat. I stagger to a halt. Victor is beside her, a stake in his hand, the tip lodged in her ribs, but not her heart. It continues to beat.

Her knees begin to buckle as she shows her fangs and grits her teeth in pain. Her eyes are large, a combination of frustration, anger, and agony.

Within minutes, Eris is on the ground, chains wrapped tightly around her. They constrict her, make it impossible for her to dislodge the iron links or the stake still planted in her ribs. But rather than scream with pain and frustration, she merely looks at me with an immense fury, like nothing I've ever seen on someone so beautiful.

Richard and Faith are going about the bodies, turning them over and crossing their arms in the dignified manner of forever sleep.

Michael and Ian are still looking among the ruins, perhaps for Day Walkers that decided to hide rather than fight. But they don't find any. Facing my friends was a lesser evil than facing a disappointed Sin.

"It looks like your plan worked," Victor says to me, in full view of Eris as though she were nothing but a beautiful rock. No threat.

"How?" she shouts.

I take off my shoe and dump the tiny microchip into my palm. The chip that would allow Victor to track the citizens of Denver. The chip designed to locate those who have not met their quota. A chip that allowed him to follow me instead.

As I explain it to Eris, she screams her outrage.

"Now," Victor says, approaching Eris and kneeling in front of her, showing no fear, no animosity. "We have a great deal to discuss."

"I'll never tell you anything," she says.

"We'll see. . . ."

Chapter 17

Victor, Faith, Richard, and I take the car. Michael and Ian each transport a carriage. Inside one of them, Eris is chained up tightly to the velvet seats she loved so much.

After we reach Valentine Manor, everything is parked in the garage and stables. Ian and Michael exchange a few words with Victor before leaving for Denver. The rest of us head inside. Once in the main hall, Victor looks toward his prisoner. Eris's chains are held by Faith and Richard as they pull her along. She takes slow and stubborn steps, her face defiant.

"Take her to the dungeon," Victor says.

Faith and Richard nod and drag her away. When she resists, they give a harsh tug, the chains rattling. She picks up her pace. Victor and I go to his study. The drapes are drawn, the room filled with shadows. A few lamps burn. A fire dances in the fireplace. I stand before it, trying to get warm.

Victor comes up behind me and puts his arms around me. "That was the longest day of my life. Did she say anything about Sin?"

"Only that he's to the west."

"Maybe she can tell us exactly where."

"Do you think she knows?"

He hesitates, then says, "No. She may have an idea, but I suspect he set up a rendezvous point where a couple of his soldiers are waiting. He wouldn't expose himself."

"That's what I'm thinking, too. That's why I didn't suggest that we wait until she had taken us to him." I turn around in his arms. "But how are we going to get her to talk? During the war, interrogation consisted of dragging vamps out into the sun, letting them burn, then dragging them back so they could heal, and doing it all over again. It was cruel, but effective." For Old Family, had any ever been caught, it would have been more horrendous. Their healing properties are more advanced. They could survive for hours in the sun, burning and healing, losing ground slowly, until eventually the sun would win out. "As a Day Walker, she's immune to that. What can we possibly do?"

"I have some ideas."

The dungeon is dank and cold. The light comes from lamps secured to the brick walls. Metal doors line the corridor, maybe a dozen in all. Our footsteps echo over the stone floor.

Faith, Victor, and I relieve one of the servants who was in charge of watching Eris. He leaves, shutting the door behind him with a resounding echo that I hope puts some fright into the beautiful Day Walker. The chains are still tightly wound around her body, only now the tail end is hooked into an eyelet on the wall, making it impossible for her to escape. She should seem helpless, but even though her body is chained, her mind isn't, and as Sin's emissary, she can be devilishly sharp.

Victor kneels in front of her, with Faith and me standing behind him, half-hidden in the shadows.

"What does Sin want?" Victor asks.

"Your death. Obviously."

"No. That's merely a step to get what he wants. What's his ultimate aim?"

Eris stares at Victor, and I'd give anything to know her thoughts. As long as they didn't match the flirtatious grin she wears so convincingly. It may work on others, but surely not on Victor.

"Sin will birth a New World Order, a Utopia that will stand for millions of years. A perfect system. A city, ten times the size of Los Angeles, made of three rings. In the center, the humans. Next, Lessers and Day Walkers. And finally, on the outside, the Chosen."

"The Infected," Victor says.

"Precisely. Three rings, each one more powerful than the one it surrounds. A perfect system. Lessers feed off humans, the Chosen off the Lessers. And Sin will rule them all."

"And what about the Old Families? Where do they go?"

Eris puckers her lips as though she were trying to kiss him and blows seductively. "They go into the wind, as dust."

"And where does that leave you?" Victor asks. "Will you join Sin? Partake in the Thirst? Become a monster?"

"No," she says. "For my years of dutiful service, I will be in charge of the second ring, the Day Walkers. I will rule over all of my kind, because I see their place in proper perspective: as a food source for the Chosen. Just as you humans are nothing more than cattle to us, so we are nothing but cattle to the Infected."

I always imagined Sin would bless Eris with the Thirst, since he considers it the highest honor. Although with her vanity, she's probably thrilled to remain a Day Walker. The Chosen may be powerful, but they lose the natural beauty of the vampires. Their teeth become maws filled with razor fangs that can't retract. Their eyes blacken, the whites and pupils giving way to the darkness unfolding within their hearts. Their gaunt faces are frightening, all glamour destroyed as though it never existed to begin with. That's the inevitable result of the Thirst, and I understand why she fears becoming that.

I'm sure Victor recognizes the reasons behind her fears as well.

"How are the Day Walkers getting into the city?" Victor asks.

"Ah, I'm afraid that little secret must remain just that: a secret."

"They aren't simply walking in. Clive has tripled the number of spotters searching the area. They would have found traces of them by now. So, tell me, how are they getting in?"

"Maybe they're invisible; did you ever consider that?" she asks with a smile.

"Last chance," Victor warns.

"What are you going to do? Drag me into the sun?"

Victor reaches out and Faith gives him a small black case. He places it on the ground. The latches *click* and echo ominously throughout the tiny chamber. Slowly he opens the lid. What's inside makes my skin crawl. When Eris sees the syringes nestled inside, her smile disappears.

Victor pulls one of them out, the vampire blood inside a dark crimson, darker than most can imagine, holding ever darker possibilities.

He holds up the syringe, the light finding the sharp needle point, making it glisten momentarily. "I wonder what will happen when I inject you with my blood."

Eris squirms uncomfortably, the first involuntary action I've ever seen from her. Her cold, calculating mind must be reeling, searching frantically for a way out of this. But it might as well be as bound as her arms.

Victor holds her chin. "Imagine all your beauty destroyed. It'll be wiped away, and you'll become one of the Chosen."

"Is this your brilliant plan? Make me into an even stronger monster?"

"How long have you been a Lesser? A hundred years?

Imagine looking in the mirror and that porcelain skin, that perfect symmetry, those brilliant eyes are all fading away. You know what I think? I think it would drive you mad."

"I won't talk."

Victor moves to her side and pinches the tissue around her shoulder, much like a doctor preparing to inject a vaccine.

"I have no idea what will happen," Victor says. "The Thirst affects everyone differently. All it may take is a single drop of blood to turn you, to make you crave more. Or it may take the entire syringe, or the entire case. It doesn't matter; I have all the time in the world to find out."

"If you stick me with that, I'll never tell you," she says, sweat beginning to form at her brow.

"You won't tell me anyway."

Victor jabs in the syringe but doesn't press down on the plunger. Eris is looking at the ground, defeat in her eyes, her curled lips baring the fangs that have brought her eternal beauty. Fangs that may change before long.

"One last chance," Victor says.

"Fuck you."

He pushes the blood into her. I expect her to lash out immediately, to react as Sin did—laughing maniacally. Instead she looks more helpless than ever. Victor calmly puts the syringe back in the case, latches it shut, and stands.

"We'll be back. And if you still aren't in the mood to talk, it'll be two syringes."

Victor becomes somber, almost mournful as we walk back to the study. What he did to her may be worse than death. Only time will tell.

"So how did it go?" Richard asks, lounging on the couch.

"She didn't talk," Victor says, putting the case onto the table. I sit in a chair. Faith drops down on the couch next to Richard.

"But then, you didn't expect her to," Richard says.

"No, I didn't."

"She worships Sin," I say. "She would die for him."

"She'll break," Faith says. "Her vanity is worse than my own."

"She may not get a chance to talk," I say. "She may be turning already."

Victor smiles. "I doubt it."

"How can you be so sure?"

He taps the case with his palm. "It's cranberry juice. Nothing more."

Shaking my head, I laugh lightly. Victor's plan is perfect. We couldn't take the chance of her succumbing to the Thirst, because then she'd be useless to us, not to mention much more dangerous. Yet without any blood at all, she'll begin to starve, and that sensation will trick her into thinking the Thirst has kicked in. I have a hunch that Eris hasn't been starved for decades, not while under the watchful eye of Sin, who rewards loyalty with lavishness.

"Unfortunately," Richard says, "even if she talks, it doesn't solve our lack of blood problem."

"No, no, it doesn't," Victor says. "Our capturing Eris was

a good faith gesture. I'll talk to Clive tonight. Tomorrow we'll start inserting the chips."

I hate that idea, can hardly fathom that he's still considering it. "Victor, you will get so much more blood if the people feel safe."

"You've always said that, but it's never worked."

"Think about Crimson Sands."

"I'm sick of hearing about Crimson Sands," Victor says. "It's a mirage in the desert. It would never work on a large scale. Too many vampires need feeding, and too many people are willing to pass the responsibility on to their neighbors."

"Because they see it as a duty, not a privilege."

Victor studies me, obviously confused by my wording choice. "We have to change their attitude toward vampires," I continue.

"That'll be hard to do when vampires in the city are slaughtering them," Victor says, frustration running through his words. Though whether it's aimed at me or the vampires inside the walls, I'm unsure.

"The Day Walkers are the enemy," I say. "Let *your* vampires be the heroes."

Victor nods. "I'm listening," he says, eyes meeting mine.

"Clive says he doesn't have enough manpower. So here's my proposal: Let the Night Watchmen guard the city during the day, and then let your Lessers guard it at night."

"The people will never allow that."

"We won't tell them," I say. "You said that you have the Lessers' loyalty. Tell them that they are to guard the people and kill the Day Walkers. It'll only be a matter of time before the Day Walkers are finished. Afterward we can tell the citizens who are the real heroes and who are the real monsters."

Victor sits back, eyes on me, then upward, looking for answers in the ceiling, contemplating all the ways my plan could go wrong. But I hope he sees all the ways it could go right. He then looks at Richard and Faith, who both subtly nod.

"I'll send Clive a letter tonight," Victor says. "Only those most loyal to me will be allowed into the city. They'll be led by Anita. None of my Lessers will question her."

"How will they get in?" I ask.

Victor just smiles. "I have a few connections among the guards, those willing to look the other way for the right price."

"No," I say. "No more secrets. Get them together, and we'll march up to the gate. I'll have Clive meet us."

Victor stands. "You're right, Dawn. Clive needs to trust me, now more than ever. We should all probably try to get some sleep. It's going to be another long night."

Upstairs, I clean up in a bathroom down the hall from Victor's room. It's all marble, luxurious but cold. Everything that can be gold or silver is. I'd love to spend an hour in the massive tub fitted with lion's feet and gold fixtures, but that'll have to wait for another time. I put on silk shorts, a tank, and a robe that Faith found for me. It feels so wonderful against my skin. Maybe she's right. I should let the flannel go. I make my way back down the hall.

It wasn't long ago when I dragged Victor down this corridor, bleeding from the strike his father delivered, a strike that wasn't fatal, unlike the one Victor gave in return. When I enter Victor's bedchamber, my heart gives a little flutter. He's waiting for me, standing beside the fireplace, where flames crackle.

I walk over, sit on the couch, and tuck my feet beneath me. "How long do you think before Eris talks?"

"Impossible to know. Sin instills loyalty in those he turns."

"How can someone so evil be so charismatic?"

"Throughout history, those who start wars usually are. Take Roland Hursch, for example. You and I both know that what he is doing is not for the greater good, and yet the citizens believe in him."

"I figured you named him delegate because you wanted to keep an eye on him."

"I did. It was poor strategy on my part."

"So we're just going to wait Eris out?"

He sighs. "I don't see that we have much choice."

"I hate the chaos that the Day Walkers are causing in Denver, but we don't need her information to destroy the V-Processing center in Los Angeles."

He joins me on the couch and puts an arm around my shoulders as he presses a kiss to my temple. "I don't like that you're going. I'm going to send some of my Lessers to watch over you."

"The others aren't bringing Lessers. And the more vampires we have, the more blood we'll need to travel with."

"Then we'll get more blood."

"Victor, if I'm claiming to be equal to Old Family, then I can't be given special treatment."

"We're going to disagree on this."

"Yes, but in the end, you'll recognize that I'm right."

"Maybe," he grumbles. He combs his fingers through my hair. I could become so lost in the gentle sensations.

"When do you think the Old Families will arrive?" I ask.

"Sometime in the next night or so, hopefully."

"Then I need to go to Denver tomorrow," I announce. "I need to let Clive—everyone—know that I'm leaving . . . and why."

He places his hand on the back of my neck, begins kneading my tight muscles. "It won't be easy."

"Nothing in my life is. Even falling for you was hard."

His eyes glitter with understanding. Having me in his life hasn't been easy for him either.

"Will you come back tomorrow night?" he asks.

I shake my head. "No. I'm going to arrange a little dinner at the apartment for everyone. I'll tell them afterward."

He cocks his head to the side. "I didn't know you cooked."

I shrug. "I've watched Rachel. You heat a pan or the oven and put stuff in it until it's cooked."

He grins. "I'm sure it will be a very special meal."

I narrow my eyes. "Why do I think you're mocking me?"

His smile widens. "I would never mock you."

"Better not." I lean into him. "I can take your message about sending in the Lessers to Clive."

"I've already sent it. I knew once you started getting ready for bed that I would have plenty of time."

I straighten. "It didn't take me that long."

"It always takes women a long time. Faith needs at least two hours."

"It took me twenty minutes, tops."

"That's all I needed." He threads his fingers through my hair, holding me near. "Your friends won't turn against you, Dawn."

He voiced one of my biggest fears: that they'll look at me differently. I remember Michael wiping his hand after he touched me in Crimson Sands. I had to fight for my place in the vampire world. Now I may have to fight for it in the human world.

Chapter 18

To my surprise, I wake up feeling fully rested. I roll over to see Victor lying so peacefully, as still as death. I listen for his breath and hear it softly flow in and out, his chest barely rising at all.

My stomach growls and I worry it'll wake him up. It's not *that* loud, but to a vampire's sensitive ears it could sound like a thunderstorm in the distance. So I slip out of bed, deciding he needs his sleep and I need breakfast.

I quietly shut the door and head toward the stairs. I don't know where the kitchen is, but I assume that it's near the dining room, the infamous place where I used to meet Lord Valentine.

Down the stairs, through another hall, and I'm greeted by the two massive Greek sculptures that flank the doors. I guess that hasn't changed. But when I open them up, I'm greeted by something new. Someone.

Eustace is setting the massive table.

"Oh, I'm sorry," I say, suddenly uncomfortable that I'm alone in a room with a vampire. Everyone else is asleep. Shouldn't he be as well?

"Ah, good day, Miss Montgomery," he says. "I heard you coming down the hall. I suppose you're here for breakfast."

"Yes, and please call me Dawn."

"Yes, Miss Montgomery. Please, have a seat, while I go inform the cook."

"Thank you."

I sit in the nearest chair, the flames crackling in the fireplace. The room, like much of the manor, has huge windows that are kept under blinds and curtains during the day. Tiny bits of sunlight slip through the bottom, but the room itself is brightened slightly by gas lamps along the wall. I always figured vampires wouldn't like windows, but I guess they like to look out at night. An oil lamp is suddenly placed in front of me by Eustace, who seems to appear out of nowhere.

"Please forgive the darkness," he says. "Normally the moon and stars help alleviate that. But I'm afraid the windows must be closed for now."

"It's no problem. I hate being a bother. I'll just take some food back to the room."

"No, no, I won't hear of it."

He continues setting the table, the napkins and silverware lined up so perfectly that I'm surprised he doesn't have a ruler to measure the exact angles and distances. I guess he's had a lot of practice. He looks to be in his late forties but could be hundreds of years old. I have no idea when he was turned, or even by whom. All I know is that once he was human.

A moment later he brings me coffee and orange juice on a silver platter. "I do hope that coffee or juice is *your thing*," he says, reminding me of our exchange about the tea.

"I love coffee. Juice? I can take it or leave it."

"Take it or leave it where?" he asks.

I fight back my laughter because I don't want to insult him. Obviously he doesn't get out much. "It's just an expression. I'll drink it."

"Very good."

"Everything smells wonderful," I say.

"You're a guest of the Valentine house. The servants are here to serve."

A female vampire sets a plate loaded with pancakes, eggs, bacon, and fruit in front of me. I quickly take a few bites, only realizing how hungry I am once the aromas hit and the tastes explode in my mouth.

"I hope this is adequate," Eustace says.

Is he joking? "More than adequate," I say. "It's amazing."

"I shall pass on your compliments to the chef."

When I finish my food, Eustace has the plates taken away and refills my coffee cup. I begin to understand what Victor meant when he once told me that the Victorian era was their glory days. This sort of pampering would have been normal for the Old Families, so they could've blended right in with the wealthy. I imagine them having house parties with humans, their guests being none the wiser that a vampire was host, a monster from books and legends. I have to ask. . . .

"Eustace, can I have a moment with you?"

"Of course, miss."

He stands by the chair across from me, hands folded, listening attentively.

"You can take a seat," I say, trying not to smile.

He looks around, maybe confused a bit, before sliding out the chair and sitting down. He takes a moment to make sure it's perfectly aligned with the table, then sits upright, everything about his posture faultlessly parallel and perpendicular.

"Were you a butler during the Victorian era?" I ask. "It's just that Old Family always talk about it, but I've only ever heard tales from them, never a Lesser. So I was just curious what it was like."

He looks up dreamily for a moment. "It was wonderful," he says. "Everyone was polite. The Old Families weren't at each others' throats. There was no shortage of blood."

"But how did they get it?" I ask. "Without donations it must've been difficult."

"There was the occasional black sheep in the family who went out and took from whomever he chose. But for the most part, it was very civilized. Most Old Family would have Lessers infiltrate the morgues as assistants or even as morticians. There, they would drain those who had unfortunately passed. Few seemed to notice, or care, that these people loved the night shift. Most gladly gave it to them. There were also doctors who took from the living so that it was fresher. Blood-letting was not for the health of humans as the history books would have you believe, but was a secret way for us to obtain blood for the vampires."

I try to imagine the entire operation of getting the blood to the vampires consistently. It must've been a real challenge.

"It just doesn't seem like it would be enough," I say.

"Remember, fewer vampires existed back then. Whereas now there are millions, back then there were hundreds, Old Family included. And the system was much better than the one before it."

"Really?"

"Oh, yes. Back when there were kings and castles, we simply had to steal villagers in the middle of the night. Sadly, there was simply no other way to do it. Oftentimes we would keep a human alive for years, draining him slowly in exchange for food and modest shelter. In reality they were prisoners, but it was better than taking their chances as a serf."

"Wait, wait, wait. That must've been, what? Eight, nine hundred years ago?"

"Hmmm, something like that."

"Eustace, how long have you been a servant?"

He once again looks up at the black ceiling, shadows and darkness keeping its true height a mystery.

"Fifteen hundred years, I suppose."

It's probably poor manners to gape at that, my jaw wide in disbelief, but I can't help it.

"Well," I say. "You don't look a day over fifty."

He laughs a little. "Thank you, miss. I was fifty-five when Leo Valentine turned me. Before that, I was his blood servant, what you kids now call blood divas. I remained loyal at that post for thirty years. This was in Eastern Europe, the heart of the Valentine holdings. Leo lived in a gigantic castle overseeing the village below. One day, a massive plague swept through the town, and I fell ill. I would have died, but Leo, in his great mercy, turned me. I have served by the Valentines' side ever since."

That's amazing. I'm talking to a walking history book, a man older than Victor.

"What happened to Leo?" I ask.

"He was killed by his son, Murdoch."

"As in, Victor's father?"

"Yes. I watched young Murdoch being born, held him in my arms, tutored him as he grew older. But I always knew, deep in my heart, that he would ascend the throne violently. It was a very bloody time for the Valentines. Murdoch killed many of his own family, all of them vying for the throne. When it was over, the Valentine dynasty was greatly weakened. It would have been destroyed by the other, more powerful families at the time. But Murdoch quickly gained a reputation for being ruthless and cunning. I think that time in his life, when he was battling constantly, stayed with him forever. Until, of course, Victor followed in his footsteps and slew him."

It seems like it runs in the family. And now, it's brother against brother.

"What was Victor like when he was young?" I ask.

"Bright. Caring. Compassionate. Not unlike his own father at the same age. When the war finally broke out, I watched him go off, knowing that he would change, just as his father had. One cannot fight for so long without the scars building on one's soul. Even if he chooses not to show them, the scars are there."

I think of a young and happy Murdoch Valentine, something I never even imagined was possible; but it was. Then I see him changing, becoming bitter over time, killing his own father, ascending, and then finding that the world is much more difficult and unforgiving than his idealism made it out to be.

"But Victor's different, isn't he?" I ask.

Eustace smiles, knowing that this question means more to me than I care to admit. "In more ways than you can ever imagine. And please tell me if I speak outside my bounds, but do you know what the biggest difference is?"

"What?"

"You."

Chapter 19

After I finish breakfast, I get dressed and go into Victor's room. He's still sleeping. I'm not surprised since the clock in the hallway indicates it's only two in the afternoon. Before we went to bed, he told me to take his car to Denver. I give him a light kiss on the cheek, grab his keys, and head out.

I consider paying Eris a quick visit, see how she's holding up—or not holding up as the case may be—but decide her isolation will do us more good. She's accustomed to being the center of attention. Being deprived of it is probably as tortuous as the belief that she's going to become one of the Infected.

The drive into the city is lonely with no passengers in the car and nothing but my own thoughts bouncing around my head. The last time I drove was the day after

Victor overthrew his father, and I had to get back to the city to tell Clive what had happened. Now I have something else momentous to share, and I'm dreading it. My thoughts center around how I'll break my news, what I should emphasize.

I *am a vampire.*

I am *a vampire.*

I am a vampire.

I'm a dhampir. Oh, what is that? you ask. Well . . .

Say, Clive, how well did you really know my father?

Guess what?

Maybe I should start with a joke, lighten the mood—

So a vampire and a delegate walk into a bar . . .

Nothing seems adequate. There's just no easy way to say this.

I'm grateful when I see the wall so I can start thinking about something else. I spot smoke billowing out in a couple of streams within the city. Day Walkers are still wreaking havoc.

At the gate, I show my credentials and am waved through. Encountering the destruction again makes me wish that I'd taken time with Eris and forced her to tell us what she knows about the Day Walkers in the city. Fewer people are out. I can't blame them for staying indoors, and my anger is renewed. We shouldn't have to live like this.

Crossing over trolley tracks, I turn down a street—

Crash!

A Day Walker lands on the hood of the car. Revealing his fangs, he pulls his hand back to smash through the window.

I swerve and he goes sliding off. Reversing, I run over him. The action won't kill him, but it's bound to break bones and slow him down while he heals. I floor the pedal and race down the street. Glancing in the rearview mirror, I see him squirming. I should have stopped to finish him off, but it could be a trap with his friends lying in wait.

I take evasive maneuvers, going around one corner and then another. I should have asked for an escort at the gate. Hindsight is always better. In hindsight, we should have staked Sin the day we met him. Too bad we didn't know what he was.

I come to a screeching stop outside my apartment building, jump out, lock the door, and race up the stairs. In the lobby are two additional guards, stakes drawn. Extra precaution is being taken. Good.

"Is everything all right?" one of the guards asks.

"Yeah, just ran into a Day Walker in the city. It's getting worse, isn't it?"

"Their attacks have become random, unorganized. In some ways that makes it worse."

Unorganized because now we have Eris. I so wish that I didn't have to leave the city, that I could be here to fight.

Once I step into the apartment, I'm hit with the realization that I haven't been back here since the night I left for New Vampiria. I've changed so much and yet I relish the comfort of home. Rachel's not here, so I'm sure she's at work.

I go to my room and grab my cell phone from where I left it on my desk. I didn't take it with me. Who would I have called? I send out texts to Rachel, Michael, Tegan.

My place. 8. Dinner.

I add a note to the one I send Clive: *Bring Ian.*

I don't text Jeff. Rachel will know the invitation includes him.

I've taken two steps when I get a response from Tegan.

Coming over now.

As much as I miss her, as much as I want to see her, I need some alone time to psych myself up.

No. Don't. Planning a surprise.

Does it involve you and Victor? Wink.

I ignore her question and just reply: *See u at 8.*

I wander into the kitchen. It's always been Rachel's domain. But really, how hard can it be?

Hours later, I'm ready to scream. I used Rachel's recipes, but she must not list all the ingredients because nothing tastes the way it does when she makes it. The cake is flat. The cheese dip keeps hardening. When I take the chicken out of the oven, it is almost as cold as it was when I took it out of the freezer. Is the oven not working?

The doorbell rings and I jump. I look at the window. How did I miss night arriving? And who's here already? Tegan? I still have an hour to go.

I march to the door and yank it open. "Go away, you're too ear—"

I stop. It's not Tegan. It's Victor, dressed in jeans and a black button-down shirt. He's holding a large box.

"What are you doing here?" I ask.

He gives me a soft smile. "Did you really think I was going to let you do this alone?"

I blink back the tears. "I'm so glad you're here. What do you know about cooking?"

"That my chef is very good at it." He steps through the doorway and I shut the door.

"What's in the box?"

"Prepared food. All we have to do is put it in the oven—good God. It looks like one of the Infected came through here."

I punch his shoulder. "It's not that bad." Although it kind of is. "While I appreciate you bringing food, I really wanted to make it myself."

"You are making it. You put it in the oven, it cooks. You can even stir it if you want to get industrious." He sets the box on the counter.

"I'll show you industrious." I flick some flour at him.

"Hey! I can take my unwanted food and go."

I leap forward and grab his wrist. "No. I don't know if I'm distracted or what, but I just couldn't seem to make sense of the recipes."

"Then cook what I brought."

I nod. "You didn't happen to bring someone to clean up the mess, did you?"

He pulls me in close. "I'm sure we can work something out."

* * *

Although a little tension exists at first, when everyone realizes that Victor is here, it soon dissipates as the food is served. They've never had a meal as flavorful as the one Victor and I present. But then, Denver doesn't have any chefs. Victor explains that the chef is a French master cook. His only regret in life is serving Murdoch Valentine years ago at a party held in Versailles. The vampire was so impressed with the food that he decided to turn the cook and keep him forever.

After dinner, people congregate in little groups to talk: Michael and Tegan, Clive and Ian, Rachel and Jeff. They are relaxed and smiling.

"Your chef didn't put something extra in the food, did he?" I ask Victor. "You know, something to alter the state of their minds?"

"I think they've just had a good meal for the first time in a very long while."

Clive and Ian amble over.

"Just wanted you to know," Clive says, his voice low, hushed, "that your Lessers have been immersed into one of the Night Watchmen units."

"Was there any trouble?"

"Could have been," Clive acknowledges, "but we have a young Watchman who has considerable experience fighting alongside vampires. He convinced the others to give this idea of yours a shot."

Michael.

"I'm impressed with Anita," Ian says. "Wouldn't have

wanted to encounter her during the war."

"She's one of my best," Victor assures him.

I remember Anita. I saw her in a dream I once shared with Victor. Her hair is nearly white, and she has a striking presence, like she was cut from a beautiful block of marble.

Ian and Clive wander off to get more wine.

"I guess I need to do this." I exhale my breath.

"Remember you're not alone."

I squeeze Victor's hand. I try to imagine how I would react if Tegan told me she was a dhampir. But I just can't envision it.

"Okay, everyone," I call out, "I have an announcement to make, so if you could please gather around."

Tegan drops into a chair, pulls her feet up. Her smile is so big, her eyes so bright that I know she thinks my announcement involves declaring that Victor and I are a couple, maybe even engaged. Rachel and Jeff sit on the couch and hold hands. Clive takes a nearby chair. His feet braced apart, Ian stands at the edge of the circle as though he isn't quite sure he belongs here.

Michael's steady gaze is on me. I think he knows what I'm going to announce. He's leaning against the door, his arms folded across his chest as though he's preparing for battle.

Victor moves in behind me, places his warm hand on the small of my back, steadying me, strengthening my resolve.

Tegan gives the tiniest little squeal. She's probably envisioning what she wants for her bridesmaid's gown.

I swallow with difficulty. The words—

"Okay, there's just no easy way to say this. Michael already knows."

He unfolds his arms. "Dawn—"

I shake my head. "Sin didn't lie, Michael."

He takes a step forward. "You don't know that."

"Yes, I do." I turn to the others. "I'm part vampire."

Tegan's smile remains, but it is as though she's frozen in shock and can't get her muscles to move. Rachel and Jeff are looking at each other. Clive is shaking his head. Ian is as still as a statue.

I take another deep breath and rush on. "You know there are fourteen Old Families. Centuries ago, there was a fifteenth. The Montgomerys. I'm a descendant, the result of a vampire mating with a human." Could I get any more clinical, sound any less emotional? "I'm what they call a dhampir."

"Bullshit," Tegan finally says. "If Sin told you this—"

"He did, and I didn't believe him. But my father left me a recording saying the same thing. He had documents to prove it."

Victor slips his arm around my shoulders, brings me in close. "The Vampire Council recognized her claim when we were in New Vampiria. But it does not change who she is."

"Of course it doesn't," Rachel says, but doubt edges her voice.

Tegan pops out of the chair, steps over to me, and gently grabs my wrist. "So you've got a drop of vampiric blood in here somewhere," she says, feeling the pulse on my wrist. She then places her hand on my chest, where my heart is. "But Victor is right. Dawn is in here. And that will never, ever change."

I hug her then and there, and she holds me tight.

"You've been the best friend in the world," I say.

She pulls back and smiles that Tegan smile of hers. "Yeah, I have been pretty good, haven't I?"

Before I can respond, Rachel is skirting past her and wrapping her arms firmly around me. "Of course, you're still you."

"I guess that explains why your family has always understood vampires so well," Clive says, patting my back.

"Her heritage comes with great responsibility," Victor says. Everyone looks at him. "She proved herself worthy of a seat on the Vampire Council. Her vote broke the tie that would have prevented the Old Families from supporting a war against Sin."

"Wish I'd been there to see that," Tegan says.

"Unfortunately"—I look over at Clive—"every family is required to send a representative to Los Angeles. Since I'm the only Montgomery, I have to go."

"I'll go in your place," Ian suddenly announces.

I snap my gaze over to him. It still doesn't look as though he's moved. "Thank you, Ian. I can't tell you how much I appreciate that, but it has to be a family member."

"So adopt me. Will that work?"

Victor tilts his head back, thinking about it. "There might be a way. You could take a blood oath."

"Let's do it."

"You don't even know what it is," Victor says, smiling.

"It doesn't matter."

I clutch Victor's arm. "I don't want someone else to fight for me."

"There's going to be plenty of fighting to go around, and your place is here."

"Victor's right," Clive says. "Denver needs you."

"Besides, the Night Train is in Los Angeles," Ian says. "I was going to go back for it anyway."

Walking over to him, I place my hands on either side of his face. "Now I know why you're the greatest vampire hunter who ever lived. And it has little to do with the number of vampires you killed." Rising up on my toes, I kiss his cheek.

"You're going to make me blush."

Make him? When I step back, I see that he's already turned red.

"So how does this blood oath thing work?" he asks.

Victor withdraws his stake. "I pierce your palm, then Dawn's. She presses her palm to yours and you'll swear an oath that your blood will always spill before hers."

Ian nods. "I've got so many scars, what's one more?"

Victor digs his stake into Ian's palm until blood pools around it. I see the apology in his eyes when he does the same thing to me. It pricks, stings, but I don't let the discomfort show.

I flatten my hand against Ian's.

"My blood will always spill before yours," he says.

"I don't know what to say," I whisper. "It's too much."

"Say it will never spill in vain," Victor whispers. "That's your vow to him, a recognition that you value his loyalty."

"I promise it will never spill in vain."

"So it is done," Victor announces.

So it is done.

Chapter 20

Ian and I return to Valentine Manor with Victor. Ian to await the arrival of the Old Family. Me to help Victor break Eris.

I spend the day with Ian. He regales me with tales from his vampire hunter days.

That evening, Victor, with briefcase in hand, goes to see Eris, alone, asking if she wants to talk.

Ian and I wait in a massive office where Victor manages his correspondence. It's a show of extravagance when a room bigger than my entire apartment is used just to write notes and send them away in sealed envelopes. The two French doors, twice my own height, lead to a wonderful balcony that gives an unimpeded view of the countryside.

There isn't much there. Desolate and vast, mountains in the distance seem to breathe cold air over us. The clouds are few and far between on this night, gliding across the sky, avoiding the moon as though out of courtesy for the light it gives.

Victor strides in and sits in an exquisite iron chair.

"Any luck?" Ian asks.

"She told me to go to hell."

"That's very un-emissary-like of her," I say.

Victor flashes a smile. "Yes, it is."

"I could take a pass at her," Ian offers. "She wouldn't be the first vamp I've interrogated."

"She would be the first Day Walker."

Ian shrugs. "They're all afraid of stakes."

Victor considers it, then nods. "All right, Ian, if you want—"

The door to the office opens and Eustace steps into the room. "Lord Valentine, several guests have just arrived."

"How many?"

"I counted twelve carriages, sir."

The Council. They came through.

Victor, Richard, Faith, Ian, and I go outside to greet the arrivals. The black carriages, each pulled by powerful horses, stand like massive coffins in the night. They're ornate, each adorned with the crest of the Old Family it represents. And standing beside them are the vampires themselves.

"Victor Valentine," I hear one of them say. He's huge, pushing seven feet, his shoulders so broad they would block out the moon if I stood too close.

"Fabian Ferdinand." Victor approaches him and shakes the man's massive paw.

"Good to see you again. Ah, and Richard Carrollton."

"The last time I saw you," Richard says, shaking Fabian's hand, "you barely came up to my elbows."

"It's the Ferdinand blood; we grow like weeds. And this . . ." He looks at me and smiles. "This must be Madame Montgomery."

"Pleasure," I say, giving a small curtsy.

"Please, the pleasure is mine. I heard you made quite a splash at the Council meeting."

"There were one or two surprised faces I seem to recall."

Fabian approaches me and his size is even more evident. He gets down on one knee and I can look right into his eyes.

"I knew that one day the Montgomerys would return and take their rightful place," he says.

"Fabian, I don't know how to thank your family enough."

"Simply be proud of who you are. Every breath you take is a reminder that Errol Ferdinand was right. And now, more than ever, it is clear. The Montgomerys were not some monstrosity, nor did they signal the downfall of vampires. The Montgomerys could have saved us from such a terrible war if they had been allowed to live. And now, you can bridge the gap between humans and vampires."

I'm at a loss for words. Fabian simply smiles again and stands. He approaches Victor and Richard.

"I have brought eleven Old Family with me," he says.

"Every family is represented, except the Ashers. Each representative here is willing to die in order to stop this madness that Sin has created."

Twelve is one too many. Victor doesn't seem surprised by the number. He must have expected one family to send two representatives. I wonder what the story is.

I look at the Old Family soldiers. Each one is young and dashing, rivaling Victor and Richard in looks. But I see no women. I guess I shouldn't be surprised. Even if they are fast and strong, they're simply too rare to risk. And speaking of Old Family women, I look over at Faith to see if she's eyeing any potential suitors. But all I see is worry in her eyes.

"We brought human drivers and hunters to steer the carriages and protect us while the sun is out," Fabian continues.

I can see through some of the glass panes into a few of the carriages, their human counterparts inside, stakes bandoliered across their chests. I know Old Family at times hire humans to protect them. They demand the best and are able to pay for it. Even if some of these humans fought in the war, like Ian, they're willing to set aside their differences for the right price.

"Madame Montgomery, it is my understanding that you'll be coming with us."

"No, actually, Ian Hightower is going in my place."

Fabian stiffens, looks past me to where Ian has been waiting. "Well, Slayer, I have heard stories of your heroics. You have no need to worry about us wanting revenge, as long as you don't want the same."

"It was war," Ian says. "We were on different sides then, and we did what soldiers do. Now, it's a different war, and we're on the same side."

"Then we are of like minds. Have you a carriage? If not, I would be honored to have you ride with me."

"He's riding with me," Richard says. "But we're going by car."

I can tell from Fabian's curled lip that he finds the thought of traveling in such a vehicle distasteful. He's obviously embraced the Old Family's dislike of modern conveniences and isn't quite as rebellious as Richard and Victor are.

"Cousins!" a vampire shouts, striding toward us. From his black hair to his blue eyes and sharp royal features, he has Valentine written all over him. He stops before us. "You're looking well."

"Dawn, allow me to introduce Rayne Valentine," Victor says. "I believe you've had the honor of meeting his father, Seymour."

It wasn't that much of an honor. He is Murdoch Valentine's brother and expressed an interest in becoming head of the family once Murdoch was dead. But Victor quickly put him in his place. Diplomacy forces me to say, "I remember him well."

"He did not speak highly of you," he says. "But my father has always been a terrible judge of character, and I'm sure he made his usual mistake with you."

He takes my hand and kisses it. Then kisses it again. And again.

"All right," Victor says, playfully slapping his hand away. "I see that only *some* of the Valentines have kept their manners after all these years."

"Yes," he says, "and the other half have kept their good looks." He combs back his hair with his hands.

Victor laughs. "You're just as I remembered."

"Dashing?"

"Arrogant."

"I'll take it."

They pat each other on the shoulders in the exact same way any cousins would at a family reunion.

"Why are you here, Rayne?" Faith asks.

He appears taken aback by her question. "I came at Victor's behest to represent the Valentine family."

Faith shakes her head. "No, I'm going on behalf of the Valentines."

Uh-oh. Now I know why there was one more number than I expected.

"Faith," Victor says quietly, moving toward his sister. "We can't risk you going."

She spins around, her face livid. "What are you talking about?"

"If anything were to happen to you—"

"Do I have to remind you that I've already been to Los Angeles?"

"We didn't realize how bad it was then," Richard says.

Faith glares at him. "I held my own."

"You did."

"Then why did Victor send for Rayne?"

"Faith—"

"Why?"

Richard moves with such quickness, just a blur, and he's holding her, hands on her face, her tears running through his fingers.

"Because I can't protect them if you're with me. You'll be the only thing I care about. You . . . you *are* the only thing I care about."

"But who will protect you?" she asks, her voice just a whisper.

"They will."

She shakes her head like it isn't enough. "No one can protect you like I can."

He pulls her into his shoulder and holds her. "I know."

"I'd never hurt you."

"I know."

She isn't talking about Los Angeles anymore or protecting him from Sin's army. She pulls back, her arms around his neck. "Just return to me."

When she steps away, Victor looks at Richard and I see the loyalty—even the love—they have for each other. A hundred years of a deep connection that few vampires ever experience. They hug, and when they part, Victor gives a final nod.

Before they can leave, I rush over to Ian, who is loading up the trunk of the car.

"Ian."

He turns toward me and I can sense the bristling power, the excitement of the mission to come. But I also sense the recognition that it could be one mission too many.

"Don't say goodbye," he says. "It's bad luck."

"Then what should I say?"

Ian smiles and looks up at the sky, as if recognizing for the first time how clear it is tonight.

"Just say, 'I'll see you when you get back.'"

"I will. I'll see you when you get back."

He puts his hand on my head and rubs my hair, like a father proud of his little girl.

From the steps of the manor, Victor, Faith, and I watch the carriages roll out in a steady procession, led by the car that contains Richard and Ian.

"We need to get that Sin-worshipping bitch to talk," Faith says. "I'm in the mood to take down some Day Walkers."

Chapter 21

Faith stalks off to her room, probably to hurl some valuables around. Victor stares off into the night sky, his mind perhaps considering the methods they used during the war. What kind of things did he do then that made people talk? I have a terrible feeling in my gut that Victor can be much, much more *persuasive* if he wants to be. But will that unleash the monster within? Will Victor lose what makes him so human if he has to resort to such horrific things that he locked away long ago?

"Let me talk to Eris," I say.

Victor turns and assesses me. "All right," he agrees. "Perhaps she'll be more willing to talk if you're alone with her." We walk back into the house and continue on to the study. He opens up a drawer on the desk and pulls out a metal stake. He places it in my hand. "Just in case. She'll be weaker, but it's also possible she's been faking her lack of strength. For all we know, she could just be waiting for the right opportunity to break through the chains."

I nod, understanding that if I must, I'll put this through her heart.

In the dungeon I dismiss the guard watching her. We're all alone, the pale light from the flickering lamps casting more shadows than revealing our surroundings. Eris seems weak. The combination of blood hunger and stress is finally showing on the chained emissary. She's pale, leading me to wonder whether her beautiful skin has come from the sun or a healthy supply of fresh blood. Her hair is dirty and slick with oil and sweat. Victor's ruse is having an effect. She looks like she wants to give up. For her, the strength she would gain from the Thirst is no consolation for becoming hideous.

I soften my footsteps and kneel in front of her, trying to act more like a friend than adversary. She looks up at me, surrender evident in her eyes. I brush the hair off her face, using a gentle touch.

"I want to talk," I say.

"Then talk." Her voice has lost its luster, replaced with the cold need to survive.

"How much longer do you have?" I ask.

"You're the vampire expert, you tell me."

"I'm no expert in the Thirst. But I've heard that a vampire can feel the change coming."

She looks away, her chest rising and falling, struggling against the constricting chains.

"I don't know," she says to the floor. "I feel weak, but I also feel like I'm on the verge of something, like a terrible black void is right behind me and I'm about to slip into it."

"I wonder if that's what my brother felt."

Her head tilts up, sorrow and confusion on her face.

"My brother was just like you," I say. "He was a Day Walker, turned by Sin."

"I know," she says quickly. I imagine she knows just about everything Sin does, which is I why I need her to talk. Even if I have to confess things I'd rather keep bottled away.

"Did Sin tell you how Brady succumbed to the Thirst?" I ask.

"No."

"Brady refused to drink from humans. He didn't want to hurt them, so he fed on vampires, thinking that would sustain him. It didn't. The Thirst took over his mind."

I wait in the silence, my delegate training telling me she wants to speak, but I have to give her time, give her a chance.

"Sin never wanted Brady to become one of the Infected. He hoped to gain another ally, much like myself. Of course, when your brother's change was complete, and Sin saw how powerful he was, it gave him the idea for the Chosen. Infected Day Walkers, the most dangerous creatures to ever walk the earth—and Brady was the first."

I pause for a moment, preparing my next statement carefully. "And soon, you'll be another."

She releases the tiniest of squeaks. "I know."

"But you still have a choice. For you, there is still a fork in the path and a direction to choose. Just tell us how the Day Walkers are getting into the city, Eris, and all of this will stop. It isn't too late."

"You don't know that."

"Maybe not, but I know what the alternative is, and I know why you fear it. The Chosen aren't blessed like you. No, they're cursed. They may be powerful, but they trade everything for that power. The Day Walkers right now don't realize that until it's too late, but you've witnessed it firsthand, you've seen Sin's army of the Chosen begin to form, and you know the madness and darkness that grows in their souls."

Eris's eyes betray her now: They speak to me, revealing her fears. I reach down and find her hands, bound at the wrist to her body. I hold them, knowing that even in a weakened state her strength could crush the bones in my fingers. But I know what I'm doing.

"I don't want to become one," she says, her voice just above a whisper, as if it escaped from her throat when her consciousness wasn't looking.

"I know. And you don't have to. Just tell us how the Day Walkers are getting into the city."

"Sin will kill me," she says.

"He'll never know."

"Yes, he will. He always knows, and then I'll have given up the only thing he asks for: loyalty."

I tighten my grip on her hands, somewhere between violence and compassion.

"You will be dead anyway," I say, no longer sure who is the interrogator, whose soul is being peered into. "Because the Thirst will rob you of everything that you are. When I killed my brother, he looked at me, and I knew that death was a sweet release for him. His own body and mind tortured him. Don't do that to yourself, Eris."

I feel her hands shaking, I sense the walls of her will collapsing. One final push . . .

"I'm not asking you to join us," I say. "I'm not asking you to fight against Sin. And when this is over, we can protect you. But we have to know how they're getting into the city."

Eris closes her eyes tightly and I see a single tear fall to the ground, perhaps the only tear she's ever shed as a vampire. She seems so human in this harsh light, nothing like the daughter of the sun who walked into our lives.

"Hursch," she cries softly.

"Roland Hursch?"

"Yes. He's hiding them."

Over the next several minutes Eris tells me everything: When Sin first arrived in Denver, masquerading as a new student, he brought three dozen of his most loyal Day Walkers with him. They remained in Denver, watching Sin from the shadows, protecting him in case he was exposed for what he truly was. They were also told to wait. And wait. And wait.

"Wait for the signal," Eris said. "And that signal was my arrival."

Sin was very busy as a student, involved in extracurricular activities I never would've dreamed about. He met with Hursch and made him an offer: "Let my Day Walkers stay in your mansion. Protect them. And when the time comes, release them as Eris requests. They will go out into the city, slowly at first, but always to return to you. When I have conquered the world, you will rule over the humans."

I feel sick, and yet I'm not surprised. Hursch wants power, but none of the responsibility that goes along with it. His rants all along haven't been about what was best for Denver, but what was best for him. By embracing Sin's promise, he'll finally be where he wants: at the center of everything.

I'm stunned. The Day Walkers weren't finding ways to get into the city. They've been there all along.

Chapter 22

"Are you ready?" Victor asks.

The wind in the city is strong tonight, and it's cold, bringing a chill that can cut to the bone. All I can do is nod and wrap my arms around Victor's neck. We both look up at the roof high above us and the moon so much higher, clouded by the dense pollution of the Works that fuels the city. I close my eyes when Victor jumps, and I feel the wind rush through me and our soft landing as his feet find solid purchase. When I open my eyes, we're on top of the house. The owners of the very expensive, very large mansion probably won't be too happy that we've invaded their privacy and had the audacity to walk on their property. But when the news of Hursch's betrayal hits the stands tomorrow, they won't care about a few footprints on their roof.

In retrospect, I understand why the Day Walkers rained hell on the city as soon as Victor left. Hursch knew the new Lord Valentine was traveling; Victor had told him so when Hursch barged into the Agency. Hursch must have told Eris that day. How else would the timing have been so perfect?

I look out over the neighborhood, the richest and most lavish one in the entire city. All the wealth is here: businessmen and con men alike. People walk by and are envious but can't stare for long before security shoos them away, as if their stares alone could devalue the estates.

All the players are here, but they don't show their colors, not yet. Night Watchmen blend in with the shadows, their shrouded features in contrast to their intricate pendants. Michael is probably among them. I try not to worry.

With the Night Watchmen are Anita and her crew of loyal Lessers. They are dressed as Night Watchmen so no one is mistaken as the enemy.

I see a car pull up, black and familiar. It's the car that used to drive me to the Agency to give my reports.

Jeff gets out. He's traded in his normal suit and tie for something much more tactical: his old military outfit, complete with neck guard and stakes. I've never seen him wear it, but it looks completely natural, as though it were always just under his suit, just over his skin.

He looks around, and everyone moves to their positions. It's like watching a beautiful ballet that no one else can see. He then slams the car door shut as loud as possible, his signal for all hell to break loose.

I've had a lot of intense moments in my life: facing down Valentine, riding in a carriage with Sin to destinations unknown, waiting for my friends to rescue me from Eris. All of them I'll remember forever, and the emotions that they brought. This moment will definitely join the others on the top shelf of my memories.

I clasp Victor's hand the entire time. Doors are kicked in, windows broken, human and vampire screams echoing through the house and outside into the neighborhood, where lights are quickly turned on, neighbors exiting their front doors before rapidly retreating back inside. Every time a shriek fills the air, I squeeze Victor's hand tighter, unsure whether it's coming from the mouth of a friend or foe.

The takedown lasts only a few minutes, and I recheck my watch to make sure I got it right. It seems like a time warp, every second stretching into minutes, weighed down by all the lives at risk, not just inside the house but inside this entire city, maybe every city that stares up at the night sky and is afraid.

But eventually, Jeff and Anita walk out the door, Roland Hursch between them in handcuffs. And following them are the Night Watchmen and the Lessers, stakes in hand. I study them carefully, grateful when I recognize a familiar stride. Michael is okay.

Then my attention is riveted by the screeches of a girl who is very, very pissed off. A Night Watchman appears holding Hursch's squirming daughter.

"Let me go!" Lila shouts.

Lila and I have never been close. After I became the delegate, she went out of her way to make my life miserable at school: painting my locker red, starting rumors that I was sleeping with vampires, making me out to be the enemy. Ironic that her father was the true enemy.

I don't know if she was in on Daddy's little secret; it's hard to imagine she wasn't.

"Do you know who I am?" she cries.

But the Night Watchman doesn't speak, simply moves her toward another waiting car and throws her into the back with a little excessive force. Lila scrambles to the door, but it shuts in her face. And I can't help but notice that the Night Watchman who put Lila in her place is wearing red, six-inch heels.

But as much as I'd love to watch Lila be taken off to the Agency, something amazing catches my eye. The unthinkable, and the thing I'd always hoped for, the thing my parents dreamed of: the vampires and humans begin shaking hands, begin laughing, begin patting each other's backs. A job well done.

And it was.

I get the mission report from Jeff: twenty-four Day Walkers slain. On our side: four killed.

"Vampire or human?" I ask.

"What does it matter?" Jeff responds. He's right, what does it matter? They fought together, they wielded stakes against the enemy just the same, they protected one another. What does it matter whether they bore fangs or not?

"Go get some rest," Jeff says. "Tomorrow night, we tell everyone, and they better be prepared."

I don't take Jeff's advice. I'm too excited to rest, not to mention there's a party. It feels weird rejoicing, as we're celebrating a victory hard won, but we're also celebrating the end to the attacks on Denver.

The party takes place in a safe house for Night Watchmen—an old, abandoned apartment building. At least, that's what it looks like from the outside. But inside, things take a strange turn once we find the right door on the fifth floor. Labeled 504, it opens with a secret knock, and inside I can see the renovation work that's been done.

All the adjacent apartments are connected, the walls between them knocked down long ago, creating a continuous ten-bedroom, ten-kitchen, ten-bathroom apartment. Much of the space has been refurbished, designed for storage of equipment and giant maps of the city, where the Night Watchmen can plan their surgical strikes. And of course all the windows are boarded up tight, all the doors except for one nailed shut and renailed again.

"You guys made it," says a Night Watchman, shrouded

in his black balaclava. He waves us in and shuts the door behind us.

"Great job tonight," Victor says immediately, shaking the man's hand.

"It couldn't have been done without that intelligence," the Watchman admits.

I stare at the two hands in a firm grip. I see so much possibility within that bond. Does anyone else? Is this just a party or the beginning of something, a Greater World Order that counters Sin's perverse dreams?

In the mega-apartment are about thirty people, half Watchmen, half vampires. The Watchmen are in their customary outfits, their identities forever concealed, even from their friends and allies. But their masks are lifted partway up so that they can sip cold beers. The Lessers are dressed in black jeans and T-shirts, but their faces are uncovered. They talk with the Night Watchmen, both groups perfectly intermingling. I get goose bumps watching them laughing and raising glasses, giving cheers.

"Dawn, over here."

I look at the corner of the room and see a Night Watchman, mask entirely covering his face, leaning against the wall. Even if I didn't recognize Michael's voice and stance, I'd know it was him because of the person standing beside him.

"Tegan!"

She grins. "Surprise."

"What are you doing here?" I ask.

She holds up her hands. "Don't worry. I don't know where *here* is. Michael made me wear a hood on the way over."

"Figured you'd want to see her," he says, giving me a very quick hug that seems to solidify what we are now. Friends. He then shakes Victor's hand. "Thanks for the intelligence tonight. This was a real big grab for us."

"You're very welcome," Victor says. "Though I had little to do with it. Dawn was the one who broke Eris."

"Really?"

"Surprised?" I ask.

"No," Michael says, and I see the corners of his mask move as he smiles. "I'm not surprised at all."

The room begins to grow quiet. The vampires have realized who is in their midst—their lord. They move silently toward him, surround him, giving a clear message that they will protect him at any cost.

The group is divided again. The vampires in the center, the Night Watchmen around its edge. The camaraderie I witnessed at Hursch's was just an illusion, a moment of victory that wasn't as grand as I thought.

"I appreciate the loyalty, but I don't need protection here, Anita," Victor says. "As a matter of fact—"

He moves beyond the circle, then turns and holds his hand out to me. I place mine in it and step up to stand beside him.

"Night Watchmen," he begins, "you hide your faces,

you keep your identities secret because you fear retaliation from vampires. But Dawn Montgomery has always dreamed of a world where vampires and humans live together. Tonight is the start.

"Just as I don't need protection from you, so you no longer need protection from us. Remove your masks, walk proudly among your citizens, let them see who guards their back, who watches over them. I am not my father. I will not hunt you for protecting the precious citizens of Denver from any who would hurt them. Those who fought beside you tonight are not the enemy. Reveal yourselves to us so we can recognize our allies."

I tighten my fingers around Victor's. Everyone is so still, so quiet. Someone steps in front of Victor. I know who it is before he removes his balaclava. Michael.

He holds out his hand to Victor. They shake. Then he begins moving among the other vampires, shaking their hands, thanking them.

Another Night Watchman steps up and removes his balaclava. I try not to show my surprise. Sampson. I know him from school. As a bookworm, a geek, a kid that other students made fun of. I wonder how long he's been risking his life for those who never appreciated him. He shakes Victor's hand, then mine, giving me a shy smile.

"Thank you, Sampson," I say.

He nods before moving on to be embraced by the vampires.

Two more Watchmen step forward. Then three, then

six, and it's obvious that many are as surprised as I am to see who they've been fighting beside. How unfair that they've had to hide, even from each other.

When everyone is revealed, I spot Anita in a corner and . . . and is that a Night Watchman hitting on her? And is she blushing?

Victor slides his arm around me. "As I said, it's only a start."

"But it's a start." I meet his gaze. "I wish the Vampire Council could have seen this."

"You can tell them all about it when we return to New Vampiria after we defeat Sin."

"I wish we had a way to know how things are going with Richard."

"He'll send someone back with news when he has some. It'll be another couple of nights before they get to Los Angeles."

"Long nights."

"Hey, you two," Tegan says, interrupting us. "That was awesome. I had no idea some of these guys were Night Watchmen."

I grin. "Yeah, me either."

"Here you go," Michael says, handing Victor and me each a beer and clinking his bottle against ours. "To Crimson Sands."

"To Denver," I say. "They showed us what was possible, but we made it happen."

"To Denver," everyone repeats.

We chug down the beer. Then stand around embracing the atmosphere.

"So I need to go put on some fresh lipstick," Tegan says to me. "Why don't you come with me?"

"You can't put on lipstick by yourself?" Victor asks.

"That's chick code," Michael tells him. "Tegan wants to talk to Dawn where we can't hear. Which means she probably wants to talk about us."

She punches his shoulder. "Don't be such a smarty."

I can see a light dancing in his eyes, and I realize she's here not so much for me as Michael indicated, but for him. And I'm glad, so very glad.

"Come on, Victor," he says, "let's go grab another beer."

As they walk off, Tegan says, "That's something I never thought I'd see."

"I know. It's wonderful, isn't it?" I turn back to her. "So you and Michael—"

"We're just friends," she says hastily. "Okay, maybe a little more than friends. He just . . . I don't know. He just always makes me feel like everything will work out. We'll defeat Sin, and the Day Walkers, and the Infected. We'll be safe." She gives me an impish grin. "And he's gorgeous. Even with the scars. As a matter of fact, I think they make him sexier." She nudges my shoulder. "So you and Victor . . ."

I shrug. "I don't know. We haven't had a whole lot of time to actually be together when some crisis isn't breathing down our neck."

"But he's way hot."

I laugh loud and long. The old Tegan is definitely back, thinking about guys and how hot they are. Seeing her like this gives me hope that soon everything will be better.

After a while, Victor and Michael rejoin us. I relish the fact that there's no awkwardness between us. Eventually Michael and Tegan wander away, and I figure she's looking for a quiet corner where he can smear her lipstick.

Faith strolls over, but she hardly looks happy. No doubt Richard is on her mind. She's back in her signature red leather. "Everyone's acting like we've won already," she says.

"For tonight we have," Victor tells her. "Even though you weren't supposed to be involved."

"I don't know what you're talking about."

"You went into Hursch's residence with the Night Watchmen," Victor admonishes her.

"And dragged out Lila," I add.

"You're wrong."

Victor sighs. "Faith, no other Night Watchman would dare go into battle wearing red heels."

She shudders. "I just couldn't put on those hideous boots they wear."

"You're not supposed to be placing yourself in danger."

"But it's all right if Richard does?"

"He's a soldier."

"So am I."

"You're next in line for the Valentine throne."

That seems to bring her up short.

"If something happens to me—" Victor begins.

"Nothing is going to happen to you," she interrupts.

"I'm not planning on it, but you also need to step back."

"While Richard risks his life?"

"I admit what he's doing is dangerous, but he's not going to battle Sin. It'll be a covert operation. Destroy the V-Processing center, stop Sin's ability to mass produce the Chosen, and return here."

"Sin hates you. He's not going to leave Denver alone."

"No," Victor agrees. "He won't leave Denver alone."

"Now that we've dealt with the Day Walkers," I say, "we need to start preparing for Sin."

Victor nods. "I'd hoped we'd have a few days, but until we can figure out exactly where Sin is, we have to be ready."

"I can do that," Faith declares.

My eyes widen. "Do what?"

"Prepare Denver."

Victor gives her a kind smile. "Faith, you've never been in a real battle, like we had during the war. You're not experienced—"

"I know how to throw a hell of a party. How is this any different?"

He shakes his head. "It's different."

I know she needs a distraction from her worries over Richard. "Not really," I say. "I think she can do it. It's scavenging, getting everything organized. I think she'd be great at it."

"Then it's settled," she says. "I'll work with Anita, get a

list of what's needed and get things organized here. When Sin arrives, I'll throw a surprise party for him."

I can tell that Victor is going to object again. I squeeze his hand, communicate with my touch that he needs to let her do this.

He nods. "All right, then. You'll represent us here in Denver. I'll talk to Clive and Jeff—"

"I can handle that." She turns her attention to me. "Thanks for believing in me, Dawn."

"Anytime."

"Don't expect me at the manor. I'm going to stay in the city." She strolls away.

"What am I not understanding?" Victor asks.

"She's worried about Richard. She needs to do something, to have a distraction." I glance around. "Until Sin arrives, she should be safe here."

"Everyone should be safe."

As the party progresses, Victor and I find our place on a couch. I watch the groups move like a single organism. Without the masks, it's impossible to tell who is a Night Watchman and who is a vampire. Fangs aren't being lowered. The most beautiful sound, though, is their laughter. Despite what happened tonight, despite the years of hostility, despite the war and the bloodlust and VampHu, they can laugh together.

The room slows down and I marvel at what I'm seeing: humans and vampires having fun together. With every handshake I see potential for change. I remember standing atop the Agency in Los Angeles, looking down at all the Day Walkers that surrounded us on the streets below. I remember Sin saying we were looking at the New World Order. And I compare that fear and grandiose design to what's in here. One is created through blood, the other through laughter. I know which one I want.

"What are you looking at?" Victor asks.

"The future."

Chapter 23

The next evening Clive gives a speech from a makeshift platform just outside the Agency building. A crowd of citizens has gathered. Rumors have been spreading all day about the great betrayer Roland Hursch. TV cameras are locked on Clive. Reporters are anxious for details. I wanted desperately to be there, but everyone convinced me that it was too dangerous, there was simply no telling how the crowd would react. So instead, Victor and I are watching it from my apartment.

Sitting on the couch with him, I'm suddenly glad I didn't go. I want to support Clive in whatever happens next, but I also can't deny the simple pleasure of being here, with Victor by my side.

On the screen I see Rachel sitting in one of the chairs lined up in a row behind Clive. She'll be taking over the delegate position once again now that Hursch has been ousted, so she needs to show her loyalty. Beside her is Jeff, doubling as both date and bodyguard.

"You should have gone," I say to Victor.

"I want the Lessers to be shown without Old Family beside them. I want everyone to see that they are loyal and tame, they can control their bloodlust without an iron fist ruling over them."

"Roland Hursch's crimes are unforgivable," Clive begins. "He hid the Day Walkers in his home, sheltering them from discovery when they returned there from attacking our own. He toyed with our lives, using his fellow humans as pawns in a game that none of us were aware he was playing. He sold his soul to the devil, and he signed his name in the blood of those taken from us."

I sometimes forget how good of an orator Clive is, how passionate he can sound when he believes deeply in what he's saying. I always see him behind closed doors, where he's the tired leader, the exhausted man who's weary of looking for the right decision among so many bad options. But up there, in front of the crowd and cameras, he's completely in control.

I wish I could see the crowd, but their perfect silence may tell me more than their faces. No boos, no jeering, no rushing to the aid of their beloved anti-vampire delegate.

"Remember this day and remember it well, citizens," Clive says, hands held up high as though in praise. "Behind me sit several of our Night Watchmen—unmasked at the invitation of Victor Valentine. From him, we have no need to hide. Because of him, you can now know who has been keeping you safe.

"Last night, the Night Watchmen delivered us from evil yet again, but their eyes were not the only ones watching over us, nor were their hands the only hands at work. They were helped, every step of the way, by the Lesser vampires loyal to Victor Valentine."

A low gasp comes from the audience, and I feel Victor tightening his hold on me, his tension matching my own.

Behind Clive a Night Watchman stands up from his chair, as does the vampire next to him. He's wearing a suit and looks like any other employee of the Agency, which is perfect. He isn't threatening or menacing. If anything, he's a bit cute. And then they shake hands.

"Let this be the new model for all to follow," Clive says. "These Lesser vampires have proved themselves not only to Lord Valentine, but to us human beings. They protected *you* while you slept. They lost their lives, lives that were once human, lives whose hearts beat just the same. Let their sacrifice and cooperation serve as an example.

"They need our blood," Clive says, putting emphasis on each word. "But they are willing to protect us all from those who would take it by force. For that, we must be both grateful and giving to our friends. It is time we roll up our sleeves and show our appreciation . . . by donating."

Cameras flash as Clive waves goodbye and everyone retreats back into the Agency. For a moment I fear a riot may start out of nowhere, the hushed tones during the speech nothing but anger waiting to be unleashed. Instead, there are quiet murmurs and then a slow dispersion of the crowd.

I turn off the television and call Clive. It's his voice mail, like I expected, but I tell him he did a great job and he looked ten years younger on camera.

"Tomorrow will be the real test," Victor says.

"I know. If they give blood, it'll be the start of something new. If not, it's back to the beginning."

A knock sounds. I unfold myself, go to the door, and peer through the peephole. Faith.

I open the door.

"I'm looking for Victor," she says, before I can greet her. "Thought he might be here."

"Yeah, he is. Come on in." She seems a little unsettled as she glides through in her characteristic red.

Victor is immediately on his feet. "What's wrong, Faith?"

"Something strange happened." Sitting in a chair, hands between her knees, she's having a hard time meeting our gaze.

I return to Victor's side on the couch.

"What happened?" he prods.

She licks her lips, looks around. "I'm not sure how to say this, but, well, I had a dream. I . . . I dreamed of Richard, but it was like I was *with* him."

I catch my breath. Dream-sharing between Old Family vampires supposedly only happens when the vampires are in love. She's finally truly opened herself up.

"Faith, that's wonderful!" I assure her.

She nods, but her reaction doesn't seem so wonderful. "I've never dreamed before. It was a strange experience, frightening even. I don't know how you humans put up with it."

"You'll get used to it. But what was the dream about? What happened?"

Faith rubs her hands together nervously, completely out of character. "Richard showed me where they were. In Crimson Sands."

My heart lurches. "Is the town all right?"

"Seems so, from what I saw, but here's the thing. Some old guy named George told Richard that his scouts spotted Sin and an army of Day Walkers heading into the mountains. Richard thinks they were looking for someplace to rest before moving on to Denver."

Victor scoots up to the edge of his seat. "Richard isn't thinking of trying to take them out, is he?"

Faith shakes her head. "No, he knows that they are outnumbered and wouldn't stand a chance. He's following through on his orders to destroy the V-Processing center."

Victor is visibly relieved. "Good."

"Did Richard say anything about Ian?" I ask.

Faith's lips flatten. "Yes. Unfortunately, the vampires dislike him even more than they did during the war."

"But why?"

"Apparently, whenever they've taken time to rest the horses, he's won a good deal of money off them playing poker."

I laugh, imagining how much Ian would enjoy beating

his former enemies in so civilized a manner. "They're Old Family. They can afford it."

"Still, no one likes to lose."

I grow somber. We certainly can't afford to lose against Sin.

"How much time do you think we have before Sin gets here?" I ask.

"A couple of days, maybe," Victor says.

Faith stands. "I guess I'd better get to the Agency and start working with Jeff and Rachel to devise a plan for organizing the city."

Victor shoves himself to his feet. "Clive's message tonight was a good start. I think the people will be receptive to working with vampires just as the Night Watchmen now are."

"I hope so. I'll stay in the city, get things mobilized."

"If you need a place to stay—" I begin.

"I'm using Victor's theater." He used to live in an abandoned theater in the city. Its absence of windows makes it a perfect hiding place. We once watched an old movie there together. "But thanks, anyway," she says, before taking a step toward the door.

Victor touches her arm, stilling her. "Richard will be all right."

"He'd better be. If he dies, I'll kill him."

With her head held high, she strides from the apartment. I lock the door behind her. When I turn around, Victor is standing on the balcony, gazing out on the night.

I join him and say, "It's been a while since there's been

a feeling of peace in Denver. Maybe never."

"And Sin will be here soon to shatter it." I expect him to go on, but he doesn't. He turns to me and I see the desire in his eyes burning stronger than ever, so strong that it's almost overwhelming. I realize he doesn't want my *blood*, he wants *me*.

"How would you like to go on a picnic?" he asks.

"Tonight?"

He smiles. "Tonight."

"But Sin—"

"He's not here yet. And when he does get here . . . we may never have more than tonight."

I don't want to acknowledge what he's saying. As confident as he always seems, he's recognizing that he might not be able to defeat Sin, that he might fall. Any of us might fall before that monster.

I step into his embrace and wrap my arms tightly around him. "I'd love to go on a picnic with you."

We stop by the manor. When Victor tells Eustace that he's taking me on a picnic, the old vampire takes control and sends servants scurrying about to gather the necessary items: an old quilt, a fine bottle of wine, a wicker basket that contains delicacies to "delight Miss Dawn." He seems pleased that he has a role in ensuring that all goes well for his young lord.

An hour later, Victor and I are sitting on the blanket, gazing out on a lake reflecting the silvery moonlight. It's peaceful out here, with the insects chirping an unfamiliar cadence. Perhaps because of their nearness to the water, trees are actually flourishing. I hear the occasional hoot of an owl.

"I'm sorry we can't do this during the day," Victor says.

I give him a soft smile. "I like the night."

He pours deep red wine into a crystal goblet. "Do you?"

"Until recently it was more of a love-hate relationship," I admit. "I hated it because it brought out the monsters and yet I felt drawn to it, to the peacefulness of a star-filled sky."

Victor hands me the glass, pours one for himself. Then he stretches out beside me, raises up on an elbow, and taps his glass against mine. "Here's to the end of all monsters: those that haunt the night and those that roam the day."

I sip the wine. It's rich and smooth. "I guess vampires always dreaded the arrival of daybreak."

"We still do. That'll never change," he says. "But hopefully the sun is all we'll fear. We won't have to fear being hunted anymore."

He offers me a strawberry dipped in chocolate. I bite into it. It's delicious, decadent. I'll have to remember to compliment his chef.

"So now you believe vampires and humans can live together?" I ask.

"Based on what I've witnessed the past few days, I think it's a definite possibility."

"As long as we defeat Sin."

Reaching up, he strokes my cheek. "Tonight, let's pretend he doesn't exist. Tonight, it's just us."

Just us. We've had so few moments of it being just us, even fewer when there were no worries at all. I finish off my wine, feeling lethargic and relaxed. I lie on my back and stare at the stars scattered across the black heavens like tiny diamonds.

"I miss your theater," I tell him.

He skims his fingers up and down my arm. "I do, too. Maybe I'll renovate it, make it a working theater, open it to the public."

Rolling my head to the side, I look up into his face. "That would be cool."

"Once this is all over, Richard wants to go back to Los Angeles, return it to its glory days, to what it was before the war: a place that recorded dreams and fantasy."

"Do you think that's possible?"

"Since you came into my life, I think a lot of things are possible."

Tears sting my eyes. "You once told me that I was your greatest weakness."

"I was wrong. You're my greatest strength, Dawn. Sending my Lessers into the city to work with the Night Watchmen as you suggested changed everything. I can see now that I was still viewing humans as part of the problem. You helped me to see that they can be included in the solution."

"What if they don't give blood?"

"We'll find another way." He cradles my cheek and

leans in. "Vampires and humans can live together. They live together in you."

He lowers his mouth to mine. For the first time I recognize, truly recognize, that Victor unconditionally accepts me as I am: a dhampir. I've been so worried that as a lone dhampir, I would be isolated, would fit in neither world, but as he deepens the kiss, I realize that he's never turned away from me.

What courses through my veins doesn't make me what I am or who I am. I was forged by my parents' love—and my brother's. Their deaths shaped me further, but the foundation that they gave me provided the strength to not only survive but to follow my heart.

And that led me to Victor.

Whether he is a vampire or human, I would feel this strong attraction toward him, this unyielding love for him. Why did I doubt that he would feel the same toward me?

I stroke my hands over his broad shoulders, his powerful back, and I feel desire such as I've never known. He means everything to me. It's terrifying to admit, but I'm willing to embrace the possibility of hurt for the reality of now.

My life will be measured in years; his will be measured in memories. I'm determined that whatever time we have together will never fade from his mind.

He skims his warm lips along my throat, slides his mouth across my crucifix tattoo. His tongue circles the shell of my ear. He whispers low, "I love you, Dawn."

Rising above me, he holds my gaze. I look deeply into

his eyes. "I love you, Victor, forever."

"Forever," he repeats before once again capturing my mouth.

As the moon shines down on us, I know that the night has never been more beautiful, more perfect.

Chapter 24

The next morning, I awake in Victor's bed, his warm body nestled against mine. I feel so incredibly close to him, closer than I've ever felt to anyone.

I get up and put on a silk robe, the red double V stitched into it, and a pair of slippers. I leave Victor to rest and head down the hall. Hopefully Eustace will be in the dining room and I can get some breakfast.

The euphoria of last night fades slightly when a cold draft comes down the hall. I quicken my pace, my feet slapping noisily on the tile. I can't shake the feeling that I'm running from something. Certainly not from Victor, and *certainly* not from last night. But . . .

A sudden fear clenches me and I turn around—but there's nothing except emptiness. I shake my head, trying to get rid of this strange aura. The hallways seem darker, the statues more looming, the walls moving in. It's like Murdoch Valentine has reclaimed the manor and transformed it back to what it once was.

Maybe some coffee and juice will help settle me.

I open the door into the dining room. The curtains on the windows are open and light is pouring in. I've never seen it like this, so bright and revealed. The colors have changed dramatically under the sun, and artwork on the walls, once entirely hidden in shadows, now dominates.

That's when I realize why fear is gripping me. It's too quiet. In fact, it's dead silent. None of the servants are walking about, completing their daily tasks. No one dusting, no one cleaning up, no one rushing about with laundry. It's been nothing but the soft sound of my feet on the floor.

I go over and begin shutting the curtains, wondering if the other vampires will praise me for blocking out that dreadful sun. *Ha.* That's probably the word Eustace will use. "Dreadful." He's so cute in a superpolite old-world-servant kind of way. I wonder if he ever—

Crunch.

I stop. There's broken glass beneath my slippers. Slowly lifting my gaze, I see the window it once belonged to is shattered.

It's so strange, this tiny destruction in an otherwise perfect room.

I turn around and quickly, very quickly, walk out of the dining room. Something's not right. I need to talk to Victor. I'm nearly at the end of the hallway when something stops me. A song. A piano playing from the music room. The melody is soft and sad, as if scored on the coffin of a dead loved one.

I creep toward the piano room. The windows on the side of the hallway are wide open, the thick drapes pulled back, and the thin silk curtains waving like ghosts from another plane, reaching out to grab the light as though it may bring them back to life.

The melody is so beautiful, and I'd love to rest my head on the door frame and listen, afraid to disrupt the performer. But when I turn into the room, I truly am sorry that I disrupted him.

The piano player continues striking the notes, playing to his audience of dead servants splayed on the ground with throats gouged out. Some are sitting in chairs like grotesque marionettes, their eyes wide open but not seeing the musician at his keys. Others lie on the floor, their limbs intertwined, placed without care. Eustace is among them, glassy eyes looking at me as though pleading for one last chance to straighten the glassware before finally retiring.

And the music keeps playing. Even as the man turns his head toward me, his fingers never leave the ivory keys, tapping them with an unnatural ease. His eyes are black through and through, and if I look closely, I can see my distorted reflection in them. He smiles, or maybe he can't help but spread his lips wide because his teeth are so large and fanged.

One of the Chosen. That's what I'm staring at. Just like my brother, though nothing like him. Whereas good always resided deep in Brady's heart, there's nothing like that in this vampire.

He pounds the piano with all his fingers as a final crescendo, then slowly rises.

I run.

I have no idea what he plans; all I know is that if he wanted me dead, I'd already be dead. I can't fight him. So I just keep running. I take sharp turns, hoping that he's lost sight of me and knowing that he could easily find himself trapped in this maze of hallways and doors. I climb the stairs, not daring to look behind me because what good would it do if I saw him?

Victor's door is in sight and I push myself, feeling my feet slamming against the cold-hardened floors but not caring about the pain that sends shocks through my body. I practically break the door in with my shoulder, turning the knob just enough for it to swing open. Once inside, I shut it and lock it.

"Dawn!" Victor says, no grogginess, no sleep in his voice. He's awake instantly, as though the sun has already set. Instead it still has many hours left in the sky.

"Victor, the Chosen, they're here!"

His vampire speed carries him to the door in a single blurred motion. He's pressed against it and I keep quiet while he listens.

"How many?" he asks.

"I just saw one, but, oh God, Victor, all the servants are dead." Poor Eustace. He didn't deserve to be slaughtered. None of them did. But I have to hold off mourning until we're out of here.

Victor gets dressed in jeans and shirt while I watch the door. He places several stakes in his belt, then it's my turn to change and arm myself. I make it quick.

"Ready?" he asks, leaning against the door.

"Yes."

He opens it slowly, calmly, and steps outside. I follow right behind him, watching his back as he moves forward. I keep one hand on his shoulder, my head turned, the hallway lengthening behind us.

It takes us several minutes, and every few steps Victor stops to listen. I gain my own courage through his bravery, and we feel like a single unit as we slowly move down the maze of hallways.

"What's the plan?" I whisper.

"Get out of here. If we can make it to the garage, we can take the car."

Too bad it's on the other side of the manor, giving the Chosen plenty of time to spring an attack, which I'm sure is coming. I'm also sure that they'll take their time, stalk their prey, just like every other vampire. No, worse than the others. The Chosen are battling their own insanity, and every one I've seen shares the lust not only for vampire blood, but for the sadism of the hunt as well.

We try to keep our pace slow enough to mask the sound

of our feet but eventually give in to a near sprint. We're on the second floor and begin crossing the great entryway, the massive marbled stairs leading to the front door in sight. But as soon as we enter the threshold of that expansive room, terror strikes.

Victor growls and jumps back, sunlight pouring in across the floor. Our backs against the wall, we look out at the unfamiliar sight. All of the windows, many stretching up from floor to ceiling, have had their drapes slashed and torn down, the glass shattered. The front door itself, once a mighty oaken slab, is torn asunder, resting on the ground in pieces of splintered bark. The great wolf's-head knocker, the symbol of the Valentine family, lies helplessly in the sun, staring up at the unwelcome guests who have caused all of this.

Three of them. Three Chosen. One in the doorway, his dark silhouette sharpened by the blazing sun. His friends, one in each window, sit and stare like this is some casual gathering and the guests have just arrived. They begin laughing softly.

"You are not welcome in the House of Valentine!" Victor shouts.

"You hear that?" the one in the doorway asks, obviously the leader. "We aren't welcome. Well, we better make ourselves welcome."

They all start laughing like hyenas, thoroughly enjoying the strength the sun provides them and the weakness it causes the Old Family Valentine. No doubt in their minds

Victor is the symbol of all they hate. Born a powerful vampire, he started the war and caused the deaths of so many. To them, all Old Family deserve to die horribly. All except for their savior: Sin.

"Get to the garage," Victor whispers to me. "Take the car, I'll hold them off."

"Victor, no!"

"Just do it!"

"You might want to rethink that plan, pal," the Chosen leader says, his vampire ears overhearing even our faintest whispers. "Show him, John."

John, the Chosen sitting in one of the windowsills, reaches behind him and pulls out a block of machinery, wires and tubes connected to it, and throws it across the room, where it lands with a loud thud, much heavier than it appears.

It's a part to the car. I'm not sure which one, but looking up at Victor, I can tell it's vital. Of course they wouldn't let us escape that easily. The thrill of the hunt. They let me run to him. Why not? They had disabled the car as soon as they arrived, maybe before even dealing with the servants. We were never leaving this place.

"Why are you here?" Victor asks, having retreated away from the direct light of the sun. I can sense his uncomfortable stance, though. He isn't used to seeing it, and he certainly isn't used to fighting near it, if this all comes to a clash.

"For Eris," the Chosen says.

"Then take her and be gone."

"Ha! We weren't here to take her. We were here to kill her."

"Why?" I ask.

"Once she was captured, we knew she'd talk. We were under orders to take her out. So we did. Catching you two here, though, is a bonus."

"Is Sin not man enough to fight us himself?" I ask. "He has to send his dogs to do it for him?"

They laugh again, deep and demonic, like the world was a cruel joke that they had orchestrated all by themselves.

"Sin wants results," the leader says. "That's all. He doesn't care who kills Victor so long as it gets done. We thought you'd have retreated to the city walls by now. But no, your arrogance knows no bounds. The Day Walkers are here, the Thirst is in your countryside, and still you remain in your stone house that falls so easily in the daylight. Sin will be very pleased to hear of Victor's death and your capture, Dawn."

"I'd rather die than go with you!"

"That won't be a choice you get to make, girl. You may have thought your boyfriend would protect you no matter what. Well, you're about to see how wrong you are. You will see the true power of the Chosen. You will understand why *we* are the next evolutionary step."

The Chosen up high in their windows jump down, landing twenty feet below with a loud thud, nothing like the soft landing of most vampires. But they aren't fazed by their jarring impact, and as they approach, their silhouettes fill out and I see the monsters as they truly are: hideous. Black eyes and jaws lined with asymmetric fangs. No beauty, no subtlety in their movements. Nothing but death and destruction.

They don't draw their stakes; they have no need for them. Instead, they raise their hands, the fingers having lengthened and the nails becoming like claws. All it would take is a single jab, a quick strike, and one of those claws could puncture a vampire's heart. Victor's heart.

"We can't outrun them," I say, drawing my stake. Victor does the same. "But maybe we can—"

A blur of motion, black eyes and bloodied fangs moving up the stairs. I can't tell if it's one or two or all of them. It's heading toward me, so I hold out my stake, adrenaline replacing any training that I had. But my stake never connects; rather it's Victor who appears in front of me, stopping the Chosen with his own strike. I don't know if it's fatal or not because the next moment I feel another attack coming.

By the time I turn to face him, it's too late. The Chosen slams into me and I'm catapulted off my feet and down the stairs. I watch Victor and his quarry grow smaller as I'm carried away from them.

Everything slows down for me, and I hope that this fall is too great for me to survive. I don't want to be knocked out, I want to be killed. If this is truly it, I'd rather die than see Victor meet the same fate, and I'd rather die than ever see the smile in Sin's eyes.

When I hit the ground, all the wind escapes from my lungs and I struggle to bring it back in. Short gasps that grab at nothing. I try to get up, and the Chosen, John, helps me by squeezing my neck and lifting me high. My vision is shattered, as though I were looking through shards of glass and mirrors. I want Victor to appear behind John and ram a stake through him, but I can still see him fighting at the top of the stairs, which seem so far away. Especially because we're separated by a great swath of sunlight. Victor is young enough, strong enough that the sun will burn him slowly as his body continually reheals. But the pain will be debilitating, unimaginable.

John throws me across the room and I hit the far wall, the back of my head slamming brutally against it before my entire body slides to the ground in a heap. My stake is out of my hand, lying somewhere between him and me. I reach for another one, but it feels like all my bones are rebelling, and I'm slow to grab it. When I finally do, I barely have the strength to stand on wobbly legs.

The other two Chosen have tackled Victor and now hold him in the sunlight. Smoke rises from his body, making him look like a demon from hell, his fangs bared, teeth clenched, and anger stretched across his bleeding face. His legs begin to give out on him, his face scorched from the sun, red and splotchy; blood runs across the furrows on his face and chest, the razor claws of the Chosen having cut deep. Then John approaches him and the others let go. With a horrendous sound, he delivers a right hook to Victor's temple, and the vampire I love falls to the ground.

The Chosen look at us. We must seem so pathetic in our beaten state. I search them, looking for any weakness. I can tell Victor's done all that he can. Some of them, the leader included, bleed from wounds received, and one yelps as he dislodges a stake deep in his ribs, just below the heart. They're weaker now, but far too powerful still.

"So this is where it all ends, Victor," the leader says. "In the sunlight."

They laugh as one, preparing for their finale—when we all hear it. A roar in the distance. Something coming this way.

I look out the window and see the dust swirling into the air and, against the horizon, a black form taking shape. It's bulky and cumbersome, flying along as though unsure if all four wheels are supposed to be on the ground.

I look at the Chosen, and they're just as mystified. So this wasn't part of their plan, this isn't their friends showing up. Then, maybe, it's ours.

When I turn back, I see exactly what it is: a black van. Not exactly the cavalry I would've called for, but I don't have much time to consider it; the van turns sharply and screeches to a dead stop.

The door immediately slides open, and a black-clad Michael steps out. And in his arms is something I've only ever seen in pictures, the thing my brother once spoke of using in the war. It was a weapon used against the vampires in the trenches. One of the few ways to kill them, and one of the most stomach-churning.

A flamethrower.

I jump as far away as possible; Victor follows my lead. Just in time. Michael squeezes the trigger and unleashes liquid hell onto the Chosen. I can feel the searing heat so acutely that I check my clothes and hair to make sure nothing has caught fire. I look to see the entire room engulfed in yellow flames, turning things black.

And I hear the screams of the Chosen. It won't kill them right away, but it will give us time.

"Get inside!" Michael yells, his finger never letting up, the fire growing across the floor, catching anything remotely flammable and igniting it.

I run toward the van; Victor meets me there. The Night Watchmen waiting inside grab our hands and pull us quickly into the vehicle. Michael jumps through the opening last, slamming the door shut. The tires spin, and we're gone.

Chapter 25

The entire ride back I'm taking calming breaths, steadying my hands. I look at Victor: His wounds have worsened, the run from where he was to the van exposing him to direct sunlight, further burning his vampiric flesh. His perfect skin is now nothing but a patchwork of various blackened shades and raised scabs, blood and pus running from them.

"I'll be okay," he says to me, his words deep and gravelly, almost unrecognizable, as though even his voice box has been singed.

"Here," Michael says, handing him a packet of blood, the Agency stamp on it.

"No," Victor says, turning it away. "I want the people to see me as I am. Let them see how vulnerable even I am to the Chosen."

The van has been heavily modified. All of the seats, except the front two, have been removed. Most of the windows have been blacked out, and metal stakes line a magnetic strip. There are four Night Watchmen plus the driver.

"How did you guys know we were in danger?" I ask.

One of them looks up. "Ever since we got your report about the Chosen, we knew that the manor could be easily compromised during the day. We've had a scout watching it at all times. He saw several vampires breaking in early this morning and came back to the city as soon as possible. We moved out once we received word."

"Well, we're extremely grateful," I say.

"We've been practicing the mission for months," he says, then pauses. "Of course, we always assumed we'd be *attacking* the Valentines, not rescuing them."

I'm not surprised that an assassination plan was always in the works in case the Valentine family got too greedy.

"You have my eternal thanks," Victor says, sitting against the thin metal wall, looking not far from death—though I know he's a long way from knocking on its door.

"We're allies in this fight now. We aren't planning on leaving you behind," Michael says.

In the director's office the thick shutters are drawn across the windows.

"Are you sure you won't take any blood?" Clive asks Victor.

"No. I'm healing."

"And what of you, Dawn? How are your injuries?"

I touch the bandage around my head, where a nasty gash had to be sewn up. I don't bother feeling for the bruises on my neck; I know they're there.

"I'll live."

Clive leans back, looking so different in this dim light that suits vampires over humans.

"Dawn," he begins, "I'd like to offer you the small apartment here in the Agency building. It'll be safer than the one you share with Rachel, and it'll be easier to contact you if needed."

"Thank you. I'd love it."

It won't have any of my things, and it won't feel like home, but that doesn't matter. Clive is right; it'll be safer, and I have a feeling I'll be in this room most of the time. I'm not the delegate anymore, but my role within the Agency, my role within the entire city, is more important than ever before. As delegate, I was the ambassador of the people to Valentine. Now I feel like the ambassador of all people to all vampires. I'm in the center of something strange and new, on the cusp of an even newer World Order. The question is whether it will be mine, and the dream born in Crimson Sands, or whether it'll be Sin's, a world of walls and monsters worse than any that have ever walked beneath the sun or stars before.

In the tiny apartment I immediately pour Victor a drink but take coffee myself.

The place is simple, sharp lines giving a perfect geometry

not often seen in the city. It's devoid of a personality. No pictures, no art, no little tchotchkes. Instead, it's clean and sanitary, a combination of dark woods and glass.

Making a quick tour, I find that the place is smaller than the apartment I share with Rachel. It's utilitarian: a basic kitchen for cooking, a basic bedroom for sleeping, and a bathroom.

"I must look horrible," Victor says.

"You always look beautiful," I say.

He laughs and then cringes, one of his many wounds reminding him that laughter is off the table for now.

"You should rest," I tell him, "so you can heal."

He glances over at the bed. "Will you join me?"

Nodding, I follow him to the bed. I lie gingerly beside him and he puts his arm around me.

"Last night, I almost forgot that we're still fighting for our existence," I say softly.

"But if we don't have moments like last night," he says quietly, "we can forget what it is we're fighting for."

For each other, a better world, a better future.

Two days later, Victor's burns have healed and he's regained most of his strength. During that time, he drank only the blood he needed to satiate himself and allowed the healing to come as naturally as possible for a vampire. I told him he should gorge, drink every drop he can to help his wounds heal quickly, but he wouldn't hear of it. There are other vampires in the city now, good vampires, who need that blood just as badly.

The Night Watchmen have taken to guarding the day, while Anita leads the new Fanged Watchmen, a group of Victor's most trusted Lesser vampires, who guard the night. It seems like Denver's protective angels have quadrupled. Before, one rarely caught a glimpse of a black-clad Night Watchman; now it's commonplace. People feel safer. Even with so much chaos beyond the walls, everything inside is under control.

Victor and I are at a warehouse, standing in the shadows, observing the drills and training exercises. Night Watchmen, human and vampire alike, have been sharing their knowledge, their weapons, their skills so they can make short work of defeating the Chosen when they arrive.

"How close do you think the Chosen are?" I ask.

Victor shakes his head. "Impossible to know."

"Maybe Clive should send out some scouts."

"I would hate for them to run into Sin and his army alone."

"The waiting is driving me crazy."

Victor gives me a small smile. "That's probably part of his plan."

At the echo of crisp footsteps I turn to see Faith walking briskly toward us. "Clive told me I'd find you here."

"How are things going with the citizens?" Victor asks when she stops in front of us.

"Good. People are stockpiling food, preparing for a possible siege, but there's no panic. We've set up emergency ration centers, hospitals. I have some Lessers examining the wall for weaknesses. If they exist, our vampires will find them. We'll stand a better chance if we can keep Sin out."

Victor grins. "Maybe you are a tactician."

"That's common sense. But I'm here for something else." She takes a shuddering breath. "Richard and I shared another dream today. They destroyed the V-Processing center, detonating it. The entire Agency building is gone. But the city was empty."

"Empty?" Victor repeats.

"No one was there. The Inner Ring, you remember it, Dawn. It was so full of energy and people, well, Day Walkers. But when I saw it through Richard's eyes, there was no one."

"So Sin took all his Day Walkers with him," I say. "We knew he was on the move."

She shakes her head.

"I relived it all through Richard. He held my hand and we walked through the empty streets. Everything was so fuzzy, like one of those old films you collect, Victor. And I felt it on my skin. I didn't know what it was. But now I do. It was ash. Dawn, the Day Walkers, they died."

"What! How?"

"I don't know. And neither does Richard. Some of the other Old Family wanted to go looking for them. They said horse tracks and hundreds of footprints led out of the city. But they went in all directions. Why did he leave so many behind? Why did the others die?"

Faith rubs her arms, like the ash is on them.

"I'm scared," she says. "Sin is up to something and I

hate not knowing what it is."

I share Faith's concerns. Sin has always managed to be one step ahead of us.

"How's Ian?"

"Grateful to find that most of the Night Train cars are intact."

I notice then that the warehouse has grown quiet. The practice maneuvers are over. Fewer Watchmen are standing about, and I realize their vampire counterparts have dispersed for the day, seeking sleep and protection from the sun.

"It'll be dawn soon," I say. "We should head back to the Agency."

"Come with us, Faith," Victor says. "I don't want you being alone in the city."

As we walk to the Agency, I'm acutely aware of the calm, the silence as though everyone—everything—is simply waiting. Waiting for Sin to make his move.

From time to time, I notice an amateur poster slapped onto the side of a building:

> KEEP THEM FED SO THEY CAN PROTECT US.
> NO FEAR FOR OUR FANGED FRIENDS.
> DONATING BLOOD IS AN INVESTMENT IN OUR FUTURE.

Blood donations have begun in earnest. It may just be trendy now, and soon they may return to what they were. But for the time being, we've become a city-size version of Crimson Sands. We watch each other's backs so we can live our lives without fear.

As we near the steps of the Agency, a black car comes careening to a stop. Richard jumps out. I see a blur and then Faith is in his arms.

Ian is a little slower getting out. I greet him with a quick hug. "I'm so glad you're back."

"Me too. I have to return for the Night Train, but there won't be anyone to fight me about it."

Victor shakes his hand. "We want to hear everything, but the sun's coming up. We should get inside."

Sitting in the Agency apartment, we listen as Richard and Ian pretty much tell us the same thing that Faith did.

"The other Old Family vamps headed toward their own territories to begin preparing for Sin," Richard says.

"I wish they'd stopped by here first," I say. "I think they would find it useful to see how Denver's citizens and vampires are working together."

"Faith told me some of what is going on. Incredible."

"But can it last?" Ian asks.

"It's going to have to," Victor says, "if we have any hope at all for a better world."

My cell phone rings. It's Clive. "What's up?"

"I think Sin is sending us a message. You need to see it."

Chapter 26

The messenger isn't in a carriage made of white, nor does he come in the dark of the moon. He's a vampire, lit aflame in the high sun, walking slowly toward the city.

"What the hell is that?" the guard asks.

Along with Clive and Michael, I'm standing on one of the watchtowers. Beside me is the guard who first spotted the slowly moving object, just a black silhouette with fires licking across his body, taking bits of ash into the air, where it's whisked away. I borrow the guard's binoculars and look.

It's a vampire, no doubt. Humans tend to stay in one piece when exposed to the sun, and if lit on fire, well, they die pretty quickly. But this poor soul is trekking across the wasteland, his body fuel for the inescapable flames. He's stopped trying to get rid of them but instead marches on with an unmatched will to . . . to what? To reach us?

"He's Old Family," I say.

"Are you sure?"

"No one else could survive that. Even the strongest of Lessers collapse within an hour or so."

"It looks as though he's been walking for several hours," the guard says.

"I'm sure he has."

"Go pick him up," Clive commands the guard.

"But sir—"

"If he has something important to say, I don't want him dead by the time he reaches these walls. Take Michael with you."

An hour later, I'm in Clive's office. The shutters are drawn tight, and Victor stands in the corner, arms crossed. All is quiet until a scream pierces the area outside the room. We don't have much time to react when the door is kicked open. Michael and Jeff are holding a smoldering vampire, a wool blanket wrapped around him to make his body able to be handled, but his face is black and charred, pieces of him flaking to the ground like a log left in the fire too long. I have to look away for a moment to brace myself before returning his pained stare.

And his screams keep coming.

"Calm down," Jeff says.

But his shrieks echo around us.

"What do we do, Victor?" Michael asks. "Blood?"

"No," Victor says. "It won't help him at this stage. He

won't even be able to get it down his throat."

"Kill me!" the thing shouts as he's lain on Clive's desk.

"Who are you?" Victor asks, moving toward the vampire.

"Ah . . . Ahh . . . Byron Asher. Your Grace."

Only now do I recognize the charred features of the vampire who stood around the great Council table.

"What happened?" I ask.

He looks at me, and while I expect anger, all I see is remorse.

"You were right, Lady Montgomery. Sin . . . he's insane. I . . . I tried to join him, but it was too late. He's . . . he's . . ." Asher makes a horrendous gurgling sound, inhaling the ash that has fallen from his body, breathing in his own flesh and choking on it.

"How many are there?" Victor asks. "How many Day Walkers? How many Chosen?"

"N . . . no . . . none."

"What?"

"None. Sin. He . . . he killed them all. Those who survived fled. I don't know where, but somewhere far away."

I think about Faith's dream she shared with Richard. The footprints leading outside the city. They went in all directions, a mass exodus of fear.

"Why did he kill them?"

Asher calms himself, pushing the pain out, and I can tell there isn't much time left for this once great vampire. I move forward to thank him. "You were very brave, Lord Asher, to come tell us."

Victor shoots me an approving look before turning back to Asher. "This was in Los Angeles?"

He shakes his head. "I met him in the mountains. He had a few followers with him. But then . . . the Thirst." Asher's voice grows steady as though he is determined to give us this vital information. "Sin's wish has come true. He's become Infected. He's . . . oh, Lord Valentine, you've never seen a monster like this. His need for vampire blood is inescapable. It's never ending. He . . . he drank from those around him . . . without any regard to his master plan. He no longer cares. The Thirst . . . it's . . . it's taken over his mind, his entire being."

"My God, Asher, you saw this?"

"Yes, my lord." Asher grabs Victor by the collar and pulls him close. "He'll never stop. He'll never be satisfied. He'll drink forever and ever until no one is left. He can do it, Victor. He . . . he can't be stopped."

"Where is he?"

"He . . . he wants to kill you most of all, Victor. He says that . . . 'It must end where it began.' Those were his final words before the Thirst tore his mind apart once again, and he slaughtered three vampires, feeding on every ounce of their . . . of their blood. His own kind. How could he . . . How could . . . How could any of us . . ."

His final words may have been spoken, but only in his mind. They never escape his lips. The fires of the sun have caused too much damage. Asher's heart stops.

* * *

I watch Victor throw several more stakes into his leather duffel.

"Are you sure he'll be there?" I ask.

"I'm sure. It's the only place that makes sense."

An hour ago, Victor showed me on a map where he thought Sin would be, where he thought "it all began." On the folded paper, marked with roads and cities, it was just a forest. Nothing more. But for Victor, it's home. The old Valentine Manor, erected before vampires were ever known to exist. It's where he spent his early years; it's where Sin grew up under the oppressive weight of an abusive father.

"I'll need three stakes," I say. "So make sure you have enough for me. One of them has to be small, though, so I can strap it inside my boot." Victor stops. "And make sure they're razor sharp and steel. None of this wood crap."

"Dawn—"

"We should probably wrap tape around the grip, make sure our hands don't slip."

"Dawn—"

"Maybe I should go get my metal collar."

"Dawn!" I look up at him, knowing what he's about to say. "You won't be coming."

I open my mouth to speak, but he shoves more stakes into the bag, making a loud clanging noise and cutting me off. "It's not negotiable."

"I'm a delegate. I negotiate."

"Ex-delegate."

"Maybe to the city. But to you, I'm more than that."

"I know. Which is precisely why you're not going. It's too dangerous."

"And that is *precisely* why I *am* going. To protect you."

Victor looks up at the ceiling, his grip tense around the leather bag that carries his weapons of war. "I have no idea what I'm going to be facing. Sin could rip me apart in a few seconds, and it'll all be over. That's why Faith is staying behind. If something happens to me, she has to step up and become head of the Valentine family. And I'm not willing to risk you being another victim. No. I'll fight better knowing you're here, safe and sound."

"That isn't true," I say. "Remember when you fought your father, when you . . . when you killed him. You said to me that I was the reason you drove the stake through his heart. Looking at me gave you that strength. The same with Brady. Our toughest battles have always been fought together. We . . . we fight as one."

"Please, Dawn, not this time. If something happens to me . . . No, if something happens to *you*—"

"Then let it," I say. "Because I . . . don't make me say it, Victor."

"What is it?" he asks. When did the distance between us close? When did he place his hands on my face?

"Because I can't live in a world without you."

"And I can't create a new one without you."

I want this new world that we've both dreamed of, but I want him more. "I hid in a closet when Sin took Brady. I was safe at home asleep in my bed when he killed my parents. I can't—I won't—let him have you. I love you too much."

Raising up on my toes, I wrap my arms around his neck and kiss him, conveying with my lips and tongue everything that I feel for him. Victor Valentine. Vampire. I risked loving him. I'm not willing to risk losing him.

Victor draws back and studies the determination in my eyes. Tenderly he brushes back my hair. "So, that's three stakes, right?"

"And make sure they're sharp!"

A black car sits ominously outside the building. Leaning against it are several of our friends.

"About time," Michael says, a black duffel bag in his hand. He shakes it, and I can hear the metal stakes.

"I'll drive first," Richard says, his elbows on the roof of the driver's side. "We'll need a speed demon if we're to get there in time, and frankly, Victor, you drive like my grandmother."

"This will get us there and back, with plenty to spare," Ian says, loading four orange gas canisters into the trunk.

Rachel is there, a big bag in her hands. "Now, I've packed all of you lunches. Let's see, there's turkey sandwiches, roast beef, um . . . what else? Ooh, I've got a few slices of pie. . . ."

As she rattles off the rest, I slap myself out of the shock I feel and look up at Victor. He appears as surprised as I am: stunned at our gathering of friends and allies.

Faith is standing beside Richard. I wish I had vampire

ears to hear what they're saying to each other. Or maybe not; they deserve their privacy. But my human eyes catch Faith trying to wipe away a tear without anyone noticing. Hundreds of years of practice and still not sly enough for me.

Tegan is holding Michael's hand, and he reaches down and gives her a quick brush over the lips. I'm so glad they have each other.

"Everything looks good," Jeff says, shutting the hood of the car. "Just go easy on the brakes, all right?"

I'm grateful Jeff isn't suited up to go with us. The city needs him now more than ever. And as he rejoins Rachel, I can't help noticing his hand lying gently on her stomach. Maybe it means nothing. Maybe it means everything.

Faith walks over to Victor. "I want to go, but . . ."

"A Valentine needs to be here in case things don't go well," Victor finishes for her.

She nods, swipes at another tear. "Just make sure things go well."

He hugs her hard. "You're a great sister."

"You're an okay brother."

Laughing, Victor leans back and she turns to me. "Don't let anything happen to him."

"I won't," I promise.

Richard gives us our boarding call. "Let's go, guys, plenty of night left."

Victor, Michael, and I jump into the backseat. Richard and Ian take the front.

As we drive through the streets, I know that in the

distance Clive is watching us go toward the walls, toward our final confrontation. I close my eyes and think about him and my parents and everyone I'm doing this for, and our road has never felt more straight.

Chapter 27

It isn't at all what I expected. The Valentine Manor built outside Denver held such opulence, such dark grandeur. But this, the first Valentine house built in America, is held up only by haunted memories now: three stories tall, but the walls are buckling; a roof made of fine timber, eaten away and letting the rain pour into the house's interior; a massive door that once would have stood as the pride of the wealthy Valentine immigrants now hangs off the hinges, termites having made their home inside.

"This is the place," Victor says. "I remember the gardens. They looked so beautiful at night."

"I imagine this place has seen better days," I say.

"It was once the biggest estate in the Northeast. Now it's just a shell. My father let it rot away for some reason. Maybe he just grew bored with it. Once he and the servants left, nature did the rest. We vampires are well aware of what time can do to things built by hand."

"And this is where it all began?" Michael asks.

"I lived here for only a few years," Victor says. "But I know this is where Sin came into life, where he suffered, where he became twisted inside."

"It isn't your fault," I say, putting my hand on Victor's.

He doesn't agree and shakes his head. "I should have come back. I should have known that my father had changed, had become crueler than I could have imagined. I heard he hated his youngest son. I just never knew how much. Or why."

"We can't change any of it now," Ian says. "Trust me, Victor, I know this is hard for you, but you need a clear mind. We all do. If we're going in there to fight, it has to be for that and nothing else. The time for understanding is over. The time for action is here."

"He's right," Richard says. "It has to end here. Tonight. Sin can't be saved."

"I know," Victor says, rubbing my hand. "I know."

With stakes drawn, we head into the manor.

The long hallway is dark and I can see that it's cramped, a corridor meant to keep out the light, not to impress its guests. But once we reach the end and open the doors into the next room, we're all shocked by what we see.

Light. The chandeliers, the wall lamps, everything is on. Sin must have done it. He must have done it for us.

The grand central room, the heart of the house, was most protected from the elements and time. The roof hasn't caved in; the stairs haven't rotted away. It seems as though this place still beats fresh blood, while the rest of the house acts as limbs that have atrophied and died. It haunts us with its glow and its warmth, everything seeming so odd and out of place, as though we've stumbled into a dream in the midst of a nightmare.

The massive pillars that hold the ceiling in place, made of beautiful marble, show no signs of aging. Neither does the grand staircase, which is wide enough to drive a car up. A bright red carpet starts at our feet and winds through the room, up the stairs, and ends at the feet of the man who has killed hundreds and turned hundreds more into horrific creatures. He's left scars everywhere he's walked, and the shards of shattered lives surround him everywhere he goes.

Sin's back is turned to us, but there's no mistaking it's him or that he is alert to our presence. From this distance, he seems to have finally achieved what he wanted: to become a god. He appears, under the glow of the lamps in this dark house, to be the very source of its light, of its warmth. And there's no questioning his omniscience, his acute awareness of our steps and our breaths and our heartbeats. I can tell. Maybe it's because my heart beats with the same Montgomery blood. But I can tell.

In front of him is a massive portrait of the late Murdoch Valentine. It reaches up from the floor to the very top of the ceiling, something only fit for an egomaniac. Maybe Sin is seeing his own face in his father's. A man of power and action, an agent of great change. Through the weathered canvas and chipped paint, the rotting frame and running colors, his grandeur remains. Maybe it's even enhanced, as though proving that even in death he is alive and immune to the ever-moving clock.

Sin speaks. "Look at him. Look at Father."

His voice is calm, but it's a struggle, as if he were speaking out of a mouth that was no longer his.

"Such arrogance he held. Such shortsightedness. All I asked for . . . was . . . was to feel the sun. That's all. But you wouldn't give it to me. No. You had to lock me away, didn't you? Didn't you! Talk! Speak to me!"

Whether Sin thinks he's speaking to a painting or to his father, I don't know. But I'm aware of Victor moving forward and the others spreading out, taking their places.

"Why? Why didn't you love me? Why didn't you . . . see me?"

I can hear . . . No. I can *feel* his weeping.

"Sin!" Victor shouts, and the weeping stops. "Sin, it's over."

"Victor. You always were his favorite."

"You're right. I was. He loved me, and he despised you for what you are. He didn't want a son like you."

Victor wants Sin angry. He wants Sin to stop thinking and act on impulse.

"I killed them all," Sin says. "Years of planning, and all for nothing."

"You've been driven mad," Victor shouts, at the stairs now, one foot on the first step.

"No, I've been given ultimate power. Years of drinking

vampire blood, and finally the Thirst has chosen me. Finally, I've reached my full potential."

"You've reached insanity."

"I have become a god. And I will be a lonely god. For nothing will remain once I am finished."

"Sin! Face me!"

He does so. What I see is nothing like the beautiful teenager who walked into my classroom unexpectedly such a short time ago. He's a demented shadow of what was once Sin Valentine. His jaw has grown in size, the teeth inside his mouth fighting each other for space, expanding into a maw, a forest of sharpened fangs that would fit on no natural creature. His skin is stretched and bleeding, wounds that may never heal. Or perhaps he does it to himself with his hands, or, what were once hands. Now they are claws. His fingers are long and grotesque; the nails at the end have lengthened and sharpened, becoming lethal weapons.

But it's his eyes that capture souls and hold them prisoner. It's his eyes that will haunt me for as long as I live. Freakishly large, black as the purest oil, reflecting all they see like some dark crystal ball. He appears, in this moment, remorseful. Sad. Filled with regret.

But in the next moment, it all changes.

With a frightful scream through his engorged jaw, he causes the ceiling to shake and fine plaster to fall. I look to see where the others are, if everyone is as afraid of this monster as I am. And when I turn back, Victor is off his feet, Sin having hit him square in the chest, and the two fly backward onto the floor.

They slide together, nearly to the door. Sin is on top, one hand around Victor's throat, the other in the air ready to bring down a terrible strike. Victor acts first, shoving his stake into Sin's side.

The Thirst-infected Valentine doesn't even flinch.

Victor scrambles for his other stake as a blur tackles Sin, throwing him off and onto the floor. It's Richard, his own metal stake lodged into Sin. But the monster doesn't care and tosses Richard off as though he's little more than a pillow.

Michael and Ian charge in, one from the back, the other at the front. But Sin's speed is too much, and even though Ian is able to land a solid blow with his stake, he misses with the other and is quickly flung across the room. Michael, for his efforts, receives a blow to the stomach, and I hear the air leaving his lungs. Sin merely shoves him to the floor, as though insulted that a human would have the audacity to face him.

Victor is up now, another stake already in his hand. Sin has three stakes in his body, but he doesn't bother removing them, shows no signs of slowing down. Instead, his eyes narrow in anger, and the blackness within is a rage that has built over years, over decades. And it's all focused on his half brother.

In a flash, Sin appears in front of Victor, his frightening claw raised upward. Victor was fast, but not fast enough, and a trail of blood spurts from his chest in a misty spray. The strike wasn't fatal, and Victor moves in. But Sin grabs his hand and twists and squeezes until Victor falls to a knee and the stake rolls out.

That's when I run in, and I pound my metal stake into Sin's back with both hands and all my weight. But I can't believe it. It barely pierces at all, the Thirst having thickened his gray skin until it stands like leather stacked on more leather.

He turns and looks at me and I think I'll fall into the voids of his eyes never to escape. He raises his hand to strike at me, but he's pushed aside by a thunderous clap as Richard drives into him.

They hit the wall so hard I see it crack, an imprint of Sin placed into it. The master of all the Chosen, the New World god, kicks Richard off before slashing his beautiful face, spraying the wall with deep crimson. Richard staggers back.

Ian and Michael rush in, but Sin delivers a well-placed strike against each and I hear the crunch of bones, the loss of breath. They stumble back. And Sin looks up, no longer enjoying the game, wanting to end this forever. He sets his eyes on Victor.

And Victor wants the same. To end this.

All things stand still, save the two brothers. They move as one, nothing but a blur; hints of their existence dance around the room. And in a brief moment that seems meant only for me, I see Victor, and he looks at me, at Dawn, and I know he draws strength from me, as he always has.

The movement stops, and I see Sin's eyes over Victor's shoulder. I expect them to be wide, pained from the death blow delivered. Instead, I see them carry a hint of joy, a sign of the smile on Sin's face. I look down and see Sin's claws sticking out of Victor's back, having gone clean through his stomach. They drip Victor's blood onto the floor.

But I don't scream; instead, I draw another stake.

The others, Richard, Michael, and Ian, begin to move.

And Victor . . . he grabs Sin's wrist but doesn't remove the claws deep within him. Instead, he holds them tightly, not allowing them to leave, not ending the pain he feels. Only then do Sin's eyes go wide, as he realizes what is to come.

Sin screams and pulls back, but Victor has both hands tightly wrapped around his half brother's arm, and it goes nowhere. I see the blood running from Victor's mouth, I see his body convulsing, but still he remains a statue, Sin's hand stuck within him.

Sin has raised his other arm, ready to strike, when Victor pushes forward with all his strength. Sin trips over himself, stumbling backward, until Victor slams him into one of the marble columns that hold the mansion together. It shakes violently, more plaster raining down.

Sin lets out a short scream but then looks at Victor with confused eyes, questioning if this was his great plan. Sin again raises his other claw, ready to bring it down.

It's just a blur, but it's Michael who delivers the blow deep into Sin's ribs, the deepest strike yet, aimed true and unimpeded. It stuns the vampire just long enough for Richard to swoop in and grab the monster's raised arm and twist it back until it is flush with the marble column. Ian does the rest, hammering his stake through the arm and into the marble, which cracks.

Sin screams, and Victor puts his foot on his half brother and pushes away, dislodging the claw within him. But he doesn't rest. His hand still on Sin's wrist, he pins it to the other side of the column, where Richard brings another stake down, nailing it in place.

The beast stands with his back against the cool, cracking marble, a stake in each arm, pinned, four in his body, and still he fights and struggles.

We all stand back, looking at him. His wide eyes, pathetic; his gaping jaw, weak.

Victor takes one final stake from his belt and approaches Sin.

"Don't do this," Sin says, looking Victor in the eyes for maybe the first time in his life, really looking into the soul of this man. "We could have the world."

Victor looks at him and turns toward me. "I already do."

With those words, he pounds the stake into Sin's chest. The Thirst has thickened his bones, creating a nearly impenetrable breastplate. Sin screams, but he isn't dead, and Victor pushes. But I know he's holding back, know that he's hearing the cries not of Sin, but of the child he should have saved from his cruel father, the child who cried while locked in the basement when all he wanted to taste was the sun.

But that child is gone now, and only the soulless monster remains.

I approach Victor, place my hands on the stake, just as

I had done to the one hovering over Brady. Only this time, it's Victor who needs to let go.

Victor gives Sin a final look before whispering, "Embrace the dark."

I push the stake, feel our strength together, and it ends a life that has ended so many. I feel the stake vibrate with his heartbeats.

Once.

Twice.

Thrice . . .

No more.

Sin's head collapses onto his chest, and Victor closes his brother's eyes, knowing they will never open again.

Epilogue

Year One of the Greater World Order

Standing on my balcony, I watch the sun turn the sky into a brilliant red. Soon he'll come to me. He always comes at night.

How much has changed? What remains of the old world? I search the horizon for the wall that once surrounded Denver. Not a single brick remains, not a single stone is left standing. A dozen roads now weave their way into the growing city, letting in strangers, both human and vampire.

Human and vampire. Finally.

"I did it, Mom," I say. "I did it, Dad."

Between my hands I hold the photo of us all that I found in the documents my dad left me. I wonder if he did it so I wouldn't forget who I was deep down.

"I did it, Brady."

We look so happy around the table. But I no longer yearn to go back to those days, to change the things that have shaped me. My past has already been written, and my future awaits.

"The sunset was beautiful. I wish you could have seen it," I say.

"You're getting better," Victor says, moving from behind me, joining me on the balcony, the night sky above us.

I can never hear his footsteps approaching, but I always know when he's near.

"How is everything?" I ask.

"Blood donations are overflowing. No sign of the Thirst in months. With the Lessers now helping out with the Works, the entire city will be lit before the year is over."

"That's good," I say.

His elbows on the railing and the wind running through his hair, he laughs.

"But that's not what you were really asking, was it?" he says.

"No."

We both look out at the city. I wonder what he sees. Is it what I see? A future? One that started in a trolley car after two girls tried to leave a party?

No. It started before then. Before my parents, before the war. Before anyone I've ever loved was even born. It started in vampire blood and death warrants signed. And it ends here: human and vampire, leaning against each other, looking at a world unafraid of the night.

"I love you, Dawn."

I hold his hand, and feel his pulse. It beats for me.

"I love you, Victor."

Beneath that night sky, somewhere between here and the oceans, blow the winds that carry dust and sand. And in those winds lie everyone who helped shape this world. They go, from one place to the next, and it matters not whether it is the sun in the sky or the moon. They go together.